He drew her towards him and lowered his face to hers. His lips were on hers before she could protest, and his arms were holding her so close against him that she could feel his thighs against hers. Her body tingled with anticipation and she put her arms up and round his neck, returning his kiss. She wanted him, there was no denying it; the fire he had kindled in her in Trieste was still there, still waiting to be fanned back into flame. But it was madness. She twisted her mouth away and pushed against his chest, but it had no more effect than a puff of wind. 'Let me go, Leo.'

He still held her, though he leaned his head back to look at her. 'You want me to let you go?'

'Yes.'

'For ever? Never hold you again?'

Her hesitation was only momentary, but he saw it and smiled, and it seemed to Stella that it was a smile of triumph. He could have her whenever he wanted and he had to give nothing in return—neither love, nor fidelity . . .

Although born in Singapore of a Dutch-South African father and English mother, Mary Nichols came to England when she was three and has spent most of her life in different parts of East Anglia and now lives in Ely, Cambridgeshire. She has been a radiographer, school secretary, information officer and industrial editor as well as a writer. Her writing career began in her teens with short stories and articles and more recently, novels. Mary Nichols' first Masquerade Historical Romance was *In Love and War*.

Mary Nichols has three grown up children and four grandchildren.

THE HEART OF THE LION

Mary Nichols

MILLS & BOON LIMITED
ETON HOUSE 18–24 PARADISE ROAD
RICHMOND SURREY TW9 1SR

*First published in Great Britain 1988
by Mills & Boon Limited*

© Mary Nichols 1988

*Australian copyright 1988
Philippine copyright 1988
This edition 1988*

ISBN 0 263 76128 2

*Set in 10 on 10½ pt Linotron Times
04–0788–79,250*

*Photoset by Rowland Phototypesetting Limited
Bury St Edmunds, Suffolk
Made and printed in Great Britain*

HISTORICAL NOTE

THE CHARACTERS in this novel, Leo, Stella, Carson, Pablo, Jimmy and Josephina, are purely fictitious, as are the events in Yucatan, but the story of Maximilian's troubled reign is not.

The struggle between Liberals and Conservatives in Mexico had been going on long before the arrival of Maximilian. Benito Juárez seemed to be winning, but he found himself President of an impoverished nation which could not pay its debts to the Europeans who had invested heavily in it. In late 1861, Spain, France and England agreed to a military expedition, not, so they said, to acquire new territory or to intervene in Mexico's internal affairs, but simply to collect their debts. The French, intent on vengeance after a humiliating defeat, together with certain exiled Conservative Mexican leaders, suggested that Mexico needed a monarchy, preferably headed by a European prince, and Maximilian, then Archduke of Austrian Italy, was approached.

Many of his followers had grave misgivings, and Maximilian himself could not make up his mind but he agreed at last, in 1864. He was backed by French money and troops, although it was always understood that the troops would leave after two years.

Juárez left the capital to await his opportunity to return to power. Almost from the beginning there were problems with the *Juáristas*, who maintained a guerrilla warfare. The American Government, watching developments with special interest, were worried that the large colony of ex-Confederates who had made their home in Mexico would ally themselves to the French and become strong enough to threaten the peace of the new United States, and began supporting the Liberals clandestinely.

Maximilian eventually decided to leave, but was persuaded to change his mind. He returned to Mexico City, and the French troops moved out, leaving him with the support of only a few thousand loyal Mexican troops. After three months of siege, their headquarters were over-run, and Maximilian surrendered. He was executed on 19 June 1867. Juárez governed as President until his death five years later.

CHAPTER ONE

VERA CRUZ, viewed from the steamship on which Stella had travelled from New Orleans, was a dismal-looking place, enough to discourage any traveller from setting foot on Mexican soil. The coastline was flat, broken only by a few spindly palm trees, and an island in the harbour seemed to house nothing but a graveyard. The passengers had been warned not to linger in the town, which was full of yellow fever, but to take a train as soon as possible to a higher, healthier climate, and this advice was reinforced when they were rowed to the shore; the air was filled with the stench of stagnant water and rotting vegetation. But, on dry land again, they wished themselves once more at sea. In the oppressive heat, they felt the energy being drained from them as they straggled along the waterfront looking for a carriage or someone with a cart to convey their luggage to the railway depot.

Stella, leaving her trunk and basket where they had been landed, followed hopefully, but all the carts and carriages seemed to have been taken by the earlier arrivals on the French steamship *Empress Eugénie*, which had been unloading when they steamed into the harbour, and she went back to sit on her trunk and wait patiently until one returned empty.

It was not a very auspicious beginning to her stay in Mexico, but then she had hardly expected anything else: Jimmy did not know she was coming, and she was not at all sure he would be pleased to see her. But what else could she have done? She could not remain in London after the house had been sold; she had no income of her own, and the tiny inheritance from her parents would not keep her until her husband returned. And there had been the debts she had known nothing about. There had been nothing for it but to sell everything and use the proceeds to pay off the debts and finance her journey to Mexico.

Oh, how she wished she had never gone with her parents to Trieste in that spring of 1864! Then she would never have fallen in love so disastrously, her father would never have met the Archduke Maximilian and taken up the appointment in Mexico, and Jimmy would not have gone with him. A year later, her father had died in an accident here that no one had seemed able to explain properly, and, surprisingly, Jimmy had stayed on. She had considered coming out to Mexico then, but she could not leave her mother who, without the will to live, had succumbed to a severe chill and had died four months ago. Not until Stella had met her lawyer to talk about her future did she realise that she was almost penniless, and the reason Jimmy had stayed in Mexico was to escape his creditors.

But it was no good dwelling on it, and sitting still under her parasol, fanning her flushed cheeks with her landing documents, was no way to get things done. She stood up, intending to resume her search for a conveyance, and it was then she noticed a pile of boxes and bags not ten yards away, and leaning against them, a canvas-wrapped picture, whose covering was slightly torn. It looked curiously familiar. She moved over and pushed the torn material aside, and found herself staring in astonishment at the portrait Leo Manfred had painted of her in Trieste.

'Oh, no,' she murmured aloud. 'Dear heaven, have I not enough problems without that?'

Memories of Italy flooded back and, try as she might, she could not drive them away. She felt again the pressure of Leo's body against hers, his lips bruising hers, but now the feeling was not one of anger or outrage, simply of desolation, of something beautiful spoiled, of longing for what might have been. And although she had persuaded herself that he was a deceitful, conceited man without the manners to apologise or the grace to be ashamed, she had had to concede that he was a talented artist. He had brought out all her good features—the high cheekbones, expressive grey eyes and firm mouth, and the sunlight in her hair so that it looked like gossamer-fine auburn thread—and he had captured her spirit, caught it in the sparkle of her eyes, the curve of her lips and the way she held her head. In the picture's background, Miramar Castle was shrouded in a mist that gave it an air of unreality and a kind of sweet sadness, which clutched at her heartstrings. Over two years later it could still do that, could still make her want to cry.

In the space of a few seconds, that first meeting was brought forcefully back and she could not move from the spot. The torrid heat of Mexico in September was replaced by the gentle warmth of Trieste in April; the calling of seabirds became the raucous cries of a peacock she had disturbed.

She had backed away and then, as the peacock continued to advance, turned, picked up her skirts and run across the grass towards the safety of the summer-house, with the bird's cries of alarm ringing in her ears. She paused, breathless, at the corner of the beautiful building, then ran round the side of it and the next moment was sprawled across the grass entangled with an overturned easel, and nursing a wet canvas in her lap.

'You clumsy child! See what you've done!'

She looked up at the speaker. Even if she had been standing, he would certainly have been much taller than she was, but from her position near the ground, he seemed to tower over her like an angry giant, with his voluminous paint-stained smock blotting out the April sun. He sounded angry, but in his cornflower blue eyes she detected a hint of amusement, and her apology died on her lips. Pushing the canvas away, she scrambled to her feet, stretching to her full five feet two inches.

'I am not a child!'

He smiled. 'My mistake, ma'am, but you must admit

an understandable one; adult ladies rarely, if ever, run.'
He was laughing at her, which was annoying, but she
could not turn away; his gaze held hers with an almost
mesmeric quality. It was as if he were dissecting her
piece by piece: her hair, falling from its pins, her hands,
her tiny waist and neat feet peeping from beneath her
printed muslin skirt.

'Do you always stare at people like that?' she demanded, determined to keep the initiative and put off
the moment when she would have to apologise for
spoiling his picture.

'Only when they are as beautiful as you are.'

'That is a most improper remark!'

He threw back his head with its mane of raven-black
curls and laughed aloud. 'And are you a very proper
miss? I'll wager not.'

Unwilling to answer, she turned away to pick up her
hat, and caught sight of the picture. He had been
painting Miramar, with its pointed turrets, rounded
minarets and terraced roofs lined with statues, which
gleamed like a fairytale castle on the other side of the
park.

Straightening her back, she heard his soft voice
against her ear and felt his warm breath on her neck.
'Tell me your name.'

She hesitated, toying with the idea of inventing an
identity, but decided against it; if she were to regain her
dignity and his respect, the truth would be best. She
turned to face him. 'It's Stella Gardiner; Miss Gardiner.'

'And what are you doing trespassing in the grounds of
the Archduke's home, Miss Gardiner?'

'I am not trespassing,' she retorted. 'If it is any
concern of yours, my father, Sir Peter Gardiner, the
botanist, is visiting the Archduke on a matter of
business. I am just passing the time until he leaves.'

'Creating havoc would be more accurate.'

'I'm sorry,' she said contritely. 'I didn't mean to spoil
your picture.'

'I wasn't thinking about the picture.'

'What else have I done?'

'Ah, if you only knew.'

'You are talking in riddles. Tell me, what have I done?'

He smiled. 'No matter.' He stooped to right the easel, and picking up the canvas, set it back in its place.

'Is it completely ruined?'

'No, but it wasn't very good. I doubt if I'll finish it.'

'Oh, but it is good,' she said.

'Are you a connoisseur?'

'No, but . . .'

'Then don't presume to judge. I do not need flattery.'

'Then I shall not flatter you. You are a rude, boorish man with no manners at all!'

She turned to leave, but he put a hand on her arm to detain her. 'Don't go,' he said. 'It's my turn to apologise, and I do so most humbly.'

She smiled. 'Then I accept your apology, if you will also accept mine.'

'Good.' He paused to regard her with his head on one side, as though sizing her up, and she felt herself colour again. 'I should like to put you in my picture.'

'You said you wouldn't finish it.'

'I've changed my mind. Will you pose for me?'

'But we haven't been introduced.'

'Let's say Mr Peacock introduced us, shall we?'

She laughed. 'And what name did he give you?'

'Leo Manfred.'

Except that his mare was black and not golden, he was well named, she decided, and, like a lion, his movements were deceptive. There was grace and suppleness there, but strength and power too, and it made her shiver a little.

Taking her hand, he led her to one of the many beautiful conifers that graced the park. 'Now the formalities have been disposed of, come and stand over here, with your back against the tree and look towards the castle.'

'I—I don't know that I should.'

'Why not? Where's the harm? I am an artist, Miss Gardiner, not a ravisher of women.' He smiled easily and, taking her shoulders in his hands, put her in the position he wanted. For a moment he stood looking down into her face, almost as if he were going to kiss her, and she wondered what she would do if he did, but all he said was, 'Hold that position.'

'I should tell you it's impossible for me to keep still for two minutes together.'

He laughed. 'That I can believe!'

Adjusting the easel and retrieving his palette from the stool where he had put it when she had arrived so unexpectedly, he dipped his brush in colour and looked up to scrutinise her. Then he began to make deft strokes on the canvas, concentrating on his task, apparently to the exclusion of everything else. Stella ventured to tilt her head to look at him overtly.

'You moved.'

'Sorry.'

'How old are you?' he asked suddenly.

She was prepared to be offended by his bluntness, but his open smile melted her annoyance. 'Nearly twenty-three.'

'And not yet married? How sad.'

'It is not sad. I shall marry when I fall in love, and not before.' She paused, remembering her grandmother's comment when she had made that same remark to her some months before. 'Fall in love!' she had scoffed. 'Love is not something you fall into like stumbling into a puddle; it grows with two suitable people being together, sharing their life. I don't know where you learned such modern notions.'

Stella had never been timid or afraid of adventure. Her father had taught her to ride astride, to shoot and fish and walk for miles with him in his search for botanical specimens; in her grandmother's opinion, frequently voiced, her parents were making her into a misfit in society, almost unmarriageable, at least to anyone of any standing. Grandmama would have seized the invitation to Miramar Castle as a wonderful opportunity to have Stella seen and noticed; she would have made endless enquiries about all the eligible young men attached to the court and made it her business to see they were introduced. But her grandmother was at home in England, and Stella was thankful her parents did not share her views.

'You truly believe that?' Leo asked softly. 'You believe that for every woman there is a man who is just right for her and that no other will do, like two halves of a whole?'

'Now you're making fun of me,' she said, wishing she had not spoken.

'No, indeed I am not. I believe it too.'

'And have you met the woman that's just right for you?'

'Oh, yes,' he said lightly.

'You are married, then?'

'Not yet.'

Suddenly it seemed as though a cloud had passed overhead, although the sun still shone. 'Does your future wife pose for you?'

'Yes.'

'Are you English? You speak it fluently.'

'Half of me is.'

'And the other half?'

'Austrian.'

'Do you live in Trieste?'

'No, I'm visiting friends at the castle.'

'Oh, how fortunate you are! Is it as beautiful inside as it is outside?'

'The parts of it I have seen certainly are.'

She assumed that he meant the servants' quarters, for the Archduke's guests were usually from the royal families of Europe, or aristocracy at least; they dressed magnificently and were always followed by a retinue of servants and bodyguards; they did not roam the grounds alone in paint-stained smocks.

'I don't know how anyone could bear to leave it, even to become an emperor.'

'Archdukes and emperors cannot always please themselves,' he said laconically.

'Does the Archduke really mean to accept the throne of Mexico?' Stella had been intrigued by the story, rife all over Europe, that Maximilian, Viceroy of Austrian Italy, had been offered the throne of Mexico and was on the point of accepting it.

'If he can be convinced it's what the people of Mexico want, I believe he will, though it has to be said that most of them had never heard of him six months ago.'

'Then why ask him?'

'In the fifty years since Mexico broke away from Spanish rule, there has been one president after another; either they've been shot or banished into exile, and the country is verging on anarchy. Some of the exiles decided that what Mexico needs is a European prince, and Maximilian has been approached.'

'Do you think he'll go?'

'I don't know, but he has been planning his government, the institutions he means to set up, the museums, schools and colleges. He has been working on court ceremonial and regulations and designed his new livery. I believe he already thinks of himself as Emperor of Mexico.'

'How do you know all this?'

He paused to stand back and look at his work with half-closed eyes. 'It's common knowledge up at the castle.'

'Do you think he should go?'

He shrugged. 'It's of no consequence what I think. Maximilian is an idealist, who imagines himself as a knight in shining armour, going to rescue the country from ruin and misery.'

'Is that such a bad thing?'

'No, but it ought to be tempered with realism.'

'Will Miramar be shut up when he goes?'

'Possibly. Why do you ask?'

'I wondered what the servants would do,' she said, probing. 'Will they go with him?'

'Some might; others might stay to look after the castle.'

'And you?'

He looked up at her sharply, as if he resented her question, but then he smiled slowly. 'My plans are uncertain. It depends on the turn of events. In the meantime, I paint.'

She fell silent, conscious that he did not want to answer her questions, and she supposed it did seem as if she were prying. But how else could she find out more about him? And, she had to admit, she wanted to know more. 'The Archduke has sent for my father to ask his professional advice,' she said.

'And left you to wander around Trieste un-accompanied?'

'You could hardly call a walk in Miramar Park wandering round Trieste. Besides,' she added, unable to resist the temptation to boast, 'I am used to much more adventurous expeditions. Jungle, desert, mountain, it makes no difference. I have frequently been exploring with Papa.'

'A veritable amazon,' he murmured, and then laughed. 'An amazon afraid of a peacock.'

'I wasn't afraid of him; he just startled me, that's all.'

'Do stand still. How can I work when you keep moving?'

'I warned you I couldn't keep still.'

'I'd like to paint you in the middle of a rain-forest with a snake about your neck and a leopard at your feet.'

'Not a lion?'

He smiled, understanding her teasing reference to his name. 'A lion, if you like.'

They did not speak for several minutes, then he said, 'Such a life can't be easy for you. Don't you miss the social occasions, the balls and receptions, meeting other young people?'

'But I do meet other young people. I've met you.'

'But I am old as Methuselah.'

'How old?'

'Thirty-two.'

'And do you make a living at your painting?'

He seemed to be considering his answer carefully, then said, 'I'm still struggling to earn a crust.'

'I'm sure you'll be very rich and famous one day.'

'Thank you for your confidence.'

'Will you sell that one?' She nodded towards the canvas.

'No.'

'Why not?'

'One day I'll tell you.'

'Tell me now. We might never meet again.'

'Oh, indeed we shall. I cannot paint a likeness with only one sitting. You must come again.'

'I'm not at all sure that would be proper.'

He grinned. 'But we have already established that you are not a proper miss. In fact, you are very different from any other young lady I have ever met. Surely someone who has crossed deserts, climbed mountains and explored jungles is not afraid of coming to Miramar Park to meet a lion?'

'I am not at all sure Papa would approve.'

'Shall I ask him?'

'No,' she said quickly, and wondered why she said it. Was it because she knew her father would forbid it, and she did not want to risk that?

He put the palette down on the stool and walked over to where she leaned against the tree and stood looking down at her, smiling. She became suddenly aware of a quickening of her heartbeat, which left her flushed and breathless as if she had been running or riding hard.

'I can't make up my mind about you,' he said, putting his hands on the trunk above her head and imprisoning her between his arms. 'You are either an innocent child, younger than your years, or you are . . .' He paused, to brush away a strand of hair which had fallen across her forehead. 'Or you are a very experienced temptress.'

The amused look went from his face and there was a softness about his eyes that disconcerted her. She became aware of his powerful masculinity; it seemed to fill the air about them. Afraid of her own emotions, she wanted to turn and run, but she could not move. Her pulse raced and she felt like a terrified mouse trapped by a cat. He took her hand and lifted it to his lips, then murmured softly, 'And, make no mistake, I am sorely tempted.'

She found her voice at last. 'Mr Manfred, please let me go. Papa will be worried.'

He laughed and took a step backwards. 'Did you think I would . . . Oh no, my dear Miss Gardiner, I wouldn't dream of it. Go home. Go home before I have an irate father on my heels.' He dropped her hand, and added softly, 'If your courage returns, come back tomorrow at the same time. I shall be waiting.'

She had fled to where her father waited with the brougham at the gates of the park to take them back to the villa they had rented in Trieste. Leo had been going to kiss her, she was sure of it, and she wondered what she would have done if he had gone even further than that and tried to seduce her, and the thought made her limbs tremble with a kind of wild excitement. If he had, she would have no one to blame but herself; she had flirted outrageously. And he was only amusing himself with her because he had told her he had already met the woman he wanted to share his life with. It would be tempting fate to return.

But she could not banish him from her mind, and his image floated in front of her whenever she shut her eyes, his smile teased, his voice called her. Was he really as handsome as she had imagined? Did he really find her attractive? Did he mean it when he said he would be at the summer-house the next day? She knew she would have to find out. But what could she tell her parents? They would almost certainly want to know where she was going and why, not because they did not trust her, but for her own protection.

It was strange how that same fate had played into her hands, though she had wished a million times since that it had not. Maximilian had asked her father to go again the following day, saying he wanted to continue their discussions, and as her mother already had a visiting engagement, Stella accompanied him as far as the park gates, where she left him and walked across the grass to the summer-house.

Leo Manfred was there before her, filling in some detail of the background of the picture while he waited. His greeting was natural and relaxed, as though they had known each other for years, and she forced herself to sound calm as she answered him and resumed her pose.

For several minutes, neither spoke; he worked with a concentration which seemed to shut her out, and yet he studied her as closely as before and it was as unnerving as before.

'We are going home to England soon,' she said, to break the long silence. 'Then we shall probably go to Mexico. The Archduke has asked my father to help the Director Designate to set up a natural history museum there.'

He dabbed his brush on to his palette before replying. 'Mexico is hardly a safe place to be at the moment, what with Benito Juárez and his Liberals fighting the Conservatives for power.'

'Oh, we shan't go immediately. Archduke Maximilian told my father that he means to settle the unrest in the country first, then he will send for him.'

'That won't happen in a day.'

'My father told me that Maximilian's brother, the Austrian Emperor, has insisted that he renounce all claim to the Austrian throne if he goes to Mexico. Is that true?'

'Yes. Francis Joseph arrived by train yesterday to obtain Maximilian's signature to the document.'

'It can't have been an easy decision.'

'It broke his heart,' he said, and for a brief moment she thought he sounded angry. 'But he did it.'

'Does that mean he will be leaving for Mexico soon?'

'Tomorrow or the day after, I think. A Mexican deputation arrived this morning to offer him the crown in an official ceremony. We shall know it has been accepted when the Mexican flag goes up over the castle and the ships' guns fire a salute.'

He had hardly finished speaking when the boom of cannon echoed from the bay, and, looking towards Miramar, they saw the new flag fluttering in a light breeze on the highest turret of the castle.

'It is done,' Leo murmured softly, and Stella thought she detected a note of sadness in his voice. It was strange, when everyone else in the town was treating the imminent departure of the royal couple and their entourage as cause for celebration. For days banners and flags had been flying on all the public buildings, while out in the bay, the Austrian ships *Novara* and *Themis* lay at anchor, ready to bear them away. She had a terrible feeling of unease, a fear of the unknown, which affected her so strongly she had to remind herself that it had nothing to do with her and she was merely an onlooker.

She looked towards Leo, but he appeared to be concentrating on putting the finishing touches to the picture, and the expression on his face did not invite conversation.

'Not at all bad,' he murmured, just as she was beginning to wonder if he would ever speak again.

'Let me see.'

'In a minute.'

He took two or three paces back, and regarded his handiwork with his head on one side. 'There, now you may look.'

Eagerly she went to stand beside him, and what she saw took her breath away.

'It's beautiful,' she whispered. 'I had no idea . . .'

'You didn't know you were so lovely? You have only to look in the mirror. I paint only what I see.'

'And that is what you see?'

'It's a great pity I can't also paint what I feel. Mere paint and canvas cannot do justice to that.'

She looked at him sharply. 'What do you mean?'

'Don't you know?' He smiled slowly and took her in his arms, crushing her against him so that she could feel the hard contours of his body against hers, and pressed his lips to hers in a long, hard kiss.

She should not have been shocked, not when she had earlier been thinking, even hoping, it might happen. For several long moments she allowed herself to be submerged in their mutual desire for one another, but a little voice inside her sounded a warning note. She began struggling in his arms, trying to push him away. He moved his hands to grasp her more firmly and, in doing so, ripped the bodice of her gown. The tearing sound brought him to his senses, and he let her go, so suddenly that she almost fell.

'If that is how a man behaves who has pledged his love to another,' she said, recovering her balance, if not her dignity, 'I am glad I am not the object of your devotion!' Then she turned and ran from him towards the safety of the gatehouse.

He chased after her and took her arm, pulling her round to face him. 'I'm truly sorry,' he said contritely.

'Sorry for kissing me?'

She had the most disconcerting way of coming to the point, he decided. 'Not at all,' he said, smiling. 'Not for that; it was far too enjoyable to regret. But what did you mean, you are glad you are not the object of my devotion?'

'What I said,' she said, angry with herself as much as with him. She had wanted him to kiss her, had wanted to be held in his arms; she had been playing with fire, and it was her own fault if she was burned. 'You told me yesterday that you had already met the woman you loved . . .'

'Does that make any difference to how we felt just now?'

'Of course it does!'

'You are not being honest, Miss Gardiner. Admit it. You wanted me to kiss you.'

'You are insufferably conceited!'

'Am I? If you thought that, why did you come again? A young lady concerned for her reputation would not have come within a mile of Miramar Park today.'

She did not answer, and he went on, speaking gently and no longer teasing. 'Stella, my sweet, my lovely star, didn't you realise I meant you?'

'Me?' In her surprise, she forgot to be annoyed. 'But we only met yesterday.'

'Was it only yesterday? But how long does it take to fall in love? You are the one who will hold my heart into eternity; I knew it the moment you tumbled into my life.'

'How could you possibly know that?'

He put his finger under her chin and raised her face to make her look at him. 'Chemistry, alchemy, call it what you will. But I thought you were just amusing yourself with me, that's why I behaved so badly. I won't kiss you again unless you want me to.'

Even two years later, she still felt hot with embarrassment when she remembered how she had put her arms up and round his neck and pulled his head down to hers. He had kissed her tenderly and then more hungrily, holding her closely against him. His hands had moved over her body, finding the split in her bodice, searching inside for her bare flesh. She had shivered with delight, wanting it to go on and on; her legs shook so that they would hardly support her and, half-eager, half-afraid, she had leaned against him. 'Leo! Oh, Leo!'

Her voice seemed to startle him, as though she had woken him from a trance, and he had pulled himself together and let her go. 'I must be mad. You are a witch, do you know that? Half-child, half-woman. Go away and stop tempting me.'

'If that's what you want.' She made no move to leave him.

'No, it's not what I want.' He drew her to him again. 'I want you, but . . .'

'But what?'

'What have I to offer in exchange? Only the nomadic life of an artist. Hardly the credentials your parents would wish.'

'They will understand when we explain.'

He smiled, and kissed the tip of her nose. 'You think so? They will be furious, and if they aren't, then they certainly ought to be. I would be, in their shoes.'

'They have to be faced,' she said. 'That is, if you want to see me again. I can't go on deceiving them; it would be cruel and wrong.'

He had not answered for several interminable moments, then he had stooped to put a kiss lightly on the top of her head. 'Very well. I'll ask your father's permission to court you in the manner etiquette demands.'

'When?' She did not care that she sounded over eager.

'When Maximilian leaves for Mexico. I'll contrive to be given the official task of escorting you and your parents down to the harbour to watch the royal couple begin their journey. That should be a suitable occasion, don't you think? I'll call at your villa.'

Before leaving him, she had given him the address and clear instructions how to find it. She had looked back once; he was standing beside his easel, brush in hand, watching her. She had waved, and he had blown her a kiss from the tips of his fingers. It was a scene that was to remain locked for ever in the secret recesses of her memory, however hard she had tried to eradicate it.

For the next two days she lived in eager anticipation, nursing her secret to her, saying nothing to her parents; it would be better for their peace of mind if they did not know that she and Leo had already met. Their love must be seen to blossom slowly, out of his official duty. She did not know how he would contrive that, but she did not doubt for a moment that he could do it. Nor did she doubt that he would keep his word. Foolish, foolish girl!

When the time came to leave for the waterfront to watch the departure of Maximilian and Carlota, and Leo had not yet put in an appearance, she had declined to go and her parents had left without her. Alone in the villa, she tried to make herself believe he had been delayed and would soon appear. The sound of music and the cheering of the crowds as they jostled for the best vantage-points stirred her impatience to be on the scene, but still he did not come. When the boom of guns from the frigates in the harbour was answered by salvoes from Miramar Castle and the band began to play the newly composed royal Mexican anthem, she knew that the new Emperor and Empress had put in an appearance, and they were already too late to see anything.

Had something dreadful happened to him? Was he lying dead or injured somewhere? What other reason could there be for his non-appearance? She began to wonder if it had all been an impossible dream, and from there her thoughts moved slowly, very slowly, towards an awakening. Small things he had said, and others left unsaid, had come back to her and convinced her he had not been sincere, that he had never intended to come. After all, she knew nothing about him, and he was probably one of those undesirables Papa had warned her about—feckless young men who made a living by their wits, pickpockets, pedlars of shoddy merchandise, sailors from the many ships in the bay, more of such riff-raff than usual because of the comings and goings at Miramar.

She had moved at last when she heard her parents returning, and was glad she had not told them about Leo. She would never tell them now, and she would have to learn to live with the disappointment and the humiliation. She could not forget how gullible she had been, how easily he had taken her in, but neither could she stop herself wanting him, and many a night she cried into her pillow with an aching heart.

They had returned to England soon afterwards, and the pain of rejection had gradually died. Trieste seemed so remote from London, which was a cold, fog-shrouded, down-to-earth world. Miramar and its castle were all part of a dream, and it behoved her to rouse herself and make something of her life. Leo was part of the past, who had no relevance to her life in the present, or in the future.

She began helping her father in his work, and that was when James Wainright came into her life as his assistant. Tall and dark, with deep brown eyes and soft expressive features, he began paying her attention when everyone had convinced her she was fated to remain a spinster. Her grandmother's assertion, that love came with two people sharing their life and not in some great explosion, began to make more sense. She told herself that she had stumbled into a puddle at Trieste, but having climbed out of it without too much damage being done, she ought to pay more attention to her elders.

She and James had been married just six months before the call came for her father to join Maximilian, and she had been totally taken aback when Jimmy said he was going too, telling her it was an opportunity he could not miss. It had seemed such a sensible idea at the time.

The tropical heat of Mexico forced her back to the present; her skin was sticky beneath her heavy mourning gown, and the flimsy parasol she carried did little to protect her. She began to wish she had accepted Colonel Carson's offer of a ride in his carriage, but he had gone now and so had everyone else. Everyone except the owner of the picture. Had Leo sold it, even though he had assured her he never would?

Suddenly she felt herself being pulled away so violently that her parasol flew from her hand and she almost fell. When she recovered her balance and turned to face her assailant, she found herself looking into the bright eyes of a half-naked Mexican boy, brown as a berry, with high cheekbones and mongoloid eyes. He could not have been more than fourteen years old, but he began berating her in a mixture of Spanish and French with an accent that made it impossible for her to understand. He was standing beside an empty handcart, which he had obviously brought up to carry the painting and its accompanying luggage into the town.

Intent on trying to understand him and protest her innocence of whatever he was accusing her of, she did not hear someone else approach until a laughing voice at her elbow said, 'He has been well paid to convey my belongings to the train, and he takes his mission seriously enough to protect them from would-be thieves.'

She whirled round to confront the speaker, and found herself looking into the smiling face of the man she had been thinking of only moments before.

CHAPTER TWO

LEO MANFRED had not changed in the two and a half years since she had seen him; his figure was just as slim, and his mane of curly hair, the only slightly unruly thing about him, was just as striking. He no longer wore a painter's smock, but a well-cut frock-coat, a plain shirt and a silk cravat fastened with a diamond pin. His blue eyes regarded her for what seemed an age before his lips twitched into a half-smile, which unnerved her so much she was forced to turn away. 'My parasol,' she said lamely.

He signalled to the boy without turning his head, and the young Mexican ran to retrieve it, stooping to pick it up just as a gust of wind caught it and sent it tumbling over and over into the bay. Before she could stop him, he had dived into the filthy water after it.

'Oh, no!' she cried, concerned for the child's safety. 'Do tell him not to go after it, it's not important.'

But Leo appeared to be amused by the incident and encouraged the Mexican to swim faster. 'Go on, Pablo,' he shouted, running past Stella and standing with the waves almost lapping at his feet. 'Go on, before the wind catches it again.'

'No, don't,' she called, as the boy swam towards the parasol, which was bobbing out to sea like a toy ship in full sail. 'Come back! Oh, please come back!'

He took no notice, and a moment later caught the flimsy sunshade and was swimming strongly back, holding it aloft. He was such a comical sight that Leo laughed aloud and even Stella found herself smiling.

Leo reached down, took the parasol and gave it to Stella, then held out his hand, grasped the lad's wrists and hauled him on to dry land.

'Now I wonder how much you think that little escapade is worth?' he said, still laughing, and surveying the dripping boy with his head on one side. *'Cuánto?'* He turned to Stella. 'How much do you think? Bear in mind that he is wearing only a thin pair of trousers, he has hardly spoiled his Sunday best clothes, and on such a hot day the water must have been pleasantly cool.'

There were a thousand questions whirling in Stella's brain and a confusion of emotions she did not want to acknowledge, but she did not want him to see the effect he was having on her, especially as he seemed so unconcerned. She tried hard to sound normal, although she could not help the slight note of acrimony that crept into her voice. 'Do you make a commercial transaction of everything?'

He laughed. 'No, but Pablo does, you can be sure.' He turned to the boy again, who was shaking himself like a wet puppy and grinning from ear to ear, revealing beautiful even teeth. 'Well, my fine friend, name your price.'

'I come with you,' the boy said in English.

'To the train,' Leo said. 'Thank you for reminding me. We mustn't miss that. I don't want to spend a night in this fever-ridden place, and I'm quite sure the young lady doesn't. Come, on to the cart with the baggage.' He strode back to the handcart and bent to the handle of Stella's trunk, motioning the boy to take the other end.

'Thank you,' Stella said, still holding the parasol which was quite ruined; not wanting to hurt the boy's feelings, she shook the surplus water from it, shut it carefully and laid it on her trunk, as they lifted it on the cart.

When all their bags, boxes and trunks and the picture had been loaded, they set off through the town to the railway depot, with Pablo pushing the cart. It left Leo and Stella to walk side by side along the dusty road, which seemed to bounce the heat back up at them like a furnace. She stole a look at him from beneath the brim of

her feather-trimmed hat. He was still physically attractive, bronzed and smiling; that was what she remembered
most about him, the way he seemed always to be
laughing, as if life itself was one big jest. Did he treat
love in the same way, she wondered, not worth taking
seriously?

Away from the sea's edge, it seemed hotter than ever
and she was finding it difficult to breathe. Despite her
intention to be strong and independent, she was
prompted to ask, 'How far is it to the train?'

Leo stopped and turned towards her, as if noticing for
the first time how the climate was affecting her. 'Not far,
but in this heat it seems like miles. Would you like to
wait here while I search for a carriage?'

She looked about her. There were no public buildings
that she could see, and the squat, white-washed adobe
houses seemed deserted. There was nowhere she could
rest out of the sun, although a little way off she caught a
glimpse of a square surrounded by a few spindly palm
trees. She shook her head. 'No, I shall walk.'

'As you wish.' He offered her his arm and she took it,
knowing it would be churlish to refuse, but his nearness
was making her heart pump uncomfortably fast and she
felt hotter than ever; the road before her began to swim
and then a blackness closed in on her.

'Oh!' she murmured, and fell against him.

When she felt herself being lifted, there was nothing
she could do to prevent it, and she knew no more until
she found herself sitting on a stone bench in the shade of
one of the palms that bordered the square. Leo was
sitting with his arm protectively over her shoulder, and
beside him stood the little Mexican boy, fanning her face
vigorously with Leo's curly-brimmed hat. She felt weak
and stupid and annoyed with herself, and tried to
rise.

'Sit still until you feel better,' Leo ordered.

'I'm quite recovered,' she said, but her feeble legs
defied her will and she was obliged to obey him, realising
that the look of concern she thought she had seen in his

eyes when she first opened hers had been imagination on her part.

'She fine now,' Pablo said. 'We go on, eh?'

'No,' Leo said firmly. 'You stay with Mrs Wainright till I come back, do you hear? If you leave her, there will be no money—*no pesos*—understand?' He repossessed himself of his hat, replaced it on his head and strode off across the square. It was not until he had gone that she realised he had used her married name. How did he know it? she wondered.

It had only been a momentary fainting fit, and Stella felt ashamed of her weakness. After a minute or two, she stood up and shook out her skirt. 'Come,' she said to the boy. 'We shall go on.'

'The *señor* said to stay. He will be very angry.'

Stella had already started in the direction in which Leo had gone and the boy was obliged to pick up the handles of the cart and follow, though he protested volubly in a mixture of several languages.

They had not gone far when they were met by a coach and pair, which stopped when it reached them. Leo emerged from its interior and jumped down to help Stella into it. Although it was hot inside, it did afford some shade, and she was glad to sit back against the cushions and relax, while he turned to transfer the luggage from the cart. He was met by determined resistance from Pablo, who tugged at the opposite handle of the trunk he was trying to lift.

'I take cart to train,' he insisted. 'You give me *pesos* to take trunks to train. Pablo good porter boy. Pablo take to train.' Then, as Leo took a purse from his pocket and opened it, 'I want no more *pesos*. I come with you. You say "Yes", so I come with you.'

Stella leaned forward to speak to Leo. 'Why don't you tell him to take the cart and meet us at the station?'

'What, and never see him or the luggage again?'

'He seems honest enough to me, in fact, very conscientious . . .'

Pablo had been looking from one to the other, and although he was still smiling broadly, he was obviously determined to complete his mission.

Leo sighed. 'Very well, young shaver, help me to load it, and then it's up beside the driver with you.' He pointed to the driver's seat.

'*Si, Señor.*' The boy obeyed with alacrity, honour satisfied, and they were soon on their way, with Leo sitting opposite Stella, his head leaning back against the squabs, scrutinising her down his long nose. Hot though she was, she felt herself colour even more.

'I'm sorry to be so much trouble,' she said. 'I have never fainted in my life before.'

He smiled slowly, but it was a smile that did not reach his cornflower blue eyes. 'Have you any idea what you are letting yourself in for, coming to this country just now? The situation is far from stable, with bandits everywhere.'

'I had little choice,' she replied. 'I have come to join my husband in Mexico City.'

'Does he know you are coming?'

'I don't know. I wrote, more than once, but received no reply.'

'Perhaps he is no longer in Mexico City. Had you thought of that?'

'It's a possibility. When I last heard from him, just after my father died, he was considering an expedition into the countryside, but when exactly I don't know.'

'Then how are you going to find him?'

'I'll go first to the rooms he shared with Papa at Chapultepec.'

'If he isn't there?'

'I'll set out to look for him.'

'Quite apart from the political situation, which is bad enough, Mexico is a vast country and much of it mountain and forest. You surely do not intend to conduct a search yourself?'

'Why not?'

'At the risk of stating the obvious, Mrs Wainright, you

are a woman and not up to the rigours of such an expedition . . .'

'I shall not faint again.'

He smiled. 'Perhaps not, but there are other hazards . . .'

'Mr Manfred,' she said, matching his formality with her own, 'if my grandmother could not dissuade me from making this journey, you will certainly not persuade me to abandon it.'

He did not speak for some time, and then completely disconcerted her by saying softly, 'I had forgotten how beautiful you are. Paint and canvas cannot do justice . . .'

She wished he had not used that particular phrase; it reminded her of the first time he had said it, that day in Miramar Park when he had finished the painting, the day he had declared his love for her. Oh, what a simpleton she had been to believe that! Why, oh why, had fate dealt this blow to her? Surely it was enough to lose both parents and have to come searching for a lost husband, without meeting this ghost from the past!

'What are you doing in Mexico?' she asked bluntly.

'I am returning from a mission in Europe.'

'Returning?'

'Yes.'

She wanted to ask if he had been with Maximilian's entourage when it left Trieste, it might explain his disappearance at that time, but it made no difference to the fact that he had deceived her and left without a word of explanation. He had been reluctant to tell her anything about himself then, so he was hardly likely to do so now.

'Why did you bring the picture to Mexico?'

'I like it. It's one of my best. I might even sell it.' He paused, watching her face for a reaction to that, but she had learned to control her features since Trieste. 'On the other hand, I might give it away.'

The coach slowed to negotiate the traffic round the

railway depot and then drew to a stop, effectively putting an end to the conversation, and she was glad. Leo Manfred made her feel uncomfortable with his steady gaze and amused smile. It was almost as if he were deliberately trying to provoke her, and she was determined he would not succeed. He jumped down to offer his hand, and she took it and stepped carefully down. The touch of him could still send a tingle of excitement running through her body; it was most unnerving, particularly when she had long ago convinced herself that he was objectionable and hateful and not worth breaking her heart over. She had been right: she must stop thinking about it and remember her husband and the reason she came to Mexico. She thanked him, and turned towards the station building where Europeans, Americans and Mexicans crowded and jostled to buy their tickets and take their seats in the train, which was already noisily getting up steam.

Colonel Redford Carson detached himself from the crowd and hurried towards them. He was tall and well built, wearing a light-coloured cutaway suit, a snow-white shirt with a black string tie, a broad-brimmed felt hat and patent leather boots. His eyes had a fleck of gold in them and his small moustache enhanced his bronzed complexion. He was travelling with his sister, a waspish spinster who had little to say.

Stella had met them in New Orleans when she had been waiting for the steamer to carry her on to Mexico. He had taken her under his wing and showed a keen interest in her journey and her reason for making it, which, when she thought about it afterwards, was more than mere politeness demanded. It made her feel uncomfortable and, because of that, she had tried to avoid them on the short voyage to Vera Cruz and declined his offer of transport to the railhead when they arrived.

'Mrs Wainright,' he said, doffing his hat. 'Fully recovered, I hope?'

'Yes, thank you, Colonel, but how did you know . . .?'

'I borrowed the Colonel's carriage,' Leo said.

Stella looked puzzled, and the Colonel added, 'When I went to New Orleans, I left it here to be ready for my return.'

'Oh, then I thank you,' she said. 'It was the heat, you know.'

'Of course. Please allow me to fetch your ticket and escort you to a seat.'

'That won't be necessary,' Leo put in quickly. 'Mrs Wainright is travelling with me.'

Bewildered, she turned from one to the other, sensing their antagonism towards each other and wondering what had caused it, but before she could protest that she was travelling with no one, Leo had turned to Pablo, who was hovering near by apparently waiting for further commissions, and ordered him to find two first class seats and hold them until they arrived to claim them, then he strode off to the booking office.

The Mexican boy obeyed instantly, and Stella turned to the American. 'Thank you, Colonel, but it appears that I am already being looked after.' She held out her hand. 'Perhaps we shall meet again.'

He surprised her by taking her hand and raising it to his lips. 'Indeed, I hope so,' he said. 'I shall be staying at the Iturbide Hotel for a few days after we reach Mexico City, to attend to some business, before returning to my home in Carlota Colony. If you should need assistance of any sort, please call on me.'

Stella thanked him, and he released her hand reluctantly, touched his hat, bowed and left her to rejoin his sister. She hardly had time to look around and take in the sights and sounds, the colourful costumes of the Mexicans, the uniforms of the French and Mexican soldiers, the crinolines of the European women, so hot and uncomfortable, before Leo returned to her side.

'Come,' he said. 'Time to find our seats.'

'Mr Manfred,' she said, speaking slowly and deliberately as though he were unable to understand plain English. 'I came to Mexico by myself, knowing I would have to travel alone and look after myself, so you need feel under no obligation to escort me.'

He laughed aloud. 'You would be the victim of robbery, if nothing worse, before the day is out, and if you swooned again . . .'

'I shall not swoon again,' she said, wishing she could disabuse him of the idea that she fainted at the least provocation. 'I can promise you that.'

'You should never make promises you can't keep,' he said, looking down into her eyes. Once again she felt at a disadvantage under his scrutiny, almost as if she had something to be ashamed of. But she had not, so she stared him out and it was he who spoke. 'Since we are both going to Mexico City, it won't hurt you to sit beside me on the journey, if only to give the appearance of having my protection. I will not bore you with my conversation if you do not wish it.'

'I'm sorry,' she said. 'I only meant that if you preferred to be alone yourself, I could travel with the Colonel and Miss Carson.'

'Him!' There was no disguising the contempt in his voice. 'He is no better than the bandits who skulk in the hills—worse, in fact, because they have a valid reason for what they do.'

'How can you possibly know that?' she asked, falling into step beside him.

'They make no secret of the fact they want a return of the Republic.'

'No, I meant about Colonel Carson. You came on the *Empress Eugénie*, didn't you? He was on board our boat from New Orleans.'

'So he was, but he is no new arrival. He goes back and forth frequently—on business matters, so he says. He is well known in Mexico City.'

'Perhaps you have misjudged him,' she said calmly. 'I found him very charming.'

'Ladies usually do,' he said laconically, as he searched along the carriages for Pablo. 'Ah, there he is.'

They hardly had time to pay the boy more than

generously for his services and take their seats before the train began to move, chuntering its way out of the unattractive town, between sandhills dotted with cacti and bone-dry little bushes, towards the distant hills.

The bench on which Stella sat was upholstered with a mat of plaited straw, a concession to the fact that the carriage was for first-class passengers, and the windows were covered with blinds to keep off the glare of the sun. As they climbed slowly, the landscape became greener and wild cattle grazed on the slopes, and at Soledad they stopped, and Stella was thankful to leave the train to stretch her legs and find something to eat. It was only a short respite, and they were soon back in their seats and on their way again. Leo sighed, leaned back and shut his eyes, feigning sleep, and Stella, in some ways glad not to have to talk to him, turned and lifted the corner of the blind to watch the landscape slide past the window.

Some time later she said, 'We're slowing down.'

'Then we're approaching Paso del Macho, the end of the line. This is as far as the English railwaymen got before they were called home. Mexico will have to wait for more peaceful times to have its railway finished.'

'What next?' Stella asked, as the train came to a halt and she left with everyone else.

'We go by road.'

The passengers stood by the train, looking up the single mud-baked village street lined with palm-thatched huts, trying to be the first to spot the new transport when it arrived and thereby claiming the best seats for themselves. Behind them there was a great deal of heaving and shouting, as the Colonel's carriage was unloaded from an open truck at the end of the train and the horses were brought up to be harnessed.

'He is very well organised,' said Stella, turning to watch.

'As I said,' Leo commented drily, 'he does the journey frequently.'

'And does he always have so much luggage?'

'I don't know.' Leo was showing an interest for the first time. 'It looks heavy too; not clothes, I'll be bound. I wonder . . .' He stopped in mid-sentence and wandered off towards the carriage.

The arrival of a battered old coach pulled by four mules coincided with the discovery of Pablo in the Colonel's carriage, and the passengers were torn between claiming their seats in the diligence and watching the action. The boy was pulled from the carriage by his thin arms and flung to the ground, where he lay a moment, winded by the force of the fall.

'I'll teach you to steal!' the Colonel shouted, grabbing a whip from his driver and raising it to thrash the boy.

Stella, horrified, ran forward. 'Don't! Oh, don't! He's only an innocent child!'

'Innocent be damned!' He raised the whip again, but it was Leo who seized his upraised arm and stopped him.

'Not that way,' he said, his face set in a mask of controlled anger.

Carson turned, and the two men faced each other, their mutual hate almost a tangible thing, and for a moment Stella thought they might come to blows.

'If the boy has been stealing, then he has to be punished,' Leo went on quietly. 'But not that way.' He tugged the whip from the Colonel's hand and threw it to the ground. 'First of all, what has he stolen? Apart from a free ride, I mean.'

'He had a pocketful of silver, and he didn't come by that honestly, I'll wager! He was using my carriage to hide from retribution.'

'Even if that were true, it's not up to you to administer the punishment,' Stella said.

'You don't understand these people.' His voice softened when he spoke to Stella. 'They need discipline, especially the children.'

Pablo had taken the opportunity to get to his feet, and now, instead of running away, he came to stand behind Stella, realising that here he had a champion. She turned to him. 'Did you steal?'

'No. Your man gave me *pesos*.'

Ignoring the implication that she and Leo belonged to each other, Stella turned to the Colonel. 'That's true. He was well paid for his services.'

Colonel Carson smiled thinly. 'Mr Manfred's generosity will be repaid in a way he hasn't bargained for, you can be sure. The Injun is yours; I give him into your hands.' He tossed the confiscated coins to the ground, where Pablo dived for them, before following Stella and Leo to rejoin the other passengers who had boarded the coach and were waiting for them. He showed no sign of going away, and Stella felt partially responsible for him, so she signalled to him to get up beside the driver and took her place inside, opposite Leo.

'That was a rather foolish thing to do,' he said, as they moved off. 'What do you propose to do with the little urchin? He will attach himself to you like a leech until he realises you have nothing more to give, then he'll take what he wants and disappear.'

'I have given him nothing,' she retorted. 'You did! You gave him money, and if what you say is true, it is to you he will attach himself.'

He laughed. 'I wonder what he'll do when we get to Mexico City and he finds we are parting company; he can't divide himself in two. Perhaps we should stay together to save him having to make the decision.'

If his voice had not held such a note of bitterness, she might have been amused, but as it was, she spoke sharply. 'How do you know he has no friends or relatives in the city and that he's not making his way there as best he can?'

Leo was still smiling. 'Then he is being very resourceful.'

'Indeed he is, and I admire him for it.'

'He knows that, and he'll take advantage of you.'

'You stopped Colonel Carson from whipping him just now.'

'Because I hate injustice,' he said. 'And no child

should be chastised in that manner. It doesn't mean I want to adopt him.'

She did not like arguing with him, it only strengthened the barrier that so obviously existed between them. She had been almost deluded in the last few hours into believing that the barrier was crumbling, that they could, perhaps, be friends. But it was an illusion, a dream. She had come to Mexico to find her husband, and she would do well to remember that.

She turned from Leo to look out of the window at the barren countryside. The road was no more than a track, and they were jolted from side to side as the four mules, goaded by whips, pulled the creaking coach at little more than walking pace. She could see its shadow outlined on the bare earth and, a little behind it, that of Colonel Carson's horse-drawn coach, waiting for the opportunity to overtake them. There was no sign of human habitation; they seemed to be the only people on earth, trapped by the heat between the cloudless blue sky and the rock-hard ground. Hills rose on either side, covered with boulders and scrub. Bandit country, Stella thought, wondering where Juarez, the erstwhile President of the Republic, was at that moment. Could he be lying in wait for them with his band of desperadoes?

But it seemed that her fears were groundless; everywhere was peaceful as they left the barren country behind and climbed into a more temperate zone. Here there were green trees and beautiful flowers, huge butterflies and exotic birds, a naturalist's paradise, but the roads were as bad as ever. Towards evening, they jolted and swayed their way into Cordoba and drew up at a small hotel.

The owner was a cousin of the diligence-driver, and so they were expected and rooms were found for them all. Pablo, who ran hither and thither earning what he could from carrying baggage, told the hotelier that Leo and Stella were together, and they were offered a double room.

'Mr Manfred is not my husband,' Stella explained,

looking round for Leo, who seemed to have disappeared.

The man did not understand, and Stella was obliged to ask Pablo to translate, adding, 'Will you please tell the *señor* I wish for a room to myself.'

He shrugged again and did as he was told, then turned back to her. 'He say, where is your duenna?'

'I haven't one. I travel alone.'

She became aware of the disapproval of the hotelier when this was translated, and was relieved when Leo appeared. 'Mr Manfred,' she said. 'Will you please make it clear to this gentleman that I am not your wife, or your mistress, and that I require a room to myself.' Then she added, as he burst into laughter, 'It is not funny.'

He made an effort to straighten his face. 'No, indeed not.'

Pablo looked from one to the other in bewilderment, then translated the hotel-owner's next words. 'He say all rooms taken; he has only one left, and it has big, big bed.'

Leo could not stop laughing, and his laugh was so infectious that in the end Stella was obliged to smile. 'Then I shall sleep in the big, big bed alone,' she said firmly, and then to Leo, 'You will have to find somewhere else.'

Leo heaved a melodramatic sigh and put his hand under Pablo's chin, making the boy look up at him. 'And where, my fine friend, are you going to lay your head tonight?'

'In the stable.'

'In the stable, eh, where it's warm and snug and you have more congenial company than human beings. Horses don't let a fellow down, do they? Horses, unlike women, aren't forever disappointing a man. I shall come with you.' He walked away with his hand on Pablo's shoulder, leaving Stella with her overnight basket at her feet, staring after them.

She bent to pick it up, but the Colonel's hand reached

it first. 'Allow me, ma'am.' He led the way up the stairs and kicked open one of the doors along the landing. 'This one, I believe.'

'Thank you.'

He put the basket on a table by the window and then turned towards her, and she realised, with a start of dismay, that he intended not to leave immediately but to engage her in conversation.

'It's my pleasure, ma'am. And I meant what I said: if you should need help, come to me.'

'Do you think I shall?'

'Oh, yes no doubt of it. It seems peaceful enough now, but make no mistake, Liberal guerrillas are everywhere.'

'Can nothing be done about them? Surely the forces of law and order . . .'

He laughed. 'The forces of law and order, ma'am, are powerless against those who are convinced they have right on their side. All the laws in the world will not defeat them. The Emperor's punitive measures only make things worse.'

'And you are in sympathy with these bandits?'

'I did not say that, Mrs Wainright. I am a businessman, nothing more.'

'What possible interest could the bandits have in me?'

'Not in you, perhaps, but in those you travel with.'

'Do you mean Mr Manfred?' she asked in surprise. 'Have the rebels some special interest in him?'

'Mebbe,' he said non-committally. 'He is Maximilian's man.'

'He is connected with the Emperor?'

'Yes, I thought you knew that. You had met him before today, hadn't you?'

'Only briefly,' she said, avoiding looking into his eyes. 'Certainly not long enough to learn anything of his background.'

'My mistake,' he said lightly. 'I certainly thought . . .' He paused, then added, 'Then I should tell you he is Maximilian's lapdog. The Emperor snaps his fingers, and Leo Manfred performs party tricks.'

'I don't think you should be talking about him in that fashion,' Stella said, some of the pieces of the puzzle of Trieste beginning to fall into place.

He shrugged. 'Just warning you, that's all.'

'Do you mean that everyone connected with the Emperor is in danger?'

'To a greater or lesser degree.'

'Even my husband?' she asked in sudden alarm.

'It depends what he's been up to.'

'He has no interest in politics, Colonel,' she said firmly, 'and neither have I. And, for your information, Mr Manfred is not escorting me.'

He smiled easily. 'I'm glad to hear it, ma'am; mighty glad.' He took a step towards her and took her hands in his. Disconcerted, she tried to back away. 'Travelling alone is a dangerous undertaking for a lady. You will attract unwelcome attention if you go on by yourself, and some men, be they bandits or so-called gentlemen, behave badly if they are frustrated.'

'And are you one of their number? Because, if so, I can tell you that I carry a pistol.'

He laughed aloud and threw up his hands in mock surrender. 'And are you also capable of firing it?'

'Of course.'

'I was going to offer you my protection, but it seems to me . . .' He stopped speaking to look at her with a smile of amusement.

'Your protection?'

'Yes. Join me and my sister for the remainder of the journey. You will be safe with us.'

'It's very kind of you,' she murmured, wondering whether he meant safe from unwelcome attention or safe from bandits; either way, she meant to maintain her independence. 'But I am quite comfortable in the diligence.' She moved to the door and held it open. 'Now, Colonel Carson, if you will excuse me, I need to wash and change for supper.'

He acknowledged himself dismissed with a slight bow.

'Think about it, Mrs Wainright. Having Leo Manfred for an escort, intentionally or otherwise, hardly helps your situation. I would not trust him with my dog.' Then, to her intense relief, he strode to the door and left.

How those men disliked each other, she thought, as she prepared for bed that night, with a chest of drawers pushed firmly against the door. They had all sat round one big table for their evening meal and there had been a great deal of jollity, but the undercurrents of mutual suspicion and attempts to score off each other were very obvious, at least to Stella. The Colonel despised Leo, and Leo distrusted the American. And beneath Leo's apparent good humour there was a certain wariness, a quickness to rise to anger, like a storm blowing up on a calm day, and just as easily spent. His eyes held suspicion, and something else she could not quite decide on, but which seemed to be hurt or sadness. Who or what had hurt him so badly that he had to build a hedge round himself, a prickly impenetrable hedge? A woman, perhaps?

Her reaction to that thought, coming to her so suddenly, took her by surprise and, taking refuge in action, she went to the window and flung it open. She stood there for a long time, looking out across the moon-bathed town, trying to calm herself, before climbing into bed and covering herself with a thin sheet. It had been a long, tiring day, and even her confused thoughts could not keep her awake. Next morning, she was not sure if she had dreamed the muffled sound of voices and horses in the middle of the night, or whether they had been real.

As soon as breakfast was over, she took her overnight basket outside to where the mules were being harnessed to the diligence and the Colonel's carriage stood ready to leave. Carson was talking earnestly to the driver of the diligence, but quickly broke off when he saw her, doffing his hat to her and smiling easily. 'Good morning, Mrs Wainright. I trust you slept well?'

'Excellently, thank you.'

'And Mr Manfred?'

She looked at him sharply, and said coldly, 'I have no idea. I haven't seen Mr Manfred this morning to ask him. In fact, I have not seen him since he went to the stable with Pablo last night.'

He recognised the rebuff for what it was, and put out a hand to touch her arm. 'I humbly ask pardon, but it does seem as though the gentleman in question has left to continue his journey by some other means. He did not spend the night in the stable, and he is certainly not here now.'

She looked round as though to conjure Leo up from empty air, but the only other person in sight was Pablo, who hopped impatiently from one foot to the other, scanning the empty road.

'Where is Mr Manfred?' Stella called to him.

'I no know, *Señora*,' he said. 'He come soon. You wait, eh?'

'I shouldn't,' the Colonel said. 'He's long gone.'

Stella was reminded of the sounds she had heard in the night. Had they been made by the departing Leo? 'It's of no consequence to me where he is,' she said. 'I shall leave with everyone else.'

'Travel with us,' the Colonel said. 'You'll have a much less bumpy ride, I can promise you.' He turned to his sister, who had just joined them. 'Martha, my dear, it seems that Mr Manfred has been so ungallant as to leave Mrs Wainright without saying goodbye. I've suggested that she would find the journey more congenial if she travelled with us.'

'Please do; we shall enjoy your company,' Martha said. 'You can tell us all about England.'

The other travellers were coming from the hotel and taking their places to continue the journey, and Stella, knowing that none of them spoke English and she would have no one to talk to, decided to accept the invitation.

Colonel Carson ordered his driver to fetch her trunk and went to open the baggage compartment to receive it. It was then Stella noticed that two of the large boxes that had been loaded on the train at Paso del Macho had gone. Before following the Colonel's sister and her elderly duenna into the coach, she glanced up at the roof; only a small box and a couple of baskets were strapped to it. But it was not her concern, and she soon forgot it when Carson joined them and gave the order to proceed.

As they moved off, Stella glanced back at the other coach, just as Leo galloped up on a sweat-lathered horse. She found herself letting out a long breath of relief, but neither Carson nor his sister suggested that she might like to change her mind and return to the other vehicle. She sat back in her seat, determined to enjoy the ride and the magnificent scenery.

Leo dismounted and watched the Colonel's coach disappearing, cursing aloud and wishing he had turned back earlier because the chase had been a complete waste of time. Now, to add to his concern, Stella had gone off with the American. Why, of all the people in the whole of Mexico to choose for an escort, did she have to take up with the ex-Confederate? Did she know what she was doing? Did she know the danger? She was new to Mexico, she did not understand the situation at all and it was more likely that the man had chosen her, picked her out for some nefarious reason of his own. But what? And why?

Standing in the middle of the road, asking himself questions he could not answer, was also a waste of time. He took the horse to the hotel stable-boy, beckoned to Pablo, who joined him eagerly, and together they boarded the diligence.

He dozed fitfully as the old coach jolted along in the wake of the Colonel's coach, but it soon left them a long way behind and they had not caught up with it by nightfall. He became resigned to the fact that he would not be able to see Stella and warn her until they reached Mexico City.

She had matured since Trieste and become a poised

and confident woman, able to hold her own with anyone. But the qualities that had attracted him to her then were still evident—her spirit of independence, her honesty, and, he suspected, her sense of adventure, which was one of the reasons he was so concerned for her now. What had begun in Miramar Park as an amusing and pleasant way to pass the time had become something much more serious. He had soon realised she was not the sort of girl you could kiss and forget. For more than two years he had tried and failed. But, he reminded himself, she had managed to forget him; she had married someone else and put herself out of his reach. That he did not think much of her choice of husband made no difference; she held his heart with chains that could not be broken by time and distance.

He was still thinking of her and only half listening to Pablo's excited chatter the next afternoon, when the coach came to a sudden halt and the shooting began.

CHAPTER THREE

As COLONEL CARSON had promised, Stella had a more comfortable ride than on the day before; the coach, unlike the diligence, was well sprung, and because they were climbing into the hills, it was cooler.

Here was a land of trees and flowers, oleanders, acacias, lilacs, orange and lemon trees in groves, pomegranates and bananas. Brightly plumed parrots swooped about, chattering and calling to each other; huge butterflies danced from flower to flower. The country could have been a paradise, but it was not; the whole area was neglected and overgrown. Acre upon acre of old coffee plantation grew wild and untended, and rows of cotton had gone to seed and not been picked. The haciendas of the plantation-owners were deserted and crumbling, their gardens a riot of untended roses, carnations and geraniums, interspersed with long dry grass. Magnificent churches, enormous for the size of the population they served, were falling into ruin, towering over pastel-washed adobe houses at whose doors women with impassive features stopped to stare as the carriage passed.

Sometimes they found themselves travelling alongside Mexican men wearing ponchos and sombreros, their high-backed Mexican saddles swaying from side to side with the movement of the horses. They had a languorous kind of rhythm, a steady pace which Stella felt would not alter for anything, certainly not to allow a coach to pass. Now and again they were held up behind men driving sheep or goats, but as soon as the road permitted, they overtook them.

The Colonel was impatient to reach their destination and they stopped only at pre-arranged places to change the horses, leaving the diligence with its mules far behind. Even after they reached the place where they stayed overnight, it had not caught up with them, and Stella began to wonder, a little wistfully, what had become of it, but as the Colonel explained, it was considerably slower and would have stopped for the night further back.

Stella found it difficult to believe the wild stories of bandits and guerrillas and people being hanged on the branches of roadside trees, because their journey was uneventful. As they climbed up to the plateau on which Mexico City stood, and the land showed signs of careful cultivation, the houses more lived-in, she became certain that the stories had been exaggerated. She had long since ceased to expect to see the diligence coming up behind them, and now they were nearing the end of their journey, she found herself dwelling more and more on the reason for her visit, wondering what Jimmy would say when he saw her. Would he even be there?

Mexico City, when they entered it on the evening of the third day, was a beautiful city, apparently at peace, with lights twinkling everywhere and people going about their business or their leisure in a perfectly normal way. Groups of *mariachis*, plucking the strings of their guitars, plied their trade of serenading someone else's love and the air was filled with music.

On the Colonel's recommendation, Stella took a room at the Iturbide Hotel where he and his sister were also staying, and they spent a pleasant evening together before the effects of the journey overcame her and she went to bed. She dreamed that night of Leo Manfred, who was beckoning to her, drawing her away from the security of her bed towards a distant forest, where it was hot and dark and full of strange noises. The man who beckoned suddenly changed into Colonel Carson, and he was smiling, making her follow him, even though she tried to resist.

She awoke with a start to find the candle she had left burning had blown out, and beyond her window, storm-clouds were building up, making the room hot and stuffy. She got up and went to the casement, flinging it open and gulping in great breaths of fresh air. Below her in the street, a rider had dismounted from a sweating mule and was hammering on the door. It was that which had wakened her, but while she stood undecided whether to put on a gown and find someone to let him in, the door was unbolted and he was admitted.

When she went back to bed, sleep was slow in returning, perhaps because the fearful atmosphere created by her nightmare still hung about her, but at last she dozed, only to wake with a start when a cock crowed from the wall behind the hotel, followed by a bugle-call not far away. Rain was drumming against the window and the air was cooler.

Stella rose and dressed carefully, then sat at the window to write a letter to Maximilian, begging an audience. While working on the museum project, her father and Jimmy had been given rooms at Chapultepec Castle, the Emperor's home near Mexico City, but she was convinced that when her father died, her husband had left. The Emperor should be able to tell her where he had gone. Folding and sealing the letter, she went downstairs to breakfast, pausing on the way to ask the hotel proprietor to have it delivered for her. Colonel Carson was at a table alone, and she accepted his invitation to join him.

'Now are you glad you were travelling with us and not on the diligence?' he enquired. 'Being neutral has its compensations.'

'I'm sorry,' she said, mystified. 'I don't understand.'

'Then you haven't heard?'

He must have known perfectly well that she had just come down from her room and could not have heard anything, and she concluded that he was enjoying baiting her, like a cat with a mouse. But her curiosity had been aroused, as he knew it would be, and she asked, 'Heard what, Colonel?'

'There is no need for such formality, please call me Redford.'

'What should I have heard?' she persisted.

'The diligence was waylaid by guerrillas yesterday.'

Stella's heart almost stopped beating, but he obviously meant to keep her in suspense until she had made some comment, so she forced herself to sound calm as she asked, 'What happened?'

'The driver rode in on one of the mules this morning to report it. He says he is the lone survivor.'

'No other survivors!' She found herself gripping the edge of the table, using it to keep herself upright. 'You can't mean that! There must be some mistake.'

'I'm only telling you what the driver said. The coach was attacked by about ten men, who killed everyone and set the vehicle on fire.' He did not sound at all shocked. 'I'm afraid this sort of thing happens so frequently that we are becoming used to it.'

Used to it! How could he be so uncaring? People were dead. She tried telling herself it meant that Leo was dead, but even though she had seen Leo climb aboard the diligence herself, she could not make herself believe it. And Pablo. Had they murdered an innocent child? They were not men, these guerrillas, but monsters.

'Why?' she asked.

He shrugged. 'Perhaps they thought the diligence was carrying money. Bandits, guerrillas—it makes no difference what they are called—always need money for food and ammunition.'

'They will be caught and punished?'

He laughed mirthlessly. 'It's highly unlikely.'

'It's monstrous!' she cried. 'What sort of a country is this, which allows such things to happen?'

'My dear Stella, you were warned what to expect.'

'But yesterday everywhere seemed so peaceful.' She still could not comprehend that it had happened, that Leo, Pablo and all her earlier travelling companions had all gone, gone for ever. Her body sagged and her vision blurred, and she knew she could not remain dry-eyed. 'Why did the driver come here to report it?' she asked suddenly. 'Why not go to the barracks?'

She saw his eyes harden momentarily and it frightened her, but then he said, 'What makes you think he came here?'

'I heard someone arrive in the middle of the night.'

'A late traveller.'

'Then how did you hear the news?'

'From the waiter, who heard it from the man who delivered the bread this morning, who heard it from the barracks, where he also delivers bread.' His answer was glib and could so easily be true, and she had no desire to quarrel with him. At that moment he seemed to be her only friend.

'I think I'll return to my room,' she said, rising, but the weakness in her legs made her sway, and he was quickly at her side.

'Let me help you.'

He put his arm about her shoulders and walked with her to the foot of the stairs, where she stopped him from going any further.

'I can manage now,' she said. 'And you must have more important things to do.'

'I can think of nothing more important than looking after you,' he said softly. 'And nothing would give me greater pleasure than to have you lean on me.'

She was shocked by his familiarity. 'Colonel Carson, you forget yourself.'

'Redford, please,' he corrected her, taking his hand from her shoulder and letting it drop to his side. 'I beg pardon; I was simply offering you my help. You are alone in this country.'

'Colonel Carson, I have a husband . . .'

'You don't know where he is.'

'I shall soon find out,' she said, wondering how he knew that. 'I have written to the Emperor requesting an audience; he will tell me where to find him.'

'You can't go wandering all over Mexico alone, it isn't safe. Surely the attack on the diligence has taught you that?'

'I won't be put off,' she said.

'Then, dear lady, allow me to be your escort. I have some business in Mexico City and I must take my sister home to Carlota Colony, then I am entirely at your disposal.'

'You are very kind,' she said, thankful for at least one friend. 'But I can't put you to so much trouble.'

'My pleasure, ma'am, my pleasure.'

She thanked him again and went slowly up to her room, maintaining her self-control until she had shut the door behind her. Then, suddenly overwhelmed by the horror of what had happened, she flung herself across her bed and wept. She wept for her mother, for her father, for Leo and Pablo, for Jimmy and all the knocks fortune had dealt her; she wept out of loneliness and homesickness.

When the summons came from Maximilian in the middle of the afternoon, the rain had stopped, and Stella's misery had turned to a firm resolve to keep her emotions under control until she had done what she had come to Mexico to do.

She repaired the ravages of weeping by splashing her face with cold water and changed from her crumpled dress to a newly-pressed grey silk. Then she went out to the hansom she had ordered and asked the driver to take her to the cemetery, where she spent a few minutes praying at her father's graveside before returning to the cab for the journey to Chapultepec.

The castle, half an hour's drive from the centre of the city, stood on a hill surrounded by a great park and gleaming lakes. The gardens were intersected by paths lined with marble and bronze statues; gilt monograms hung over the doors and windows and the ornate balconies blazed with colourful trailing plants. A servant conducted her to a small sitting-room that had french windows giving on to a private corner of the beautiful garden where Maximilian was playing with his three-year-old adopted son Augustin.

There was a child's swing near by, and sitting on it,

idly moving to and fro, was one of the most beautiful
women Stella had ever seen. She was about thirty, a year
or two younger than the Emperor, with a clear, golden
complexion and even features, and her hair, drawn
straight back into a coil at the nape of her neck, was jet
black and smooth as silk. Her green eyes were lazily
watchful. She wore a white *huipil*, a sheathlike garment
that clung to her figure and showed off the round
contours of a perfect body.

When Stella was announced, Maximilian patted the
boy's rump and gave him a gentle push. 'Go now, my
son.'

Obediently the boy left and the Emperor turned
towards Stella, who dropped a deep curtsy.

'We were surprised to receive a letter from you
written in Mexico, Mrs Wainright,' he said in English.
'But you are welcome.'

'My husband has not replied to my letters, your
Majesty,' she said, noticing how ill he looked; it was as
though he had not slept for several nights. His eyes had
an unnatural brightness, and his cheeks were hollow and
devoid of colour. He was also a great deal thinner than
when she had seen him in Trieste. He wore loose-fitting
Mexican trousers with silver buttons up the outside
seams, a frilled shirt with no cravat, and carpet slippers.
She did not know whether to be shocked or flattered that
he should allow her to see him like that. 'I believe he left
Mexico City after my father's accident. I have to find
him. I hoped you would be able to tell me where he has
gone.'

He waved her to a wrought-iron garden chair, ignoring the Mexican woman, though Stella sensed he was
very aware of her presence. 'Sit down, my dear. We are
deeply sorry about Sir Peter's accident; it was a great
shock to us all. Naturally, we shall do all we can to help
you, but as to where your husband is at this moment, we
do not know. He set off for Yucatan three months ago,
and we have not heard from him since.'

'Yucatan, your Majesty?'

'Yes, it is one of our more distant provinces, a wild, beautiful country full of ancient ruins and great forests, a paradise for a natural historian. He and Sir Peter had planned to go on a specimen-hunting expedition on our behalf, but after the accident, Mr Wainright decided to go alone.'

'Then I shall go after him.'

'It would be better, Mrs Wainright, if you stayed in Mexico City until enquiries can be made about his exact whereabouts.'

'But, your Majesty,' she said, made bolder by her frustration, 'he may be in danger.'

He looked at her sharply. 'Why do you say that? He came to Mexico at our invitation, to do work we asked him to do, so why should he be in danger?' He sounded displeased that she should even hint at such a thing. 'This is a peaceful country, and any small problems we have will soon be overcome.' He paused and turned to the woman. 'Is that not so, Josefina?'

'Oh, yes,' the Mexican said, smiling.

'But is it?' Stella queried boldly. 'Only yesterday the diligence from Paso del Macho was set upon, and everyone . . .' She could hardly bear to think of it, let alone speak of it, but she was determined to make her point. 'Everyone on board, except the Mexican driver, was killed.'

'We have not heard this,' he said sharply. 'Why has no one told us? Perhaps you have been misinformed. There are always wild rumours . . .'

'I don't think so,' she said. 'If it had not been for Colonel Carson, I would have been among their number. As it was, Mr Manfred . . .'

'Leo?' he asked, sitting forward in his chair to look into her face. 'Leo was on the diligence? Are you saying he has been murdered?'

'Yes, your Majesty.'

He slumped back in his chair and shut his eyes, and behind her, Stella heard the woman's sharp intake of breath. 'No, no, I can't believe it!' He seemed to have forgotten her and was talking to himself. 'I sent him to Europe with the Empress; I did not expect him to return so soon. Oh, my poor faithful friend.'

So that had been Leo's mission! Stella had heard that the Empress had returned to Europe and even rumours that the life she led in Mexico had driven her mad; if there was any truth in that, only someone Maximilian trusted implicitly would have been sent to escort her. Stella would never have guessed that Leo was so close to the royal family, though Carson had hinted as much. 'I'm sorry to be the bearer of the news,' she said.

'You knew him?'

'I met him in Trieste, your Majesty.'

'I am sorry,' he said softly. 'We are both the poorer. He was a faithful servant and a staunch friend, and he had been doing very valuable work for us in Mexico.'

'But the other people on the coach were innocent travellers,' she said. 'The perpetrators should be caught and purnished.'

'Mexico will punish its own,' Josefina said, from the swing. 'You need not concern yourself with our affairs.'

Maximilian turned and opened his mouth to rebuke her, but changed his mind and turned back to Stella. 'Tell me all you know.' His voice was stronger now. 'How did it happen that you were not also in the diligence?'

He was silent for a long time after she finished telling him, then at last he said, 'I shall consider what is to be done.'

'But . . .' she began, but he waved a hand, dismissing her.

'Leave us now. We have much to do.' He sighed. 'Life must go on. We must not allow these criminals to upset the normal routine of state and government; that's just what they would like to happen. We shall not allow it.'

She rose and curtsied, stifling her disappointment that he had not reacted more positively. He did not appear angry even, just hopelessly resigned.

'May I go to my father's rooms, your Majesty?'

'Of course. Josefina will take you; won't you, my dear?'

Josefina left the swing and moved towards them with the grace and suppleness of a cat and, like a cat, she had claws! Stella sensed it with a kind of intuition that told her to be wary of her, even though her smile was friendly as she said, 'Come with me.'

Stella followed her indoors, along the corridors of the castle, lined with beautiful pictures, rare vases and fine furniture, and up to the first floor.

'Did you know my father and husband, *Señor-ita* . . .?'

'Gonzales,' the woman said. 'My name is Josefina Isabella María Gonzales. And yes, I met them both while they were working here.'

'It's still difficult to believe Papa has really gone,' Stella said, with a lump in her throat. 'Were you here at the time?'

'Yes, but I cannot tell you anything about it, your husband was the only witness. All I know is that he was cutting up a specimen with a very sharp scalpel, and it slipped.'

'Have you been to Yucatan?' Stella changed the subject abruptly. She had read the account of the accident in an official letter sent to her mother and knew that the only person who could tell her the details was Jimmy. And he had disappeared.

'My home is there.'

'You speak excellent English.'

'I spent some years in New Orleans, Mrs Wainright.' She pushed open the door of a large room that looked out over the gardens to a distant lake. 'This was their sitting-room. I believe that door leads to Sir Peter's room and that one to Mr Wainright's.' She pointed across the room.

Although the room was tidy, it showed evidence of her father's occupation; a photograph of her mother, a book, a flower pressed between layers of absorbent paper, a folder of drawings, a huge wooden box, labelled ready to be despatched to England. Surprisingly, there was very little she could identify as belonging to Jimmy; it was almost as if he had never been there. She sat at a desk by the window and turned over the leaves of the portfolio. Unlike Leo, her father was no artist but he was meticulous in detail, and here were drawings of trees and shrubs, with their leaves and seeds, all neatly annotated. But one was not her father's work. It was not even a botanical drawing, but a picture of a pyramid almost hidden by the foliage of dense jungle. A broad stone stairway, flanked by two long snakes with fanged open mouths, led up to a temple. In the foreground were two huge obelisks covered with hieroglyphics.

She held it out to Josefina, who stood in the doorway, watching her. 'Do you have any idea where this might be?'

As the Mexican took it, Stella thought she detected a look of surprise on her face, but it was gone in an instant, as she said carefully, 'It could be anywhere. Mexico is full of such places.'

'But you do have some idea?'

Josefina shrugged. 'It looks like one of the drawings the earlier explorers made when they were in Palenche years ago.'

'I feel sure that this is where Jimmy has gone.'

'Why? It's just a drawing.'

'I have an intuition that it is important. Don't you ever feel things like that? As if you were being told something from beyond the grave?'

'If you don't mind my saying so, that's fanciful nonsense, Mrs Wainright. You would do better to return to Europe and not meddle in the affairs of Mexico.'

'I have no wish to meddle. I want to find my husband, that's all.'

'Take care you do not find more than you bargained for.'

'What do you mean?'

Josefina shrugged and handed back the drawing,

which Stella folded carefully and slipped into her hand-bag. 'It was a friendly warning, no more.'

'Well, you will not mind if I take no heed of it, will you?' Stella took a last look round the room, and said, 'I am ready to go now.'

Together they returned to the marble-floored hall, where they suddenly came face to face with Leo, who had just come in from outside.

'Leo!' Stella cried, moving towards him. 'Thank God you are safe!' She put out a hand to touch his arm, almost as if to reassure herself that he was real and not a ghost. He winced with pain, and she dropped her hand to her side. 'You're hurt!'

He paused and turned towards her, and she realised with a shock that his eyes were red-rimmed with exhaustion and his face was cut and bruised. 'It's only a scratch.'

'What happened?'

'Nothing of importance,' he said lightly. 'Did you find your husband?'

'No, he has gone to Yucatan.'

'What are you going to do?'

'Go and find him; what else?'

'You are determined on that, then?'

'Yes, as soon as I can make the arrangements.'

'I don't suppose it will do any good to advise you against it?'

'None at all,' she said firmly. 'Señorita Gonzales has already tried that.'

'Leo,' Josefina put in quickly, 'don't you think you should report to Maximilian? Mrs Wainright told him you were dead, and he is very upset.' It was almost as though she were accusing Stella of lying, but before Stella could protest, Josefina had taken Leo's arm and, looking up into his face, smiled and added, 'Then you can tell us all your adventures.'

'Yes, I must.' He passed his hand over his brow in a gesture of weariness and looked at Stella. 'If you wait, I shall accompany you back to your hotel.'

'There is no need; I have a hired cab waiting.'

She bade them goodbye and walked the length of the corridor to the big outer doors. On the step, she paused to adjust her hat and stole a glance behind her. Josefina had linked her arm in Leo's, and together they were walking towards the royal apartments, heads together, one sleek cat and one black-haired lion.

Josefina was pulling on Leo's arm, and he knew she was right; he must report to the Emperor, but he was reluctant to let Stella go. During the whole journey from Vera Cruz she had never been far from his thoughts, and that, he realised, could be dangerous, not only to the way he did his job, but for his peace of mind. He had been thinking of her while the diligence jolted along in the wake of the Colonel's coach, and in the half state between waking and sleeping, it seemed that she was still sitting beside him and he did not want to open his eyes. But he had been forced into action when they had come to a sudden halt and the shooting began. Now he was back at his post by the Emperor's side and he must concentrate on his work.

Much to Josefina's chagrin, he insisted on seeing Maximilian alone. She had no position in court and the Emperor did not acknowledge her in public, but in private she was his companion of the moment, and she hated being shut out of the conversation.

'We are delighted to see you, Leo,' Maximilian said, as soon as she had left them. 'Sit down and tell us what happened.'

Leo, whose legs were beginning to buckle, was glad to obey. 'I was returning to Mexico City on the diligence, your Majesty, when we stopped just after leaving Orizaba because the driver said there was something wrong with the brake. It was while he was supposedly fixing it that we were attacked. The bandits appeared from nowhere, ten of them, riding their horses round us and shooting indiscriminately with brand-new rifles. The mules broke loose, and the coach toppled over.' His account was given without emotion and gave no indication of the anger and helplessness he had felt at the time.

'I was given to understand that only the driver survived.'

Leo laughed suddenly. 'The driver took to his heels, or rather the heels of one of the mules, so fast that he had no way of knowing if there were survivors or not!'

'Go on.'

'It was quite a scrap.' Leo smiled wryly at the memory. 'Few of us were armed, and those that were had little ammunition. One by one, those who had not been killed when the coach overturned were massacred until there was only me, one other who was wounded, and Pablo still alive.'

'Pablo?'

'A little Mexican orphan, your Majesty. He seems to have appointed himself my protector. When the position was over-run, we ran to cover in some bushes a little way from the coach and lay low. We were overlooked when the attackers searched the coach and set it alight.'

'What were they looking for?'

'I was bringing gold and despatches from Europe, your Majesty. I'm sorry that I could not prevent them from taking the gold, but I still have the despatches. Everything else was destroyed.' He handed a small document-case to the Emperor, who put it to one side to open later.

'Go on.'

'After they had gone,' Leo went on, 'I sent Pablo back to a hacienda we had passed on the road to get help for the injured man, then I set off after the culprits. I wanted proof of who they were, who had told them I might be bringing the gold, and who had supplied them with their guns.'

'And did you find it?'

'No, your Majesty. I have nothing but a sketch I made of one of them, and he was not the leader, though I have a strong suspicion who was behind it.'

'Suspicion is not enough, Leo.'

'No, your Majesty, but I shall find the proof, I am determined. Mexico must be made safe!'

The Emperor smiled at Leo's vehemence, then said gently, 'Go on with your account. What happened next?'

'I went back to the diligence, hoping to find the second of the two mules and ride it to Mexico City, but it had bolted. It was while I was deciding what to do next that Pablo arrived, leading a horse he had borrowed from the hacienda-owner. He told me the last survivor had died of his wounds and he had left him to the *señor* to bury, and had come to help me.' He laughed suddenly. 'He is amazing, that one! He seems to think I can't manage without him. I had to take him up behind me.'

'Where is this young orphan now?'

'At my quarters, your Majesty, fast asleep.'

Maximilian smiled. 'You have a kind heart, my friend.' He paused, then added, 'We had a visit from Mrs Wainright today.'

'Yes, your Majesty, I met her as I came in.'

'She is a very beautiful young lady, but very outspoken. She had the temerity to suggest that *I* should hunt out the rebels who attacked your coach and punish them. She implied that we could not keep order. It displeased us.'

'I'm sorry,' Leo said, feeling he had to apologise for Stella. 'I expect she was concerned for . . .' He stopped, wondering momentarily if she had given him a thought, and went on, 'For the other passengers. She is a gentle girl, unused to such violence.'

Maximilian smiled. It softened his features and lit his eyes, so that it was easy to see why he attracted the unfailing loyalty of those closest to him. 'That is why I forgive her. But you know, Leo, she cannot be allowed to wander about Mexico by herself.'

'No, your Majesty.'

'She wants to go to Yucatan to find her husband. You

had better make arrangements to go with her.'

'But, your Majesty, she might not agree. Indeed, I am sure she will not.'

'Then you must persuade her.'

'But, your Majesty, there is so much to be done here . . .'

'We do not want to hear objections, Leo. She will need a trustworthy escort, and to tell the truth, I myself am a little curious about Mr Wainright's long absence. Go and make the arrangements and then tell Mrs Wainright.' He paused, then added, 'You can invite her to the banquet at the National Palace the day after tomorrow. It will be time enough to set out after that.'

Reluctantly Leo left the room to obey. It was all very well for the Emperor to issue him with orders, but Stella did not have to obey them, and he wondered what her reaction would be. But when he arrived at the Iturbide Hotel, he learned that she had not returned from her visit to Chapultepec. While he had been talking to the Emperor she had completely disappeared, and he was out of his mind with worry.

CHAPTER FOUR

STELLA LEANED back in the hansom taking her back to the hotel and shut her eyes, trying to shut out the picture of Leo and Josefina with their heads together, almost as if they were lovers. Yet she should not have been surprised. After all, she had found someone else since those far-off days in Trieste, so why not Leo, too?

They were on the outskirts of the city when the cab suddenly stopped and she became aware of a great deal of activity in the street. She leaned forward to look out of the window, and discovered that they were being held up by a crowd which had gathered to watch in silent hostility as a group of French and Mexican soldiers searched the buildings, herding the inhabitants into the street while they ransacked their homes.

'What are they doing?' she asked the driver.

He shrugged, not understanding. She left the cab, dismissed the driver and pushed her way through the throng to where a group of men, women and childen stood, looking lost and bewildered, outside their tenement home. Flimsy furniture and rough pottery were being hurled from the upper windows. The women were weeping, and the two men, restrained by the rifles of the Mexican soldiers guarding them, could do nothing but shout and curse. They were knocked down with the butts of the rifles.

Stella was so angry that she did not stop to think, but even if she had, it would have made no difference; she could not stand by and do nothing. She darted forward and addressed the French commander of the group, who sat his horse, watching his orders being obeyed. 'Stop that! Stop it at once! Can't you see they are only poor people? What harm have they done?'

She had spoken in English, and no one understood.

The soldiers turned to point their guns at her, while the Mexican family looked on, more bewildered than ever. Stella, faced with two rifles, halted but did not retreat.

There was a shout from inside the house, and then a soldier came out holding aloft an ancient sporting gun, which he took to the officer. The captain hardly glanced at it before giving the order for the two men in the group of civilians to be singled out. They were dragged from the arms of the hysterical women, stood against the wall of their own home, and shot.

It was done so quickly and so callously that Stella was, for a minute, dumbfounded; then, stung to action, she rushed over to the Frenchman and began berating him with a flow of English. Though she tried, her French was not equal to the task of conveying her abhorrence of what had been done. Frustrated, she tugged at his sleeve. He shrugged her off.

'I will make you understand,' she said furiously. 'I cannot believe you have been ordered to shoot people on a whim like that. Look at them! Do they look like criminals?' She pointed at the women and children, clinging to each other and wailing in their misery. 'How could you! You are an unfeeling monster!'

He was doing his best to ignore her and that made her angrier than ever. In the absence of a parasol, she set about him with her handbag, quite forgetting that it contained her tiny pistol. The force of her blow rocked his head back, and he clapped a hand to his chin where a tiny trickle of blood began to flow. It was no good apologising or maintaining she had not meant to hurt him, because she had meant it—and in any case he would not believe her. She stood her ground and glared at him angrily.

His answer to that was to order her arrest. She found herself being propelled so violently forward by a push with the butt end of a rifle carried by one of the Mexican soldiers that she stumbled and almost fell, but regaining her balance, walked with dignity to a tumbril that waited at the corner of the street. It was already half full of detainees, and when she clambered aboard, the driver flicked the reins, and the old horse set off at a walk. No one spoke. Stella, still too angry to appreciate her own precarious position, looked back to see the bereaved family dragging the bodies of the two men into the house.

The prisoners were herded into one of the city's gaols, where they were searched and interrogated. Stella's little pistol excited a great deal of interest and she was questioned by more than one prison officer, but as they spoke in Spanish, she could only guess what they were asking. She realised how foolish she had been to carry the gun; it put an end to any hope she might have had of being let off with a caution.

'Find someone who speaks English,' she said, when her attempts to explain herself in a mixture of French and English failed. '*Inglés*. Don't you understand?'

They talked among themselves while she stood waiting to see what they would do, wondering with a certain amount of bravado if they would use physical violence on her. Whether it was her manner or their frustration at their inability to communicate, she had no idea, but they gave up at last and signalled to the dour-faced turnkey to take her away. It was not until she found herself in a crowded prison cell and the door had clanged shut behind her with a noise that echoed round the stone walls that she realised the seriousness of her position. No one knew where she was.

Most of the time the cell, which was below ground level, was dark, and it was almost impossible to tell night from day. She gauged the time by the intervals between the arrival of the rancid meals and the changing of the guards. She could not eat the food, which was so highly spiced with chilli that it made her throat burn, and she was reluctant to drink the water that the inmates scooped with their hands from the bucket in the corner. She felt hungry and thirsty, but most of all filthy.

Was this how people disappeared without trace? Had the same sort of thing happened to Jimmy? Was Leo aware of what was going on? If so, he was as bad as the French officer who had arrested her. But surely they would do nothing to harm foreign nationals? There would be a hue and cry from the government back home if they did.

She tried talking to the other inmates, but no one understood her and she could not understand them. Even her few words of Spanish were useless. Sitting in the dark and the dirt, she reflected on the events of the last few days, trying to make sense of everything, but failing. This was a barbaric country, and the sooner she found Jimmy and they left together, the happier she would be. But that was a futile wish while she was locked up and there was no one to set her free. Not even Leo. With nothing else to do, she started going over their last conversation, but that left her with more questions than it answered, and she began to wonder if his appearance at Chapultepec had been a dream, a figment of her imagination. But Josefina had been no dream, and her last sight of the two of them with their heads together had not been a dream either.

For two days she alternated between periods of black despair and raging anger until she thought she would go mad, but then as if in answer to her prayers, the door was thrown open and the guard shouted, 'English *señora*! Where is English woman?'

Her neighbour nudged her. '*Señora! Señora!*'

Slowly Stella got to her feet and moved to where the guard stood, holding the door open with his booted foot, while maintaining his rifle at the ready, half expecting trouble.

'I am Stella Wainright,' she said, mustering some dignity, in spite of her unkempt appearance.

'You come,' he said, pushing her into the corridor.

She stood unmoving as he locked the door behind them and then indicated that she should precede him up the stone steps. At the top he opened a door, pushed her through it and left her. The small room was lit by a smoking oil-lamp and had a table and two chairs in its centre. She stood uncertainly just inside the door, then a movement in the room made her spin round. A cavalry officer was standing to one side of her, but this was no olive-skinned, dark-eyed Mexican; this man had a mane of black hair and blue eyes, and he wore the full-dress uniform of an Austrian Hussar with its red jacket and gold braid.

'Oh, Leo!' she cried, and without stopping to think, fell into his arms. 'Thank God you've come!'

He stood holding her without speaking, and she could feel the strong beating of his heart against her ear and felt safe and warm. Then her mind suddenly cleared and she tore herself away almost jerkily, embarrassed by her action. He was in the uniform of a soldier, and though she had never thought of him as a military man, it probably meant he was on official business. Her spine stiffened, and she spoke calmly. 'Why are you here?'

He looked at her as though surprised by the question, then turned and opened the door, ushering her out into the corridor. 'Come,' he said. 'We must hurry.'

'How did you find me?'

'I went to the Iturbide to talk to you two days ago. Carson told me you had not returned from your visit to Chapultepec. He assumed that the Emperor had invited you to stay.'

'What did you want to talk to me about?'

'I had a message for you from the Emperor, but that was before you got yourself into this pickle. Now I don't know what will happen.'

'I'm sorry,' she said contritely.

'You know,' he said, as he hurried her along the corridors, 'you make it very difficult for anyone to help you.'

She bridled. 'I have not asked for your help!'

'I was referring to the Emperor.'

'Was it the Emperor who found out where I was?' she asked. 'Surely he has more important things to do than to worry about me.'

'No, you have Pablo to thank for that.'

'Pablo?' she said eagerly. 'Pablo is alive?'

'Yes, and as undaunted as ever. I had been questioning everyone along your way and learned nothing, but Pablo heard about a family who had been defended by an Englishwoman, and from the description, it could only have been you.' He smiled wryly. 'No one but you would have acted so impulsively.'

'I couldn't do anything to help them.'

'Why should you help them?' His voice was harsh. 'The men were rebels, hiding arms against the day when they would rise against the Emperor.'

'That's nonsense!' she said. 'They were just a poor peasant family who happened to have an old sporting gun. I doubt very much if it could even be fired.'

'Owning guns without permission is against the law and punishable by death,' he said. 'They call it the Black Decree.'

'Execution without trial?'

'Yes, if the circumstances warrant it.'

'And am I not to have a trial?'

'No. Stop asking questions, and hurry.'

'You mean I'll be condemned without one? On what charge?'

'Carrying a firearm and intervening in the affairs of Mexico.'

The idea was so preposterous that she managed to laugh. 'The pistol was for my own protection, and you can't say, after the ambush of the diligence, that I would never need it. As for intervening, how can you think I would do anything against the government of a country where I am only a guest?'

'It doesn't matter what I think,' he said, as they emerged on to the street. 'There are others prepared to testify that you are in league with the enemies of the state.'

'But you can tell them that I have no interest in the affairs of Mexico beyond finding my husband and returning with him to England.'

'Your behaviour contradicts that.' His voice was clipped and impersonal.

'This is nonsense!' she said, coming to a halt. 'I won't go another step until you tell me where you are taking me.'

'The Emperor wants to question you himself. I am sent to escort you to him.'

Sent to escort her, she noted; he did not come of his own accord. The pleasure and relief she had felt at seeing him a few minutes before faded. 'When?' she asked.

'Now.'

She looked down at her grubby dress. 'I can hardly go like this!'

'I'll take you back to the hotel to change first.'

She turned from him and said sharply, 'Then let's get it over with.'

She began walking so fast that he was taken by surprise, and it was a moment or two before he made a move to catch her. 'I'm sorry, Stella, but I have to obey orders.' He indicated the closed carriage that stood waiting.

She turned back towards the vehicle, still seething. 'And does your zeal to obey orders blind you to what is going on around you, to hate and greed and fear? No, not fear,' she corrected herself, 'downright terror. You talk of terrorists in hiding in the hills. I can tell you there are greater terrorists in this city, and they wear French and Mexican uniforms!'

'Please don't speak so loudly,' he said, hurrying her into the coach. 'What you are saying is treasonable, and only adds to your offences.'

'Offences!' she cried, as they settled into their seats facing each other, and moved off. 'I am English and I am speaking in English. If you like, I'll repeat it in French.'

He looked alarmed and leaned forward to take her hand. 'No, please don't, Stella. For your own sake, have some discretion.'

'You think I should have turned away from those poor

people, is that it? I should have stood by and seen two men shot in cold blood in front of their wives and children, and then walked away as if nothing had happened? You do not know me very well if you think I could do that.'

'It would have been better for you if you had. You would have saved yourself an unpleasant stay in gaol, and not embarrassed the Emperor.'

'It was worth it!' she said defiantly. 'It was worth it if it opens his eyes to the truth. Maximilian may or may not know all that is being done in his name, but the people see the actions of the army as his actions. As far as they are concerned, the Emperor gives the orders, therefore it is the Emperor who oppresses them. Being locked in that prison cell, with a whole host of ordinary people who had probably done nothing more than make a justifiable protest, taught me a lot about how the poor people are treated.'

'Did it also teach you to mind your own business?' He laughed suddenly, and it was almost like his old humorous self breaking through. 'No, I'll wager it didn't! And just because Maximilian ordered your release, it is not the end of the affair, you know. The French officer you assaulted is furious, to say the least, and demanding your punishment.'

'Assaulted!' Her laugh was almost hysterical. 'Is that what he said?'

'Yes. You humiliated him in public in front of his men, and he won't forget that.'

'And do you believe that I, a weak and defenceless woman, who swoons when the sun gets too hot, am capable of such a thing?'

He smiled grimly. 'I can never think of you as weak and defenceless! You have your own weapons to maim and hurt, as I know to my cost, but I think the incident may have been exaggerated. Let us hope Maximilian believes that.'

He sat back in his seat and regarded her with his frank blue eyes, but she could not read what was behind them.

His moods changed like the shifting sands and she felt insecure, groping for a foothold on firm ground.

'Why are you in that uniform?'

'I am a soldier. I have a job to do.'

'In an army that shoots civilians for no reason at all!' she retorted. 'Would you ever do that?'

'They had a reason. And yes, I would if I had to.'

'Why?'

'You ask me why?' he asked in surprise. 'Maximilian is my emperor and my employer; he is also my friend. Would you have me turn my back on him? Besides, it gives me a certain authority to do what I have to do, to ask questions and insist on answers. Without it, I could not have taken you from the prison.'

'It doesn't suit you,' she said stubbornly and untruthfully. 'You look much better in a paint-stained smock with a palette in your hand, not a weapon.'

There was nothing he could say in answer to that, and they fell silent. He leaned back against the cushions and his eyelids drooped; he looked so exhausted that she suddenly felt very sorry for him. Whatever the rights and wrongs of Maximilian's cause and whatever part he had to play in it, he was totally committed and he did not deserve the complication she was putting in his way. Did he believe she had no wish to embarrass the Emperor? She decided that there was no point in trying to convince him, but she had better learn to behave with more circumspection—and she ought to apologise to the Emperor for the trouble she had caused him.

When they arrived at the hotel, he ordered the carriage to wait and escorted her inside, stopping at the desk for her key. She had no thought of eluding him or trying to escape, but he must have thought it a possibility because he took a very firm hold of her arm as they crossed the floor towards the staircase. The door to the salon was open, and through it Stella caught a glimpse of the Colonel deep in conversation with a woman who had her back to them.

He looked up and saw her and, excusing himself to his

companion, hurried across. 'Stella! You're safe! You had us all worried. They didn't hurt you?'

She smiled, 'No, I am dirty, but in good health.'

His companion rose lazily and turned to join them, and Stella realised with a start that it was Josefina. She was dressed in a magnificent deep green velvet crinoline and wore rubies at her throat and on the comb in her hair. Leo's grip on Stella's arm tightened, making her gasp with pain. She looked up at him; his blue eyes were steely and his jaw rigid as if he were controlling himself with an effort. So that was why the two men hated each other, she thought suddenly; they both loved the same woman! She felt a sharp stab of jealousy, which was like a physical pain and made her want to cry out.

'Josefina, what are you doing here?' he asked.

'I came to see if there was news of Mrs Wainright. The Colonel has been kind enough to keep me company.'

'As you see,' Leo said coolly, 'she has been released into my custody.'

'You poor lady!' Carson said, laughing. 'I can't think of anything worse.'

'Prison is much worse, I can promise you,' she said coldly.

'What did they charge you with?'

'Intervention,' she said. 'And carrying a pistol.'

'They found that, did they?'

'You knew Stella had a gun?' Leo turned on him angrily. 'You knew it, and you did nothing to warn her of the consequences?'

'I didn't know she would carry it about with her, did I? Nor that she would set about a French officer with it.'

'You should have warned her. You should have insisted that she surrender it.'

Carson laughed. 'Who am I to dictate to the lady? She would have taken no notice.' He turned to Stella, 'That's true, isn't it?'

She smiled. 'I'm afraid so.'

'What will happen to you?' he asked.

'That depends on the Emperor,' Leo put in quickly. 'Please excuse us, he is expecting us. Come, Stella.'

'Colonel,' she said, resisting Leo's attempts to make her move, 'will you do something for me?'

'Anything, my dear lady, anything,' he said promptly. 'But you agreed to call me Redford, remember?'

'Redford,' she corrected. 'If they lock me up again, will you go to the British Minister in Mexico and tell him of my plight? He will be able to put pressure on the Mexican authorities.'

'That's nonsense,' Leo said firmly. 'You won't be locked up again, unless you do something else to antagonise the authorities.'

'I'm relieved to hear it.' She turned to Redford. 'Will you take me to Yucatan?'

Leo made a sound that was almost a groan, as Redford answered, 'Yes, if you promise to come and stay with us at Carlota Colony while I make the arrangements.'

'How long will it take to get to Yucatan?'

'It depends on the vehicle and the willingness of the driver. A week or two from Carlota, at least.' He paused. 'It won't be pleasant; the jungle is uncomfortably humid and there are insects . . .'

'Oh, I don't mind that,' Stella said. 'Adversaries in the natural world don't bother me, it's men and what they do to each other that frighten me—the shooting and killing.'

He shrugged. 'A fact of life, I'm afraid, especially here in Mexico just now. But where in Yucatan do you want to go?'

'Stella, it's out of the question,' Leo interrupted, taking a firmer grip of her arm. 'Come. We are very short of time.'

She pulled herself away, angry that he should try to dictate to her. 'Palenche. That's where you said, wasn't it, Señorita Gonzales?'

Stella intercepted a glance between Redford and Josefina, a secret look which was meant to convey something—a warning, perhaps—but it was gone in an instant and she spoke pleasantly. 'I was making a guess, but yes, I think Palenche might be a good place to start.'

'Stella, please,' Leo implored her. 'You cannot afford to displease the Emperor any further by being late.'

Admitting the wisdom of his argument, she allowed herself to be led away. At the top of the stairs, he stopped to ask, 'Which is your room?'

'That one.'

She waited without speaking while he unlocked the door, pushed it open and ushered her inside, shutting it behind them.

'You're angry,' she said.

'Is it any wonder? What were you thinking of, asking Carson to take you to Yucatan?'

'Why not? He offered to help me, and I must go to Jimmy.'

'I forbid you to . . .'

'Forbid!' she interrupted him. 'Did I hear you correctly?'

'The American is not to be trusted.'

'Why not? Could it be that you're jealous because you both love the same woman?'

He looked at her sharply, then completely surprised her by chuckling softly. 'That may well be so, but this has nothing to do with a woman—any woman. It has to do with the situation in Mexico.'

'I am not concerned with the situation in Mexico,' she said, trying to control emotions which see-sawed from anger to a strong desire to fall into his arms, from frustration to the need to be reassured. 'I am entirely neutral, and so is Redford; he told me so. Besides, I owe him my life. If I had been on the diligence instead of his coach . .'

'That fact had not escaped me,' he said, striding across the room to open the wardrobe door.

'Just what are you doing?' she demanded, as he began sorting through her gowns. 'What right . . .'

'You can't go to the Emperor looking like . . .' He paused to look at her, searching for a word that would adequately describe the way she looked and the unsettling effect it was having on him. 'Like a street urchin,' he added, smiling. 'Is this all you have?'

'It's all I need. After all, I am in half-mourning for my mother, and I did not come to Mexico on a social visit. I came to see my husband, and the sooner I find him and we return to England, the better pleased I shall be.'

He took a heavy silk crinoline from her wardrobe and handed it to her. 'Wear this one. White suits you, and you do not need fancy decoration.' He turned towards her with an expression that betrayed a depth of emotion she could not understand.

'Do you enjoy being my gaoler?' she asked suddenly.

'I am not your gaoler.'

'It looks very much like it to me!'

'I'm sorry, Stella,' he said, 'but you brought it on yourself. Now take those filthy clothes off and put this on.'

'And if I won't?'

He took hold of her shoulders and twisted her round. 'Then I shall have to do it for you.'

She struggled as he began unhooking her dress, but his grip was firm enough to hurt, and when her dress fell away at her feet, she was effectively imprisoned by its folds. 'How dare you!' Her voice was low and controlled. 'How dare you behave like a common barrack-room soldier!'

'Because I am a soldier,' he said grimly, fumbling with the ties of her petticoats. 'And you are enough to drive any sane man mad.'

'Just because I dared to criticise your beloved Emperor?' She twisted herself out of his grasp. 'I can do more than that, I promise you! When Jimmy and I return to Europe, we shall tell the world what a barbaric regime this is.'

'If you go on like that, you will never return,' he said. 'Can't you understand?'

'You wouldn't . . .' She went to step out of her skirt, tripped over it, and fell forward. His arms were out in an instant to catch her, and the next moment he was holding her against him and his mouth came down on hers, silencing her. Too surprised to move, she submitted as he moved his lips slowly across her face and into the arch of her neck. She shivered as he kissed her bare shoulder and cupped her half-naked breast in his hand. 'Oh, Stella, why do you torment me so?'

She wanted it to go on and on, but there was a little voice inside her, reminding her of Jimmy and saying, 'Where is your pride?' She pulled herself away.

'Get out,' she said, controlling her voice with an effort. 'And don't ever try that again! I am a married woman, and though I may be your prisoner, I am not your whore.'

'Oh, God,' he groaned. 'I'm sorry.'

'So you should be! Now, if you want me to come with you to see the Emperor, you had better go and wait downstairs.'

He surprised her by obeying and, fifteen minutes later, she went down to join him. There was no sign of either Redford or Josefina.

Palace guards in blue and silver uniforms and wearing silver-mounted swords lined the entrance to the National Palace as Leo and Stella arrived. They passed between their ranks and were received by a Mexican-Indian footman in magnificent lace-embroidered livery with huge silver buckles at waist and knee. He conducted them to a drawing-room where a crowd of French, Mexicans and Creoles of all ranks were already assembled. The women, in elaborate crinolines in all the colours of the rainbow, and the men, in tail-coats and white shirts or the colourful uniforms of French and Mexican officers, turned towards them, just as they had to every new arrival, curious to know who was on the guest-list, ready to criticise or praise. Stella realised with a start that this was an official reception and not a private audience, and she looked up at Leo, who was relaxed and smiling.

'Why didn't you tell me?'

'I wanted to be sure you came.'

'Do you mean that the Emperor doesn't want to talk to me?'

'Indeed he does, but later. In the meantime, do you think we could call a truce, just for this evening? Your stony looks will put everyone off their food.' He smiled. 'Besides, I want you to enjoy yourself.'

'Have I any choice?'

'No.' He laughed, and his laugh reminded her of Trieste, and it was like being back there and being in love for the first time. She had to keep telling herself that everything was different now. Time had passed and they were not the two people they had been then; she was no longer free and, if her guess was correct, neither was he.

She tried to put the episode in the bedroom out of her mind but it kept intruding, and so that she would not have to speak to him, she pretended to be interested in the elegantly furnished room with its thick carpet, beautifully draped satin curtains, its magnificent chandeliers, the paintings on the walls. One, she realised with a start, was a picture of Miramar, and it reminded her of the one Leo had painted of her. What had happened to that? she wondered. Had it been destroyed, along with everything else in the diligence? It was a great shame if it had, because it was so well done, and the fact that he had thought of selling it or giving it away did not make it any less so.

The banquet lasted three hours, and throughout that time Maximilian, in the uniform of the Commander-in-Chief of the Mexican army, was at his sparkling best. Stella marvelled at his ability to laugh and joke and talk of his plans for the future of Mexico, parrying or simply ignoring any questions which touched on law and order and the inability of the army to put down the rebels. No one dared mention the diligence, the latest in a long line of atrocities, although it was on everyone's mind. Whom was he deceiving with his show of opulence and good living, she wondered—his friends or his enemies? Himself? How far could he trust those around him?

When the meal was finished, they returned to one of the brilliantly-lit salons, and each guest was formally presented to the Emperor. Stella, waiting her turn in the crush, suddenly felt Leo stiffen at her side and looked up to see him gazing across the room over the heads of the guests.

He excused himself hurriedly and left her, pushing his way through the throng. Stella, even when she stood on tiptoe, could see nothing. From the other side of the room came a shout, the sound of a scuffle, and a half-smothered cry. The crowds parted momentarily, and she caught sight of Leo grappling with one of the palace guards, then others ran to help and the crowd closed round them again.

She was standing alone and undecided what to do when a Mexican officer pushed his way through to her and introduced himself as Lieutenant Rodriguez. 'Leo is with the Emperor in the next room,' he told her, indicating a door. 'They ask that you join them.'

Stella thanked him, and made her way with some trepidation over to the door he had pointed out. A flunkey opened it, and she found herself once more in the presence of the Emperor.

Maximilian and Leo were alone in the room, deep in conversation, and did not immediately notice her. 'One of my own guards a *Juárista*?' Maximilian was saying. 'I can't believe it! Are you sure?'

'Yes, your Majesty. I recognised him as one of those who had ambushed the diligence. With luck, he'll lead us to the rest.'

'Once again I owe you my life, my lion-hearted friend.'

Stella gave a small cough to tell them she was there, and Leo turned and strode over to take her hand and lead her forward.

'Here is Mrs Wainright, your Majesty.'

Stella dropped into a deep curtsy and bowed her head,

waiting for Maximilian's greeting, half fearful, half defiant, but he silently reached out to help her to rise. When she looked up into his face, she found herself seeing past the façade of the self-assured monarch and into eyes that showed only too plainly the strain he was under.

'Come and sit by me, my dear,' he said, leading her to a *chaise-longue*. 'I want a full account of what happened when you were arrested.'

She noticed that he had dropped the royal 'we', and she relaxed a little as she did as he asked, adding, 'I have no wish to interfere in the affairs of Mexico, your Majesty, but . . .'

'But you were carried away by your English sense of fair play, is that not so?'

'Something like that, your Majesty.'

'Did you know it is punishable by death to carry arms?'

'Not at the time, your Majesty, and, to tell the truth, I had forgotten I was carrying my pistol. I was more concerned about the family whose home was being searched.'

'We have to root out the rebels wherever they are, Mrs Wainright. The soldiers were only doing the task they had been given.'

'But those people were so poor, and it was such an old gun.'

'Old guns can be fired sometimes,' he said. 'But perhaps the soldiers were a little over-zealous. I have issued an order forbidding summary execution, and in future I shall personally review all death sentences before they are carried out.' He smiled. 'So, you see, you have achieved something by your protest.'

She bowed her head in acknowledgment. 'Your Majesty.'

'But there will be no more such incidents. You have erred against the state, unintentionally perhaps, but we cannot be seen to condone it. Now, I am afraid, I cannot ensure your safety or guarantee your freedom while you remain in Mexico City. Take my advice, Mrs Wainright, and go home. I do not want to have to answer to your husband if anything happens to you.'

'Your Majesty, I must find him! If he has gone to Yucatan, I ask only that I be allowed to go there.'

'Then go to Yucatan, if you must, but leave Mexico City as soon as you can.'

'I have been invited to stay with Colonel Carson and his sister at Carlota until arrangements can be made for my journey, your Majesty.'

She could feel Leo's disapproval—it was almost as if it hung in the atmosphere—but she dared not look at him because Maximilian was speaking again. 'Good; that is a very wise move. The ex-Confederates have no part to play in the internal affairs of Mexico, so you will be safe there until Captain Manfred is ready to escort you.'

Taken by surprise, she could only repeat, 'Captain Manfred?'

'Yes. I have appointed him to be your escort and to deliver you safely into the arms of your husband.' He smiled. 'We shall say no more on the subject. You have been released, and no charges will be brought.'

Great relief was mixed with a terrible doubt. She wanted to ask if Leo had agreed willingly to his assignment, but all she could find to say was, 'Thank you, your Majesty.'

'God speed and a safe journey,' he said, dismissing them with a wave of the hand.

Stella dropped into a curtsy. It was impossible not to like him and to feel sorry for him. He was a very gentle man, a caring man, who loved his people, his home and his garden; he would not hurt a fly. How then had he come into a position where he could not guarantee her safety, and dared not put an end to the punitive measures being carried out in his name?

They returned to the crowded salon, where the heat enveloped them like a thick blanket. Stella, exhausted by the events of a long day, felt stifled and her knees began to buckle. Determined not to faint, she turned to ask, 'I am very tired, Leo. Do you think I could go back to the hotel?'

He looked down at her, and said, 'Of course.' Then he led her out through the maze of rooms to a cool hall, where he took her to one of the elegant French chairs which lined its walls. 'Sit there while I order the carriage. I won't be long.'

Gratefully she sank down, and he strode off to find a servant. Through a fog of fatigue, she waited, almost dropping asleep where she sat. She was sure Leo did not want to take her to Yucatan, and she certainly did not want his company; every step of the way would be a painful reminder of what had happened in Trieste. They had each made new lives and found new loves, and it would do no good at all to be reminded of the past.

Her eyelids had almost closed by the time Leo returned. He guided her to the carriage, and helped her in before climbing in beside her. The vehicle had hardly begun to move before her head lolled and found Leo's broad shoulder. Gently he put his arm round her and laid his cheek against her soft hair, breathing in the sweet scent of her.

CHAPTER FIVE

LEO, WOKEN by the raucous crowing of a cock, stretched lazily on a bed that was too narrow and too short for him, and yawned. There was much to be done before he could obey Maximilian's order to accompany Stella to Yucatan, but for the moment he would lie where he was and remember a sleepy head on his shoulder and a soft, warm body limp in his arms. For a brief moment he forgot she had rejected him for someone else, and allowed himself to dream.

'*Señor*.' Pablo's head appeared above the end of the bed, where he had been sleeping on the floor.

Annoyed that his day-dream had been broken into, Leo gave only a grunt for an answer.

'I find breakfast, eh? And coffee?'

The boy seemed to have appointed himself his servant, and though Leo acquiesced to that by default—he had no heart to turn him away—the little urchin's timing was not of the best. Leo chuckled suddenly; perhaps it was better than he thought. Left to himself, his dreaming might have wandered into the realms of the impossible and led to a frustration not to be borne.

'Yes,' he said, sitting up and throwing back the blanket. 'You find our breakfast while I dress.' He threw a small pouch of coins on the table. 'While you're out, take that to the family Mrs Wainright tried to defend. Nothing can replace the menfolk, I know, but it might help.'

'*Si, Señor*.' The boy scrambled to his feet, added a shirt and sandals to the trousers he already wore, and trotted away.

While Leo was shaving, Ramón Rodriguez came in and sat astride one of the chairs with its back between his legs. He was very young, hardly out of the cradle, Leo thought, but he was a good soldier and a loyal friend.

'The news of the arrest of one of the Emperor's own guards is the talk of the city,' he said. 'There are rumours everywhere—Maximilian has been killed; he has been saved; he is mortally wounded; half his retinue have been slain in a bloody battle; he is fleeing to Vera Cruz and the safety of the sea. It makes you wonder if any of them can be true.'

'You know they are not; you were there,' Leo said. 'We'll question that fellow we took last night. The only way to scotch such rumours is with an official announcement and the public appearance of Maximilian himself, followed swiftly by an execution, *after* we have learned the name of his leader and who supplied the guns and ammunition.'

'Can't be done,' Ramón said laconically. 'The fellow hanged himself in the night.'

Leo looked at him sharply, 'How did that happen?'

'I'm told he used a kerchief the turnkey forgot to take from him.'

'Do you think anyone helped him on his way to silence him?'

Ramón shrugged. 'There's no telling.'

Leo cursed. More than ever he wished he had not lost sight of the boxes the ex-Confederate Colonel had despatched from the hotel at Cordoba, and that he had managed to catch up with the bandits after the ambush of the diligence. He dared not move against Carson without proof. The worst of it was that Stella had become embroiled in it all, and he had no idea how much she knew of the truth. 'I want you to find out if they did,' he said. 'Because, if so, they will share his fate, I can promise.'

'You will not be here to do anything about it,' Ramón said. 'I heard you've got yourself a bit of leave.'

'Leave, is that what you call it? It's not my idea of leave! I was never cut out to be a nursemaid.'

'I don't see why you're grumbling; she's a real beauty. Can't think what she saw in young James Wainright,

though. Not a man I could take to.' He glanced up at the
wall in front of him, where a small painting hung. 'That's
her, isn't it? I've been in this room dozens of times, but I
never really noticed it before.'

'Yes, I did it from memory when I first came here.'

'You knew her before.'

'Only briefly. Just long enough to paint her portrait. I
brought it back with me from Europe, but it was on the
diligence and I had no time to save it.'

Ramón digested this morsel of information, and
laughed in an embarrassed way. 'Never mind, you will
be able to do another in the long evenings on the road to
Yucatan.'

'I do not want to go, Ramón. Porfirio Díaz is marching
north, and he has to be met and defeated before Juárez
decides to move south to join him. This is no time to be
away.'

The young man laughed. 'On the contrary; I would
have thought it was the best time.'

'I am not a coward,' Leo said sharply. 'I do not run
from my enemies.'

'Sorry. Just my joke, didn't mean . . .'

'I know you didn't.' Leo smiled at him. 'And I can
safely leave things in your hands, no?'

'Yes. The Empire will still be here when you return.'

'Will it?' Leo said bitterly. 'Things have a habit of
disappearing when my back is turned.' He smiled suddenly, as Pablo returned with bread, eggs and coffee.
'Have breakfast with us. It will be the last for some time.'

'When do you go?'

'The lady in question has been banished from the city
for her Liberal sympathies, and she is going with the
Carsons to Carlota City to wait for me there.'

'Carson? Isn't he . . .?'

'Yes, but Maximilian refused to see the danger.'

They finished their breakfast, and Leo spent the rest
of the day visiting anyone who could throw light on the
recent movements of the American, but he appeared
to be behaving perfectly innocently, and he learned

nothing that would help. He went back to his quarters late in the evening, to be told that Maximilian wanted to see him at Chapultepec, where he had returned after the banquet.

The Emperor was at his desk, and looked grey and drawn. He listened in silence to Leo's report of the apparent suicide of the prisoner and his subsequent enquiries. 'I am certain the Liberals are being financed by the United States.'

'That I can't believe,' Maximilian said. 'One or two individuals, perhaps . . .'

'Individuals like Colonel Redford Carson,' Leo answered. 'I swear he was behind the ambush the other day, and the prisoner we took last night might have confirmed it.'

'He is dead.'

'Yes, your Majesty. I have ordered an enquiry.'

'Good. And I suggest you keep your suspicions to yourself until we are sure of our ground. We cannot afford to make an enemy of Washington.'

The audience seemed to be at an end, and Leo, thinking himself dismissed, bowed and retreated a few steps. He stopped when Maximilian went on, 'My wife is mad, isn't she?'

Leo hesitated. 'She is . . . a little unwell, your Majesty.'

'My wife is mad,' Maximilian muttered. 'These people are killing me by inches, and I am thoroughly worn out.' He put his elbows on his desk and covered his face with his hands. From behind the long, sensitive fingers came a groan of anguish. Leo edged away, unwilling to intrude on his grief. The voice that rebuked him was muffled and choked with emotion, but it was clearly the voice of a monarch speaking to his servant. 'We did not give you leave to retire.'

Leo halted and waited.

The Emperor dropped his hands, and his cheeks were wet with tears, then he stood up and went to the window to look out over the dark landscape towards the city he had entered so optimistically only two short years before. The dream had become a nightmare. 'I am going away.'

It was the first hint he had ever given that he might give up the unequal struggle, and Leo was taken completely by surprise. Then he let out a long breath of relief. The sooner the Emperor decided to leave, the sooner they could all leave, and there was still Miramar and a private life; he would have to content himself with that. And perhaps the sight of her husband in surroundings where they had both been happy might restore Carlota to her senses.

'You are silent,' the Emperor said.

'I beg pardon, sir.'

'Am I right or wrong to go? Will I best serve the Mexican people by leaving them? What would you do in my place?'

'I would go, your Majesty.'

'Then so be it.' He turned back from the window and looked about the room as though seeing it for the last time. 'Go and fetch the chamberlain.'

'Tonight, your Majesty? It's past midnight.'

'Now,' he said firmly, 'before I change my mind again.'

'Sir, there are arrangements to make . . .'

'What arrangements? I do not go in triumph, I need no processions, no fanfares, no luggage. What few treasures I still possess have already been despatched to Vera Cruz for sending on to Miramar . . .' His voice drifted away, and Leo knew he was thinking of his old home. Then he suddenly came back to the present, and snapped, 'Do as I order, and see to your own packing.'

'You wish me to accompany you, your Majesty?'

'I promised Mrs Wainright you would take her to Yucatan, and I do not go back on my word. You had better go and fetch her. We can travel together as far as Vera Cruz.

Leo left to obey. The moment he was free, he set off for the Iturbide Hotel on the fastest horse he could find in the stables, banging on the door and rousing the proprietor from his bed at two in the morning, only to be told that the Colonel and the ladies had set out early the previous morning.

Leo hesitated in the street outside the hotel, torn between a desire to ride after them and his oath of obedience to the Emperor. As he stood there, he heard the sound of horses and vehicles, and looked up as Maximilian's entourage came along the ill-lit street. There were a few closed carriages and a handful of French and Mexican cavalry as outriders, no more. To leave now would be tantamount to desertion and, as a soldier, he could never contemplate that. Their route lay within a day's ride of Carlota Colony; he would fetch Stella then.

Stella had woken in the dark hours just before dawn, to find herself lying on her bed fully clothed and covered by a thin sheet. She had been awake when Leo carried her up to her room and put her on the bed, but she knew that if she opened her eyes, he would put her down. And she did not want him to put her down, did not even want him to speak, because that would break the spell, shatter the magic of having his arms about her, of her head nestling against his strongly beating heart. And so she had feigned sleep while he removed her shoes and covered her. Very soon after he had left, she had drifted off into real sleep.

She rose slowly and undressed before getting into bed properly, smiling to herself. It had been disgraceful behaviour for a respectable married woman, but he had behaved like a gentleman, and she did not know whether she was glad or sorry. Sleep claimed her once more, and when she woke again, it was day and the sun was beating down on streets which were already packed with people going about their business.

She washed and dressed hurriedly and went down to breakfast, to find that Carson and his sister Martha had almost finished their meal. Both rose as she approached, then Martha bade her good morning and left.

'Good morning, Stella,' Carson said cheerfully. 'Join me, please. Martha has gone to superintend her packing. We are leaving today. You do still want to come with us?'

'Yes, of course, but what about Captain Manfred? He has been ordered to accompany me to Yucatan.'

Carson smiled. 'And is that arrangement to your liking?'

'No, I would prefer you to lead the expedition.'

'Then there is no more to be said, is there? We shall leave as soon as you are ready.'

She set off with the Colonel and his sister, unaware of the feverish activity they left behind in the capital, which bordered on panic as the rumours grew. Porfirio Díaz, emboldened by his recent successes, had sacked the Emperor's country mansion at Cuervanaca, only forty miles to the south, and in no time would reach the city. And if Juárez moved down from the American border, Mexico City could well become cut off from the outside world. Europeans without a pressing need to stay, packed their belongings and headed for Vera Cruz while the roads were relatively safe.

Carlota Colony, when they reached it two days later, appeared to be a productive island in the middle of a land laid to waste. The population of the little colony, apart from the servants and the Mexican-Indian field hands, was almost exclusively American, Carson told her. They had been drawn from the Confederate armies fleeing after the American Civil War. Encouraged by the Empress Carlota, they came from all over the south, from Kentucky, Louisiana, Missouri, lured by thousands of printed leaflets proclaiming 'Ho for Mexico!' and promising rich rewards. They had been given this tract of land near Cordoba, where they built new homes in the Southern style, carved new plantations out of the soil, ploughing with their old cavalry horses. Maximilian, who liked to ape their dress when he was not wearing colourful Mexican clothes, looked on them as harmless political exiles.

'And are they harmless?' Stella asked.

He shrugged. 'Allied to the French, they could become strong enough to threaten the United States; that's why the immigration was stopped.'

Stella was on the point of asking how it was that *he* was allowed to come and go without restriction, but something told her it would be a touchy subject and, if she showed any unwelcome curiosity, his hospitality would be at an end. And once in his own beautiful home, amid familiar surroundings, he relaxed and became a charming and thoughtful host.

The next morning he drove her into Cordoba himself and supervised her purchase of a large covered wagon —a half-sized prairie schooner, he called it—two good mules and enough supplies for a month.

'You don't want to rely on buying provisions,' he said. 'The Indians in the jungle villages have little enough.'

They returned to find Martha busy superintending the work of the servants, which she complained had been sadly neglected in her absence, and he suggested a ride.

Stella agreed enthusiastically, and in less than ten minutes she had changed into a dark green riding-habit and matching feathered hat and sought him out in the stableyard, where he had picked out a beautiful chestnut mare for her. She felt wonderfully exhilarated as they cantered through plantations of coffee, cotton and sugar cane, past white board ranch-houses and Spanish-style haciendas, alongside meadows where thoroughbred horses, like the one she was riding, grazed on lush grass. But her keen eyes had detected the armed guards patrolling the fields and the occasional burnt-out barn; even Carlota Colony, professing itself neutral, had not been left untouched by the struggle. She pulled up, and waited for him to rein in beside her.

'You ride well, Stella,' he said, reaching out to take

her hand. 'You belong in a place like this.' He paused, then added. 'If you could find it in your heart to forget James . . .'

She ignored the hand, though she was conscious of it and its strength. 'I'm sure I don't know what you mean,' she said sharply.

'No? Seeing you now, sitting that mare so comfortably, surrounded by cultivated fields, and backed by green hills, makes a picture not easily forgotten.'

His mention of a picture reminded her of Leo, and she looked back towards the house, almost as if expecting to see him.

'Manfred won't come,' he said, reading her thoughts.

'The Emperor ordered him to escort me,' she said flatly, 'and I am sure Captain Manfred always obeys his orders.'

'Is that what you want, to be saddled with a man who has no real interest in your affairs? Now take me, for instance, I am totally at your service, and if anything should happen to your husband . . .'

'What do you mean? What could happen to him?'

He shrugged. 'These are troubled times. All I am saying is that if you should find yourself alone, you will have a home here with me.'

'Colonel Carson, I have no wish even to think of such a possibility. I intend to find Jimmy.'

'Then let me take you to him. I offered before, remember, and you agreed.'

'Yes, I know, but . . .'

'It may prove fatal to delay. There will be a bloodbath before long.'

'Do you think it will come to that?'

'It has already started. That's one of the reasons I know the gallant Captain will not come. The Emperor needs every man he can muster.'

She did not answer immediately, but began walking her horse forward, ducking her head as she passed beneath the branch of an oak which hung over the path. Did it matter who led her expedition, just so long as she found Jimmy? 'At the moment, my only concern is for my husband,' she told him.

'Then we shall leave tomorrow, you and I and my driver.'

'Good,' she said promptly, and before he could say any more on the subject of Leo, she nudged her horse into a canter, back towards the stables. He passed her at full gallop and was there before her, ready to help her to dismount.

He handed the horses' reins to a Mexican groom, whose face seemed vaguely familiar to Stella. He was not particularly tall or broad, and his clothes were the usual dun-coloured trousers, red shirt and embroidered waistcoat of many Mexican men. He was not a man you would notice in a crowd, and yet she was convinced she had met him before. She had no time to puzzle over it, because Carson, turning to escort her into the house, suddenly stopped and looked up at the distant horizon. Stella, following his gaze, saw a puff of smoke, as if a building was on fire on the other side of the hill.

'I think it's time to leave,' he said slowly, turning to the Mexican. 'Miguel, fetch out the big coach and harness the four best horses, then bring it to the front door.'

Without waiting for a reply, he took Stella's arm and hurried her into the house, shouting for Martha as soon as he crossed the threshold. 'Matty! Matty, where are you?'

She appeared on the landing above them. 'Redford, is it necessary to shout for me as if I were a servant?'

'Pack your things, we're leaving.'

'But I've only just unpacked.'

'Never mind. Do it. Collect up everything valuable, all your jewels, the silver—cutlery and plate—and the porcelain. Pack it carefully in plenty of straw. I'll send Miguel in to load it on the coach. If you've got room, take the pictures too; wrap them in the drapes.'

'Redford,' she said calmly, 'are we running away?'

'No, we are not running away,' he said testily. 'You

are returning to New Orleans. Stella and I are going to Yucatan.'

'You expect me to travel alone?'

'You'll have your duenna, and I'll send one of the men with you. You'll be safe enough if you go now.'

She sighed with annoyance, but knew better than to argue with him, and returned to her room to obey. He shouted for two of the maids to go and help her, and then turned to Stella. 'Put your things in the wagon, then go to the kitchen and ask the potboy to help you to load up the supplies we bought this morning. Take some pots and pans, anything we'll need for cooking and eating, you know the sort of thing. Blankets, too.'

'We are leaving today?' she asked, guessing the answer.

'As soon as we're ready.' He left her to attend to preparations of his own, and she set about doing as he asked.

For the next two hours, all was bustle and hustle as the coach and wagon were loaded. Martha, directing operations, was dashing from one room to another, picking up objects she considered valuable, and then changing her mind and asking Redford if they should go. Stella, who had less to do, tried as far as possible not to get in their way. In the middle of it all, Josefina arrived alone, driving an old-fashioned gig at a speed bordering on recklessness. It was a minute or two before Carson realised she was there, and then he did not show the surprise Stella would have expected.

'How did you get here?' he asked mildly.

'I drove myself in a gig.' She looked around at the chaos of half-packed boxes and spilling straw. 'I see you have heard the news.'

'What news?'

'The Emperor has abdicated. He is on his way to Vera Cruz at this very moment. The *Dandolo* is there, waiting to take him back to Europe.'

'You mean you've left him?' Carson said.

'No, of course not. I guessed you might be sending

your sister back to New Orleans, and I thought she could travel to Vera Cruz with me in Maximilian's party.'

'How kind of you!' Martha exclaimed. 'To tell the truth, I was dreading going alone.'

'Leo?' Stella found herself thinking aloud. 'Is Leo going too?'

Josefina turned towards her as if seeing her for the first time. 'Naturally Captain Manfred is with the Emperor; he is a member of his entourage.'

'Did he send me a message?'

She shrugged. 'No, why should he? He has more important things on his mind just now.'

Stella looked up at Carson, and found him looking at her with an expression of amusement, almost triumph. But before she could speak, he said, 'Do you want to leave with Martha, or do you want to go to Yucatan?'

'You know very well I can't abandon Jimmy.'

'Whichever you do, you must do it soon,' Josefina said. 'I heard gunfire not far away as I arrived.'

'We have nothing to fear from anyone,' he said. 'We are all neutral.'

'Neutral!' Martha cried. 'No one is allowed to be neutral. The bandits need money and supplies and guns and ammunition, and they know you have them here. If you don't give them up willingly, they will take them.'

Carson ignored his sister and spoke to Josefina. 'You had better leave at once. As far as the Liberals are concerned, you are a friend of Maximilian, and therefore a traitor; they will have no mercy.'

After a hurriedly taken meal, Martha said goodbye to Redford, called to her companion and followed Josefina out to the heavily loaded carriage. It had so many trunks, boxes and bags inside and strapped on top and behind that there was hardly room for the passengers, but they squeezed themselves in, and the driver flicked the reins. The horses strained for a moment and then the vehicle jolted forward, threatening to lose some of its load. Stella, glancing up, saw a cloth fall away from the corner of a picture, and her mouth fell open in surprise.

It was like a recurring dream, and she blinked hard to dispel it. The coach moved away through the white-painted gates and on to the road to Cordoba. Her portrait had survived the fire, if it had ever been in it, and was now in the possession of Martha Carson and the lovely Josefina. Had it been stolen? Surely Leo would have mentioned it if it had. Had he sold it, or given it away as he said he might? Josefina, she thought. Had he given it to her? 'Let's pray they arrive safely,' Carson said, watching the dust thrown up by the coach settling back on the road.

'You are in love with her, aren't you?'

He looked down at her, puzzled. 'Who?'

'Josefina Gonzales.'

'I admire her,' he said evasively, 'but she is a *mestiza* —that is to say she has a Creole father and a Mexican mother. All her life she has had to battle against prejudice, but she is a very beautiful woman. Her looks alone have gained her entry into places most women only dream of.'

'Is that how she came to be at Maximilian's court?'

'The Emperor is very susceptible to beautiful women.'

Stella was shocked. 'Surely he is above such things?'

'No man is, not even Leo Manfred. And there are enough stories going round to make it possible that some of them are true.'

'I thought she was there because of Leo. He admitted to me that you were both in love with the same woman.' She had not meant to mention Leo, but her thoughts were so full of him that she could not keep silent.

He laughed, throwing back his head and looking up at the cloudless sky. She was struck by the thought that here was a handsome man with strong lean features and a proud head. Being defeated in war must have come very hard to him. Was he also vengeful? 'Did he?' he said, still smiling. 'He is more perceptive than I thought.'

'Why are you laughing?'

'For no reason in particular. Are you ready to leave? Josefina was right in one thing. Once the news of the

Emperor's flight reaches the guerrillas, they will come out of their hiding-places, and then nothing will stop them. I don't know how long Carlota Colony will be spared.'

Almost as if to answer him, they became aware of gunfire in the distance, and Stella, looking across the fields, saw a rider approaching against the sun. She lifted a hand to shield her eyes in an effort to see him clearly. He was in a great hurry, galloping his horse straight at the white board fences and clearing them with ease.

'Leo!' she cried, as he jumped to the ground almost before the animal had stopped.

'Get inside,' he ordered, ushering her towards the house. 'You too, Carson.'

'I'll be blowed if I will!' the Colonel said. 'I take no orders from a trumped-up court painter! You are on my property, and I'll thank you to leave before I set the dogs on you.'

Leo pointed at the horizon, where a great plume of smoke indicated that a house was ablaze, and the sound of firing not far away told them that some of the inhabitants were resisting. 'You need all the help you can get, Colonel.'

'What's happening?' Stella asked. 'Are we going to be attacked?'

He smiled down at her. 'Are you afraid?'

'No, I don't think so. Should I be?'

'It's only a raiding-party,' Carson said. 'Nothing to get steamed up about. I'll go and talk to them. They will respect our neutrality.' He looked at Leo, and added, 'That is, if we have no Emperor's men among us. I suggest you leave us to it.'

Leo laughed. 'Neutrality! The Liberals don't know the meaning of the word, and if you have any sense at all, you will accept my offer of help.'

A shot that was too close for comfort put an end to the argument. Leo turned and shouted to the Mexican groom, 'Tell everyone to come into the house. Bring all the guns and ammunition you can find.' He pushed

Stella indoors, then he and Carson ran round putting up the shutters of the downstairs rooms. 'Upstairs!' he shouted, as Stella hesitated. 'Go upstairs.'

She obeyed, and was followed by all the servants, the field workers, stable lads and grooms from outside, the cook, kitchen-maids and chambermaids from below stairs. Once they were all safely in, Carson barricaded the door, then both men bounded up the stairs and herded everyone along the gallery. 'If you can fire a gun, or load one, up to the windows,' he said. 'If not, keep out of the way.'

They dispersed themselves throughout the first floor, and Stella found herself in what had once been Martha's bedroom, with two rifles and a grinning Indian potboy at her side with a box of ammunition. She flung the window up, and taking one of the rifles from the boy, she knelt down to watch and wait, resting the barrel on the windowsill. The fire in the distance was spreading. She could see tongues of red flame on the skyline, could hear the crackle of burning wood, could even smell the smoke.

'That's someone's cotton gone,' Carson said behind her.

'What do they expect to gain?' she asked. 'Surely setting fire some poor farmer's crops will not help their cause.'

'They have no cause: they are just bandits, opportunists. Juárez is not fool enough to think that, because the Emperor has fled, it is safe to emerge.' He left her, murmuring something about supervising the positions of the other defenders, and Stella went back to her watch.

She became aware that Leo had pulled a chair close to the window next to the one she was watching from, but he did not speak to her and she did not turn towards him.

'Here they come!' he said, then shouted so that everyone in the house could hear. 'Let them fire first; we don't want to be accused of starting it. Then hold your fire until they get in range, and don't waste ammunition.'

Stella could see small figures darting about in the fields

in front of the house, scuttling from cover to cover, getting nearer all the time. Two minutes later the first bullets struck the building.

Before she had time to stop and think, she was in the middle of a pitched battle, firing the rifle and handing it to the boy to reload. Some of the attackers fell, and she could hear cries and yells of pain from the people in the house, but she could not tell who had been hit.

'*Americanos!*' someone shouted from beyond the corral. '*Americanos!* Surrender!'

Leo's answer was a shot aimed at the spot where the voice was coming from.

'You missed!' The voice was full of bravado. 'Give up, or we will set fire to the house.'

Carson came into the room behind him. 'We've got a wounded man, and the women are terrified for their lives. I'm going out to talk to them.'

'The fools won't listen.'

'They'll listen to me.'

Leo glanced up at him, then turned back to the window, raising his rifle to take a pot-shot at one of the attackers who, braver than the rest, was running out in the open towards the house. The man stumbled momentarily but did not fall, and Stella realised suddenly that she had not wanted to see him killed. She turned to Leo. 'This is all so futile, so wasteful, so insane! Let's try talking, for the sake of the innocents.'

Carson pulled the sheet from the bed, tore a strip off it and tied it to the end of his rifle, then he went to the window and shouted, 'Hold your fire! I'm coming out.'

He disappeared, and a few moments later reappeared briefly in the yard, then he sprinted across to the stables and a moment later emerged on horseback and galloped away over the hill, with shots from the attackers spattering round him.

Leo laughed. 'Well, I'm not exactly surprised. He's . . .' Whatever he was going to say was cut short by fresh firing and the smell of burning wood very close at hand, and they knew the house was on fire. He turned to Stella. 'Is your wagon ready to leave?'

'Yes.'

'Can you drive it?'

'Yes.'

'Take the women and children down the back stairs and out of the side door. You'll have to watch out crossing the yard, so wait until I have their attention, then into the wagon and drive as fast as you can to Cordoba.'

'What about you?'

'I'll follow.'

She ran to obey, herding the servants along the gallery and down the stairs to the kitchen door. Two minutes later, they were behind the stables and out of sight of the house. The firing continued, and now that they were out in the open, it seemed louder and nearer. Someone harnessed the mules while she helped the little ones into the back of the wagon. It seemed to take an age, but at last they were all on board and she whipped up the animals. Without waiting to see what was happening behind them, they rattled out of the yard and along the back road to the gate in the fence that marked the Colonel's boundary. The boy who had loaded her rifle jumped down to open it and scrambled back on the seat beside her as they slowed to go through, then they were away, with the passengers in the back screaming, as they were thrown from one side to the other.

Leo saw Stella come out of one of the back doors, leading the little group, and stepped up his rate of fire to keep the enemy occupied and to give her a chance to escape. Annoyed that one man should be able to pin them down, the attackers abandoned their positions and began advancing towards the house. He kept firing, glancing every now and again towards Stella and her companions. 'Hurry! For God's sake, hurry,' he muttered, knowing he could not hold out much longer. The wagon moved off at last, and he stopped firing and gave a great cry of agony, hoping he would convince those outside that he had been hit. Then he crept down the stairs and out of the back door. Slowly he edged away, found his horse and rode off after the wagon.

She was a good driver, he had to give her that. The wagon was covering the ground at an alarming speed, and he had considerable difficulty in catching up with it. He yelled for it to stop, but if anything its speed increased. When the road took a wide curve, he turned and rode across country to head it off. Only then did Stella pull the mules to a stop.

'Oh, Leo!' She was bright-eyed and panting, but she did not appear afraid. 'I thought it was one of the guerrillas coming after us.'

Her passengers looked from her to the young cavalry officer, murmured among themselves and then climbed down on to the road. One of the women came to Stella and touched the skirt of her riding-habit. 'We go now, *Señora*. We have friends.' She pointed to the hills where the Liberals were hiding. 'We go, yes?'

'If you wish.'

When they had gone, Leo hitched his horse to the back of the wagon, then climbed up beside her. Taking the reins from her hands, he smiled down at her. 'It's all over. You did well.'

The unexpected praise made her colour, and to cover her confusion she said the first thing that came into her head. 'Do you think the Colonel got away?'

'Oh, he'll have got away,' he said calmly, as the wagon moved forward. 'He is no enemy of the *Juáristas*.' He paused. 'Where is his sister?'

'She went with Josefina before it started.'

'Josefina?' he said sharply. 'What was she doing here?'

'She came to see if Miss Carson wanted to travel with her as far as Vera Cruz. It was very thoughtful of her.'

'Yes, indeed,' he said. 'And very risky! But why didn't you go too?'

'You know why. I intend to go to Yucatan.'

'Still? Don't you think you would be wiser to abandon the idea?'

'Why?'

'Oh, Stella, do you still need convincing that this is a very dangerous place to be just now?'

'Where else could I go, except back to England?'

'Then why not do that? Things can only get worse here.'

'You surely don't expect me to abandon my husband? You know I won't do that. When he has been found, we shall both leave.'

They rode on in silence. The noise of fighting had been left behind, and the only sound was the creaking of the wagon and the clopping of the mules' hooves. Both were busy with their own thoughts, which went round and round with no beginning and no end, and could not be put into words.

He broke the silence at last. 'You really are determined to go, then?'

'Yes.'

'I still have my orders.'

'And what are they?'

'To accompany you to Yucatan and deliver you safely into the arms of your husband.'

'And you don't want to do it?'

'I most certainly do not.'

'And I do not want it either. There are other drivers.'

'You will be very lucky to find one.'

'Then I shall go alone. Perhaps little Pablo can be persuaded to come with me.'

'Now you are being ridiculous!'

'Or Colonel Carson.'

'Even after the exhibition of cowardice you witnessed today?'

'I'm sure there was a reason for it. And at least he was willing.'

'No doubt,' he said laconically, and added, 'You have your duty and I have mine, so there is nothing more to be said.'

She did not answer, because to do so would have betrayed the tears that were so close to the surface. Another word from him, and they would spill over and disgrace her.

When they rode into the outskirts of Cordoba, he stopped the wagon, gave her the reins and jumped down to unhitch his horse. She watched in silence as he mounted and rode round to where she sat.

'Drive into the town and wait for me at the Confederate Hotel.'

'Where are you going?'

He smiled wryly. 'Oh, don't worry, I'll be back. I am only going to find Pablo. We can't leave him behind, can we?' He put out a hand to touch her arm. 'Stella . . .' He started to say something else, then stopped as if realising the futility of it. His hand dropped back on to the reins.

Not until he had gone from sight did she allow herself to cry. Then she sobbed as though her heart would break.

CHAPTER SIX

THE STREETS of Cordoba were jammed with vehicles of every shape and size; anything on wheels had been brought out and harnessed to any animal capable of pulling it. Betwen them, people on foot were laden with bundles. The crowd seemed to be equally divided between wanting to go to Mexico City and making for Vera Cruz to board a ship to take them back to New Orleans. Stella drew the mules up on the fringe of the mêlée, unwilling to get caught up in the panic. But gradually the great caravan began to move, slowly making its way out of the town, guarded by ex-Confederate officers on horseback.

She left the wagon outside the Confederate Hotel, went into the lobby and sat down to wait for Leo. The immigrants had gone, and the local inhabitants had either fled, joined their compatriots in the hills or locked themselves in their homes, and before long she seemed to be the only one left in the town. It was not good to be alone. It left her with nothing to do but think, and she did not want to think; it was futile and heart-breaking because it could not alter anything. When Leo finally arrived, accompanied by Pablo, she was almost glad to see him.

'It was a storm in a teacup,' he said, removing his hat and making himself comfortable in one of the armchairs. 'The rebels have gone back to their hiding-places to wait for Juárez.'

'He is coming?' she asked.

'I believe so.'

'What are you going to do now?'

'We're going to Yucatan, you and me and Pablo. That's what you wanted, isn't it?' He laughed suddenly. 'Or are you concerned that you have no duenna, no chaperon?'

His apparent light-hearted mood lifted her spirits, and she managed to smile. 'Should I be?'

'You have nothing to fear from me, Mrs Wainright.' He looked about him. 'Is there anyone here to prepare a meal?'

'I believe there are some people in the kitchens; they've locked themselves in.'

He left the room and came back a few minutes later with a tray of cold food. 'Here, we'll eat this and then make a start. We can get a few miles on the way before dark, and besides, it would be best not to stay in the town. If the guerrillas think it's empty, they'll be in to loot before long.' He put the tray down on a table and then glanced up at Pablo, who stood by the window looking out at the deserted street. 'Come and eat, young man. There's nothing to see out there.'

Pablo turned from the window to join them. 'I see Colonel,' he said.

'You saw him out there?' Leo snapped. 'What was he doing?'

'He talk to Miguel.'

Leo got up to look. 'There's no one out there.'

The boy shrugged. 'He gone now.'

'Who is Miguel?'

'One of Carson's grooms,' Stella said.

'No, *Señora*, he drive coach from Paso del Macho to Mexico City.'

Leo, who had until then been humouring the child, was suddenly alert. 'The diligence-driver? The one who rode away on the mule?'

'*Si, Señor*. I saw him make sign to *banditos* when he fix coach.'

'Ever since I saw him with the Colonel, I've been wondering where I had come across him before,' Stella said. 'And I am sure he was the one who came to the Iturbide. I was woken in the middle of the night by someone banging on the door, and when I went to the window, I saw a man and a mule. Someone let him into the hotel.'

'Was it Carson who let him in?'

'I couldn't tell, but it would explain how he knew about it so soon after it happened.'

'He was privy to it from the start.'

'Oh no! Surely the ambush was the work of bandits, guerrillas, *Juáristas*, Liberals—they have so many names that it confuses me. How can he have had anything to do with it?'

'He bad man,' Pablo said.

'You are mistaken, Pablo. He was going to help me.'

'Señor Leo help you. He not bad.'

Leo laughed. 'Pablo, you are biased.'

'*Señor?*'

'Never mind. One day I'll teach you to understand English!'

'*Si, Señor.*' Pablo grinned happily and tucked into his food.

Leo smiled at him indulgently, and as soon as they had finished their meal, stood up and went to the door. 'Time to go,' he said.

The wagon had covered about a dozen miles, with Pablo on the driving-seat beside Stella and Leo riding alongside, when Leo called a halt. They were on the outskirts of a small village, and he sent the boy ahead on the horse to find a place to stay for the night. The light was fading, and Stella was obviously exhausted; her head was lolling and she could hardly keep upright. Once the tension of the day had passed, she had been lulled by the movement of the wagon into a kind of torpor, an attitude of not caring what became of her. She was too tired and listless to wonder why Leo had abandoned the main road to the coast, which would have been the easiest route, and struck across a countryside where the roads were dreadful, when they existed at all. They were certainly quieter, with no traffic, as there was bound to be on the road to the railhead at Paso del Macho, jammed as it was with refugees.

'Tomorrow will be easier,' Leo said, guiding the mules off the road on to a patch of sparse brown grass. 'We'll leave all the shooting and arson behind us, and the journey will be a peaceful one. That is,' he added, with a wry smile, 'if we can extend our truce until we manage to find your husband.'

'I have no wish to quarrel with you,' said Stella.

He left the mules and came to stand near where she sat, high on the front seat of the wagon, and looked up at her. 'Good!' There was a brittleness in his voice that frightened her a little. 'I'm glad we agree on that.'

The returning Pablo diverted her attention. 'The village is no good,' he said, dismounting. 'Only two, three houses. Headman say he give *señora* his bed, but he want many *pesos*.'

'I'm not going a yard further,' Stella said firmly. 'You two can go into the village, but I'm sleeping in the wagon.'

'And leave you alone?' Leo said promptly. 'Fine pair of escorts we would make if we did that! It would be a grave dereliction of duty.'

She became suddenly alarmed. Supposing he suggested sharing the wagon? He had shown he did not care for her reputation when he forced himself on her in her hotel room. He had done something very similar in Trieste, taking advantage of her innocence. She was no longer innocent in that sense, but he would not care; he cared for nothing but his own satisfaction.

He seemed to read her thoughts, because he laughed aloud before climbing into the back of the wagon. For a minute or so she listened to him moving about inside it, humming to himself. She looked at Pablo, but he was busy lighting a fire with dry grass and twigs. It was reluctant to burn, and he bent over it, blowing hard and making it smoke, apparently uninterested in what was going on.

Leo emerged, and jumped down carrying two blankets. 'It's going to be a fine night,' he said, gazing up at the clear sky, now darkening to twilight. 'I'll be comfortable enough under the wagon.'

Stella heaved a huge sigh of relief and went to help the

boy to prepare a stew of pork and beans. When it was ready, they sat round the fire to eat. Each was immersed in private thoughts and no one spoke; the only sound was Pablo noisily sucking his fingers, the distant howling of a dog and the mules cropping the grass. It could have been a pleasant interlude, a peaceful ending to the day, except for the undercurrents of tension between them, a tension Stella was loath to acknowledge, because if it was like this at the beginning of their journey, what would it be like at the end?

Afterwards, she climbed over the tailboard into the wagon and drew the canvas close before preparing for bed. Outside, Leo made a last inspection of the animals tethered to a stunted tree, loaded his rifle and joined Pablo under the wagon. There was silence, followed by their light snoring, and soon Stella, exhausted by the events of the day, drifted off to sleep.

As they journeyed on, stopping only to eat and rest the mules, Leo became on the one hand more relaxed, almost as if he were enjoying himself, and on the other more withdrawn, as if he had a problem which needed thinking through. At such times he hardly spoke, and Stella turned from him to Pablo for conversation, helping him to improve his English. He was an apt pupil, and the lessons served to keep her mind on something other than Leo, and she needed that. She told herself that her only concern was to reach Jimmy, to have his arms about her again, to feel protected and loved. Leo Manfred knew nothing of love. If her trip to Mexico had taught her anything, it was that she had been right about him all along; he was a boorish, conceited man, without honesty enough to admit his fault and apologise. He had not been worth her tears.

The following afternoon they came upon the coach being used by Josefina and Martha, which had stopped by the wayside. Both women were in the road, arguing with the driver.

Josefina looked up as the wagon pulled up beside

them. 'Oh, Leo, you are a godsend! This stupid Mexican says he won't take us any further.'

'Why not?'

'The snivelling coward is afraid of the guerrillas,' Martha said. 'He says we are royalists and he is a true patriot.'

'I've told him the Emperor will have him shot,' said Josefina. But he's more afraid of being shot by the *Juáristas*.'

Leo spoke to the Mexican in Spanish and confirmed what they said; the man had heard that the Emperor had abdicated and that the new government would punish all those who had helped him. He would not take the coach another yard. Leo sent him on his way, told Pablo to ride the horse and climbed up on the driving-seat himself.

'Get in,' he said, almost brusquely. Then, to Stella, 'Keep close behind.'

The journey seemed interminable. He would have liked to ride right through the hours of darkness, but none of the women would hear of it and they stopped for the night at a wayside inn. After an indifferent meal, Leo went looking for a new driver for Josefina and Martha, but everyone he approached held the same sentiments as the Mexican he had dismissed, and he realised how fortunate they were even to have accommodation.

Intending to check on the animals, he returned to inn by way of the stable and found Pablo climbing on top of the Colonel's coach. 'What are you doing up there, boy?'

'*Señor*, you look.' Pablo pulled aside the covering of Stella's portrait.

It was a moment or two before the implication of Pablo's discovery penetrated Leo's brain, but when it did, the puzzle of the ambush began to click into place. 'Cover it up again,' he said quietly, 'and say nothing.'

Pablo looked puzzled, but then shrugged his shoulders and obeyed. 'You sleep in stable?' he asked.

Leo laughed. 'Not this time, my friend! You sleep in

the wagon and watch over it for me. We'll make an early start in the morning.'

He went back to the inn parlour, passing a guitarist who was sitting on a seat outside, singing 'Adelita', the song of a girl who followed her lover to war, and it made him want to cry. The evening was made all the more unbearable because Stella retired early and the other two chattered interminably, covering the whole gamut of clothes, homes, men and inheritance; it was almost as though no conflict was going on only a few miles away.

'What is Maximilian's home in Europe like?' Josefina asked him. 'Is it as big as Chapultepec? Is it as beautiful as Cuervanaca? How many servants does he keep?'

He answered as patiently as he could, then added, 'Josefina, if you are harbouring any thoughts about going with him, I advise you to forget them.'

'Oh, he will not leave,' she said complacently. 'His destiny is in Mexico; it is in the stars.'

He looked at her sharply. 'Of course he'll leave! He is on his way already.'

'We shall see.' She laughed suddenly. 'But you, you don't want to go, do you? You want to stay with your heart's desire. You are chafing at the bit to be with her at this very minute, but your chivalrous upbringing will not allow you to get up and leave.'

'If you are referring to Mrs Wainright,' he said coldly, 'perhaps I should remind you that she is a married woman, and I am taking her to her husband on the orders of the Emperor.'

'She would have done better to have stayed with Redford. At least he knows where the man is.' Josefina paused, watching his expression. 'You have no idea at all, have you?'

'You know where James Wainright is? He is not in Yucatan?'

'Oh, he is in Yucatan, but that is a large area, is it not?'

'But not in Palenche?'

'No.'

'Where, then?'

'You wish me to tell you?'

'Yes, or I would not have asked.'

She laughed mischievously. 'Then I shall tell you, when we reach the Emperor. Martha and I cannot risk having you go chasing off and leaving us before that.'

'We have a long day ahead of us tomorrow,' Martha said, rising. 'I think I shall retire.' Leo stood to bid her goodnight, but as Josefina showed no sign of following her, he went to the window and stood looking out, wondering if she were bluffing.

'I didn't know the Colonel knew Mr Wainright,' he said. 'What do they have in common?'

She came over to stand beside him. 'Money, my dear Leo. Redford has it, and Jimmy needs it.'

He turned to look down at her, and she put her hand on his shoulder and said softly, 'Forget them, Leo. You have more important things to think of than a silly European woman who cannot manage to keep her nose out of the affairs of Mexico.'

'On the contrary,' he said, 'Mrs Wainright is concerned only with finding her husband.'

'Do you really believe that? She persuaded Redford to take her with him instead of on the diligence, and thereby escaped the ambush. She defended a rebel family, assaulted a French officer and had herself thrown in gaol, not to mention carrying a pistol and being very outspoken against the Emperor. Are they the actions of an innocent woman? My dear Leo, you are very naïve if you believe that!'

She was still standing with her hand on his shoulder, looking up into his face with a smile that reminded him of a contented cat. It made him so angry that he felt like shaking her. He put out his hand to remove hers from his shoulder. 'It's time we went to bed,' he said evenly.

She laughed aloud and reached up to kiss his cheek. 'Is that an invitation, Leo?' Then, looking over his shoulder towards the door, added, 'Why, Mrs Wainright, is something wrong?'

Leo spun round to see Stella standing in the doorway

with a loose robe over her nightgown and her hair falling about her shoulders like a tawny halo. It made him catch his breath.

'My room is stifling,' she said, colouring with embarrassment. 'I was looking for someone to open the window for me. I can't move it.'

'I'll do it.' Leo disengaged himself from Josefina and moved towards Stella.

Behind them, Josefina burst into laughter. 'That's one way to get a man into your room, but why bother with the pretence?'

Leo turned to retort, changed his mind and followed Stella upstairs to her room.

The window catch was corroded, but he managed to open it and then turned to leave, 'You should be able to sleep now.'

'Thank you.'

He bade her goodnight with a stiff bow, and left her.

Stella wished she had not gone downstairs; it would have been better to suffocate in an airless bedroom than witness Leo and Josefina in each other's arms, but once she had been seen, she could not retreat. She returned to her bed, and lay there looking at the sky outlined by the small window. There was a bright moon and a few patches of cloud; it was the same moon that hung over her home in England, and the thought of it filled her with a longing to be back there. But there was nowhere and nothing to go back to; everything had been sold. Oh, if only she could find Jimmy quickly, then perhaps he would make everything right again.

Her impatience was not helped when they all assembled outside the inn the next morning to resume their journey, and she realised they would all be travelling on together.

'Where are we going?' she asked, as Leo called for the horses and mules to be brought out and harnessed to their respective vehicles.

'To join the Emperor's party,' he said shortly. 'The ladies need an escort.'

'Is that on our way?'

He laughed mirthlessly. 'As it seems I do not know the way, I can't answer that.'

'What do you mean, you don't know the way? You didn't say anything about that before we set off.'

'Then I thought we were going to Palenche.'

'And we're not?'

'Señorita Gonzales informs me that Mr Wainright is not to be found there.'

'Not? How does she know?'

'She tells me that the Colonel does know, and you have chosen the wrong guide.'

'I don't remember having a choice.' She smiled, in spite of herself. 'And, come to that, neither did you.'

He did not answer, but turned and ushered the two other women into the coach and called to Pablo to ride his horse.

'You are not abandoning the search, are you?' Stella asked.

He looked down at her and grinned sardonically. 'No, I am not abandoning it, but Josefina has said that she will tell me the answer to the riddle when I have taken her and Miss Carson to the Emperor, so please be so good as to follow with the wagon.'

They caught up with the royal party at Aculcingo, where it had taken over a local hacienda. The Emperor himself, they were told, had gone butterfly hunting.

'Butterfly hunting?' Leo repeated in annoyance. 'His empire is falling down about his ears, and he goes chasing butterflies!'

He left the women at the house, where they all declared they were going to enjoy the luxury of a bath, told Pablo to find Lieutenant Rodriguez and, taking his horse, rode across the fields to look for Maximilian. He found him with Father Fischer, a new adviser, and Dr Bilimek of the Museum, whose cork helmet was covered with the impaled bodies of dozens of exquisite butterflies.

'Leo!' the Emperor called, waving his butterfly-net. 'Look what we've caught!'

Leo dismounted. 'Yes, your Majesty, they are very beautiful.'

'And did you catch your beautiful butterfly?'

'I left Mrs Wainright in the town with Miss Carson and Señorita Gonzales, your Majesty. But, as I feared, she won't leave Mexico without her husband.'

'No matter, we do not think we shall leave, either.'

'Not leave?' Leo could hardly believe his ears. 'But, a few days ago, your Majesty was determined to go.'

'We can change our mind, can we not?'

'Yes of course, your Majesty, but why?'

'You are paid to draw pictures,' Fischer snapped, 'to record the events of history, not to change its course or question the decisions of your Emperor.'

Maximilian waved a dismissive hand at the priest, and smiled at Leo. 'It is my duty to stay. Besides, I do believe the people want me to. When I entered Orizaba yesterday, there was a great welcome for me. The streets were thronged with people, all cheering and shouting: *"Viva el Emperador!"* They threw flowers at me and reached out to touch me, and all declared their undying loyalty. It is the *pantalons rouges* they do not like, not me.' He paused, then added, 'Why so glum? Is it not a cause for rejoicing?'

'Yes, your Majesty,' Leo said, though he could not bring himself to smile. The Emperor's account of his welcome was at variance with what he had gathered from the people he had talked to at the inn.

'You have doubts?'

'Your Majesty,' he said, pleading, 'I beg you to continue your journey and leave Mexico without delay.'

'I delay because I am having second thoughts. If I flee, I will be going back on the promise I made to my people, when I first came to Mexico, that I would never desert them. The Habsburg honour is at stake.'

'Besides, the Emperor is ill,' Fischer added silkily, realising that it would not be easy to turn the Emperor against the young Hussar. 'The countryside here is beautiful and healthy. He needs to relax and recoup his strength.'

Leo did not like the man; he was an opportunist, and it would not surprise him to learn that the priest had paid for the rapturous welcome in Orizaba. 'And the *Juáristas*?'

'A handful of dissidents,' Fischer said. 'We shall soon have them scuttling back to their rat-holes.'

'That handful of dissidents has already taken Tampico, Monterrey, Mazatlan, Saltillo and Guaymas!' Leo rounded on him. 'We are short of men and money, and the Liberals are being financed and armed by the Americans.'

'Do you have proof of what you say?' Fischer asked coolly.

'Not yet, but, given leave, I shall get it.'

'Then I suggest you go and find it before you make accusations of that nature,' Fischer said. 'Such statements could have far-reaching diplomatic consequences.'

Leo looked at Maximilian, who nodded in agreement. 'Go, Leo, hunt your own butterflies. We shall return to Mexico City.'

'Yes, sir.' Leo clicked his heels to attention and inclined his head in a stiffly formal bow. 'Does that instruction countermand my previous order to escort Mrs Wainright to Yucatan?'

'It does not.'

Leo backed away, before mounting and returning to the town in search of Ramón Rodriguez and a little congenial masculine company. The royal military escort was housed in what was normally the building used by the ranch-hands, spartan, but comfortable enough. Ramón was sprawled across his bed, reading a pamphlet.

'Heaven preserve me from a gaggle of women!' Leo said, removing his jacket and sitting on the next bed. 'One is enough, but three is more than a body can stand.'

Ramón laughed. 'What are you going to do with them all?'

'Two of them I intend to pass on to you.'

'Me?' The young lieutenant sat up. 'What am I supposed to do with them?'

Leo shrugged. 'That's up to you, but I think Miss Carson will want to continue on to Vera Cruz if you could find an escort for her, and as for Señorita Gonzales, she will almost certainly choose to remain at the Emperor's side.'

'You know he's changed his mind about leaving?'

'Yes.'

'What are you going to do?'

'Take Mrs Wainright to her husband, as soon as I can find out where he might be, then I shall return to normal duties. That can't happen too soon for me!'

He lapsed into a broody silence, and Ramón knew better than to question him. He went to the door and shouted for an orderly to find some food and washing water, then returned to sit at the table, where there was a decanter of wine and some glasses. 'Here,' he said, pouring it, 'this will wash away the dust of the journey.'

'Ramón, my friend,' Leo said, 'you can do something for me.'

'Anything.'

'You remember my mentioning a certain painting I had on the diligence?'

'Of the beautiful Mrs Wainright? Yes.'

'It wasn't destroyed. It's turned up again on Colonel Carson's coach.'

'How did he come to have it?'

'That's a question I have been asking myself. The last time I saw it was when it was loaded on to the diligence along with my luggage at Paso del Macho. I am sure it was still there when we stopped for the night at Cordoba.'

'It was stolen?'

'I think so. It confirms what I have suspected for some

time, but could not prove—that Redford Carson has been helping the Liberals. The pieces of the puzzle are beginning to fit together. He had brought two heavy wooden boxes with him from New Orleans, and had left his coach at Vera Cruz ready to take them on. I'm sure he intended to go home to Carlota Colony the next day, but when Mrs Wainright asked him to take her to Mexico City, he would have been left with the problem of ridding himself of the boxes. He would not have wanted to take them to Mexico City.'

'Why should Mrs Wainright ask to ride with him?'

Leo shrugged. 'I don't know. I don't know how much she knows or how much she is implicated.' He spoke wearily. 'Nor do I really wish to know.'

Ramón looked at him sharply, wondering if that were true. 'I still don't see what the picture has to do with it. Is it valuable?'

'Only to me.' The shadow of a remembered pain crossed Leo's face, but it was gone in an instant, and he went on, 'I was sleeping in the stables, and was wakened about midnight by a great deal of activity around the Colonel's coach. I went to investigate, just in time to see the second of the boxes being transferred to another vehicle by two men I had never seen before. They drove it out of town, and I borrowed a horse to follow but lost sight of it in the vicinity of Carlota Colony. Though I searched for some time, I couldn't pick up the trail again. It seems obvious that the portrait was taken from the diligence at the same time, because, now I come to think of it, there was nothing in the ashes of the diligence, when I went back to it, to suggest there had been a painting on board.'

'And you think Carson is behind it?'

'I have yet to prove it.'

'Where is the man now?'

Leo laughed. 'When last seen, he was galloping away from a fight! God knows where he is now. But if he should turn up again while I'm away, I want you to watch him carefully. Make a note of everything he does. And if you can find out what his connection is with James Wainright, so much the better.'

'Of course. You can rely on me.'

'Will you also take the picture back to Mexico City when you return? You'll find it on Carson's coach.'

'Yes, if the Emperor doesn't change his mind again and decide to go on. Am I right in assuming that you are setting off with Mrs Wainright straight away?'

'At first light tomorrow, provided Josefina Gonzales gives me some answers. One minute I am convinced she is lying and has no more idea where Wainright is than I have, and the next that she is telling the truth. Either way, I need to know, or we could be traipsing all over Mexico for months on end. And that is something I could not endure!'

'Then let me wish you luck, my friend.'

Stella was ready to leave almost as soon as the sun came up, and was outside the stables, refreshed after a comfortable night and a good breakfast, when Leo, in workaday civilian clothes, put in an appearance. His uniform had emphasised his slim figure and broad shoulders, but the rough trousers and open shirt he wore now made him seem much taller and broader, with a raw masculinity she found most unsettling.

'Good morning, Stella,' he said cheerfully. 'Your punctuality does you credit.'

'I am impatient to be on the way.'

'Indeed, so am I. The sooner we start, the sooner we shall finish. Pablo is already aboard the wagon, so if you join him, we can be off.'

She watched him as he swung into the saddle of his horse, unable to stifle a little sigh of admiration. He was so handsome and self-possessed, and he ought to make a gallant escort, except . . . No, she would not think of all the reasons that made the prospect of several days, perhaps weeks, in his company an exquisite form of torture.

They left the mountains behind on the first day, the

grazing cattle on the lower slopes on the second, and on the third they passed by fields of corn and after that a barren land with prickly thorn and thickets of yellow mimosa, filling the air with its scent. Now that they were no longer in the mountains, the heat became almost unbearable, even in the shadow of the canvas covering the wagon. It must have been worse for Leo on horseback, but he did not complain. Every now and again they came upon a clearing where two roads met, where there would be a village of small whitewashed huts with palm-thatched roofs and a tiny square planted about with scarlet hibiscus and geraniums. The entourage attracted considerable interest from the villagers, as they stopped to buy fresh fruit, goats' milk and bread, but they did not stay very long at any of them. Leo seemed to be in great haste, and Stella herself had no wish to prolong the journey.

Occasionally Leo hitched his horse to the back of the wagon and took over the driving, to allow Pablo to rest. At such times Stella would sit beside him, trying to talk normally and ignore the fact that her cheeks were burning and her heart was beating a little faster.

'Mexico must be a beautiful country in peaceful times,' she said one day, when they had just passed through a particularly attractive village. 'It's such a shame that so much of it has become overgrown and neglected. Papa was particularly upset by that.'

'Your father was a fine man, Stella. I was proud to call him my friend. His death was a terrible tragedy, not only for you, but for everyone concerned with natural history.'

'Did you know him before he came to Mexico?' The question seemed innocuous enough, but he knew why she was asking it.

'You mean, did I meet him in Trieste? The answer is no. My first encounter with Sir Peter was when he came to Chapultepec.'

'Did you tell him that we . . .' She paused, and swallowed. 'That we had met?'

'No, Stella, it seemed to me that if you had wanted him to know, you would have told him yourself; it was not my place to mention it.'

His voice was clipped, as if he did not want to talk about it, and she decided to change the subject. 'Can you tell me anything about his accident? Jimmy was so upset that he could hardly write more than a few lines.'

'I'm afraid not; he was alone at the time. I believe he was using a scalpel, which slipped in his hand. He died from loss of blood before he was found.'

'Oh, but Señorita Gonzales said that Jimmy was with him.'

'You must have misunderstood. Jimmy found the body.'

They were silent for some minutes, and then he said, 'Since we are in the mood for question and answer, tell me how long you have known James Wainright.'

'Oh, ages. He was one of my father's pupils.'

'Before we met in Trieste?'

She turned to look at him sharply, but he appeared to be concentrating on the road ahead. 'We had met before that, but I can't say I really knew him. It was after we returned to London and I began helping my father, and he became his assistant, that we met again.'

'And you decided he was the only man for you? That there could be no other?' She blushed at the memory of that conversation in Trieste, and did not reply. 'Why don't you answer me? Have you forgotten your girlish dreams?'

'That's all they were,' she said, trying to sound light-hearted. 'Girlish dreams. I was young and foolish then, but I'm wiser now.'

He smiled a little lopsidedly. 'I'm glad to hear it. And has this marriage of yours been all you hoped it would be?'

'Of course,' she said quickly. 'Jimmy is a very affectionate husband.'

'How long had you been married before he came out here?'

'Six months.'

'Six months! Still in the first flush of being newly wed, and he leaves you. If it were me, I don't think I could . . .' He stopped suddenly. 'No, we won't pursue that. Did he and your father get along?'

'Yes, of course. What a funny question! Otherwise, they would never have come out here together.'

'No, I suppose not. And did either of them ever mention Colonel Carson in their letters to you?'

'No, why should they?'

'No reason. No reason at all.'

'Leo, why are you asking all these questions?'

'Just to make conversation. It's better than riding along in stony silence, though if that is what you want, I will oblige.'

'Then let me ask you some questions. How long have you known the Emperor Maximilian?'

'Ever since we were boys together. Our families have always been friends, and when my father died, my mother was made a lady-in-waiting to the Archduchess Charlotte, that was the Empress's name then. She only became "Carlota" when they came to Mexico.'

'And you came to Mexico at the same time.'

'Yes, both Mother and I are part of the Emperor's household.'

'And how long have you been a Hussar?'

'Since 1861.'

'Five years.'

'Is that significant?'

'No.' She smiled. 'I was just making conversation.'

He laughed. '*Touché!*'

'*Señor!*' Pablo's voice came to them from where he was sitting on the tailboard of the wagon. 'I see the sea.'

'Good,' Leo said. 'Stage one of our little journey is almost at an end. We should be able to hire a boat to take us and the wagon on to Carmen. A little voyage along the coast will be very pleasant and cool after the heat of the land.'

But he was wrong; there was no boat to be had. It seemed that every available craft had been taken by its owner to Vera Cruz, where there were passengers in plenty willing to pay exorbitant prices to leave a country that had proved so inhospitable.

'Now what shall we do?' asked Stella, as they stood at the quayside, gazing out over the almost deserted harbour. The only boats left were either too small or too derelict for their purpose. 'Surely there must be one suitable craft left in the town?'

'Look!' Pablo pointed to the far end of the quay, where a small fishing-vessel was just putting up sail.

Leo sprinted over to it, closely followed by Pablo and Stella. He called out to the man who was preparing it for sea, 'Is this boat for hire, *Señor*?'

'No, it is not,' said a voice in English. 'Unless the little lady cares to travel with me instead of with the Emperor's nursemaid.'

Startled, they looked round to see Carson taking hold of the rope that anchored the boat to the shore. He was smiling easily. 'Well, Stella?' he added, when no one answered him. 'Shall I cast off, or wait for you to come aboard?'

Stella looked at Leo and then Pablo, and Pablo said, 'He bad man! You stay with Señor Leo, eh?'

'Cast off, damn you!' Leo said. 'Mrs Wainright is in my care.'

Carson laughed as the rope snaked away and the sails filled. 'She may live to regret that!'

Stella had no idea why she had not seized the opportunity to go on with Carson. Maybe it was Pablo's assertion that he was a bad man, maybe it was the memory of him galloping away from a fight, maybe it was because of his almost triumphant laugh—but it was not, most definitely was not, because she wanted to stay with Leo.

In the town, they found a hotel with vacant rooms, where Stella enjoyed the luxury of a proper meal that had not been cooked over an open fire and did not taste of woodsmoke, and afterwards she went up to a comfortable bedroom, stripped off all her clothes and washed herself in a large earthenware bowl before stretching out on the bed. She had no idea what the morrow would bring, but so long as Leo was taking her towards her husband, she would accept it and make the best of it, and would try her hardest not to think about Trieste and his reasons for leaving her then. She had almost asked him that afternoon and she might have done, too, had Pablo not called out when he did. She was glad of that, now; Trieste was in the past, and it did no good to dwell on it.

CHAPTER SEVEN

THERE WAS nothing for it but to continue overland, and the next day, after buying more supplies, Stella and Leo set off in a south-easterly direction, moving away from the cool air of the coast to the uncomfortable heat of forests of pine and cypress, interspersed with bougainvillea and begonias.

Two days later the road, if it deserved the name, cut through dense jungle festooned with climbing greenery and interwoven with the thick cable-like stems of the liana twisting from tree to tree. It all joined into one dark green umbrella above their heads, cutting out the sun. Monkeys swung from branch to branch, filling the dark cathedral with their chatter; tree-frogs and brightly-plumed parrots, suddenly taking wing, added to the eerie noise. The wagon was often ankle deep in mud and at other times halted by the roots of trees pushing their way up through the road.

'Where are we making for?' Stella panted, as they rested after manhandling the wagon over one particularly bad patch. She was bathed in perspiration, and her hair stuck to her cheeks and neck in wet strands. Her serviceable brown cotton skirt clung to her legs in damp folds, and her sturdy shoes had disappeared beneath the mud that caked them. She had tried, but it was impossible to keep clean.

'Had enough?' Leo asked, daring her to say yes. He had been pushing her to the limit of her endurance, but she was determined to keep going. It was no longer a simple mission to find her husband, but a battle of wills between her and Leo, and it was a battle she meant to win.

'No, certainly not,' she said. 'I ask because I noticed

you had changed direction. We are no longer moving east but nearly north.'

'How very observant of you!'

'You forget I am not unused to moving across country.'

'And you are convinced I could not lose you?' he taunted.

She looked at him sharply. 'Do you intend to try?'

He laughed. 'No, of course not.'

'Then, where are we going?'

'To the coast?'

'Why?'

'To get out of the jungle, for a start, but also because there is a small fishing village called San Josef where we might find a boat.'

'And if we miss Jimmy by doing that?'

'Your husband is nowhere near here.'

'Are you sure?'

'Of course I'm sure! Goodness, Stella, do you think I want to delay your reunion with your darling husband? The sooner we find him, the sooner I can return to other duties.'

'I know you did not want to come with me, any more than I wanted it,' she said with some asperity. 'But you need not be so blunt about it!'

'I am a soldier, used to being blunt, and there are more important tasks.'

'Not for me.'

He laughed, but there was no humour in his voice. 'Then be so good as to put your shoulder to the wheel and save your breath for pushing.'

She did as he asked, not because she wanted to, but because it was expedient. In spite of her bravado, she knew that if he left her she really would be lost, but inwardly she was fuming. He had no right to speak to her as though she were a child who had displeased him. It was not her fault that he had been ordered to accompany her. She was beginning to wish she had boarded the boat with Carson, but she had no idea where he was going; it might be nowhere near where Jimmy was. She stepped back from the creaking wagon and stood, heaving for breath, watching it lurching slowly away from her. Leo was tugging at the head of one of the mules; he was bathed in perspiration, but the sight of him could still quicken her senses and the last few days had been a special kind of torment, because she was slowly coming to realise what she had lost. She needed her husband; she needed him to shut out thoughts of Leo, to give her some sense of normality. None of this was normal; it was like a bad dream and she longed to wake up and find herself at home in England with her mother and father and husband, cool and cosseted.

She stopped suddenly and let out a sharp cry of fear as a huge snake slid from beneath the undergrowth at the side of the path and slithered towards her. She was frozen to the spot, and Leo and the wagon were fifty yards ahead. 'Leo!' Her cry sounded weak, but she dared not look away from the reptile to see if he had heard. It moved nearer and nearer.

'Stand still!'

She did not need his command; she was petrified, but at least he had come back for her. The shot echoed through the forest, sending the monkeys into a frenzy, making the birds leave their perches, uttering squawks of terror. The snake jumped, writhed, and then lay still. Stella found herself trembling uncontrollably and her legs began to buckle beneath her.

'It's over now,' he said gently, putting his arm round her shaking shoulders to support her. 'It's dead. Look.'

Suddenly her whole body was racked by sobs, and she could not stop herself. His grip on her tightened, and his hand moved up behind her neck, holding her head so that it rested against his chest. She could feel the strength of his arms about her and hear the strong beating of his heart, and she did not want to move. His face was very close to hers, and in a moment their lips would meet. She pulled herself away and fished in her pocket for a handkerchief. 'How silly of me,' she said, falsely bright. 'It was a reaction, I suppose.'

His eyes clouded, and he kicked at the dead body of the snake, sending it back into the undergrowth. 'No doubt.' His voice was clipped, impersonal. 'Do you want to stop and rest, or are you ready to go on?'

The moment of intimacy had passed, and everything was back to what it had been, except . . . except that she could not forget the concern in his voice, the tenderness of his embrace. But she had to forget it; she had to put it from her mind. 'We'll go on,' she told him, walking to the wagon.

'We'll stop soon,' he said.

'Please don't stop any earlier on my account,' she said. 'I am as anxious to reach our destination as you are.'

'Very well.'

'Do you think they might have news of Jimmy in this village?'

'Perhaps.'

'If not, I'll show them the picture I took from my father's room. Someone might recognise it.'

'I doubt it. The coastal people never travel very far inland, for the sea is their highway. In fact, the natives in these parts stick pretty close to their own patch.'

'But they do get news of the outside world?'

'Yes, it comes by sea.'

'You will be anxious for news of the Emperor, of course.'

He returned to the head of the mule, tugging at the harness to get it going again, and did not reply.

It was so dark beneath the trees that it was almost impossible to tell night from day, but when the few blue patches they could see between the branches disappeared, they stopped in a small clearing beside a pool and made camp.

It had become a ritual, and each had a job to do, either fetching firewood, lighting a fire, cooking or looking after the animals. When all was done, they sat to eat corn *tortilla* and black beans fried in garlic-flavoured fat, washed down with bitter black coffee, while their aching muscles relaxed. Bed was the wagon for Stella and a patch of dry ground near the fire for Leo and Pablo, and she was so tired that not even the buzzing, tormenting insects could keep her awake.

Halfway through the next day the jungle thinned, then became scrub, then fields of sweet corn interspersed with beans, sweet potatoes and casava. Suddenly they found themselves on the edge of a palm-fringed beach, and the cool blue sea was lapping only yards away.

With a cry of delight, Stella, who had been on the driving-seat, scrambled down from her perch, kicked off her shoes and plunged into it, fully clothed. She heard Leo laugh behind her and then he, too, was in the water, throwing handfuls of it over his head and letting it run down his sweat-streaked face, then slapping the surface to splash it over her. She moved away and he followed, laughing. She stopped and turned, and threw handfuls of water over him until his hair was soaked and hung in tight little curls over his forehead. The privations of their journey were forgotten, the reason for it gone from their minds; this was heaven. It was cool and invigorating, but she knew she would have to leave it before long. And that posed a problem. Her clothes were heavy with water, and clung so closely to the contours of her body that she might as well not have been wearing any.

'Leo,' she said pleasantly, 'please get a towel and a robe from the wagon for me.'

He suddenly realised her predicament and sat down on the sand, half submerged in water, and laughed until the tears ran.

'Oh, dear, the very proper, the very self-possessed Mrs Wainright is in a pickle!'

'I am not in a pickle!'

'You dare not come out.'

'Of course I dare.'

'Come on, then.' He scrambled to his feet and backed up the beach, beckoning her to follow him. 'Come on.'

'Later,' she said. 'It's too nice to leave.'

'I shall go on without you.'

She dared not call his bluff, and left the water, emerging, so he said, 'like Venus from the waves, except that Venus was naked'. He ran towards her, laughing boyishly, and, picking her up in his arms, carried her to the wagon, where he stood her down beside the tailboard.

'You know,' he said, reaching out to touch her wet cheek, 'there are times when you tempt me sorely . . .'

'I have no idea what you are talking about,' she said, trying to sound cool.

'Don't you? Come, Stella, you are not as naïve as you pretend! You knew perfectly well what would happen when you ran into the water like that. You know how to tease a man, how to kindle his desire, until he is almost beside himself, as I know to my cost. You could make me forget you are a married woman . . .'

She was shivering, but why? The sea had not been cold and the sun was as hot as ever. 'I don't know what you mean.'

'Then I shall have to show you.' He drew her towards him and lowered his face to hers. 'Like this.' His lips were on hers before she could protest, and his arms were holding her so close against him that she could feel his thighs against hers. Her body tingled with anticipation and she put her arms up and round his neck, returning his kiss. She wanted him, there was no denying it; the fire he had kindled in her in Trieste was still there, still waiting to be fanned back into flame. But it was madness. She twisted her mouth away and pushed against his chest, but it had no more effect than a puff of wind. 'Let me go, Leo.'

He still held her, though he leaned his head back to look at her. 'You want me to let you go?'

'Yes.'

'For ever? Never hold you again?'

Her hesitation was only momentary, but he saw it and smiled, and it seemed to Stella that it was a smile of triumph. He could have her whenever he wanted and he had to give nothing in return—neither love, nor fidelity. 'Yes,' she said, hoping she sounded calm, but afraid she did not. 'And I would rather you did not spoil what is, after all, a perfectly ordinary business arrangement by talking in that fashion.'

'Ordinary!' he repeated. 'There is nothing ordinary about it. It is slow torture.'

'You don't have to insult me! I know you would rather be with the Emperor, living in luxury, with good food and wine and silk shirts, instead of having to put up with the hardships of an expedition through the jungle. But if I can stand it, I don't see why you should not.'

He threw back his head and roared with laughter. 'Oh, Mrs Wainright, you are priceless! Get back in that wagon and change into dry clothes before I forget myself entirely and . . .' He smiled at the look of horror that crossed her face. 'Perhaps it would teach you not to play with fire.' He put his hand out to help her up, but she shrugged him angrily away and climbed up unaided.

It did not take long to change, and she was soon back in her seat at the front of the wagon. There was no sign of the Mexican boy, and she realised suddenly that she had not seen him since they had entered the water.

'Where is Pablo?'

'I sent him on ahead to find accommodation for us and the animals.'

High on the seat, she noticed something she had not seen before. Half a mile away along the shore was a small fishing village where boats, moored against a little jetty, bobbed up and down on the calm water, their red and brown sails furled. Far out to sea a steamship could just be seen, heading east. Leo, who had also changed, climbed up beside her and raised his binoculars to look more closely at it.

'That's the *Dandolo*,' he said. 'Bound for Europe.'

'And you are wishing heartily that you were on board.'

'No, but I wish the Emperor were.'

'Perhaps he is.'

'No, he has new advisers who think he should stay, and the Mexican generals need him as a figurehead.' His tone was flat, but she detected a note of frustration. He sounded as he had in Trieste when Maximilian had been persuaded to accept the throne.

'Why are you so sure he ought to leave?'

'Because he does not have the support of enough of the people, and when the French forces leave next year, he will be unable to defend himself against the Liberals who want a return of the Republic.'

'But you are loyal?'

'I have sworn an oath of allegiance, but even without that, I would follow him. He is my friend, and the loyalty of a friend is greater than that of a servant. The one is bought, the other given freely.' He put the binoculars away and looked down at her. 'But you don't understand that, do you?'

'Of course I do.'

'Then why did you . . .' He broke off suddenly, realising the futility of mentioning his reasons for leaving Miramar, and shrugged his shoulders. 'It does not matter.'

They sat without moving until it had gone from sight and only a tiny puff of smoke on the horizon marked its passage. It made her want to cry, to cry for the Emperor, for all those who had supported him so loyally, for Leo, but most of all for herself, for dreams that had been shattered, for hopes never to be realised, for love unfulfilled, for a husband who was no more than a half-remembered dream.

Leo picked up the reins and called to the mules, and they resumed their steady plod. 'We'll stop in San Josef and make some enquiries about your husband,' he said. 'We also need some supplies, and you need to rest.' He was again the hard, cold soldier, and in truth, she preferred him that way, he was easier to deal with.

Pablo met them on the outskirts of the little port and led them to a two-storey house near the waterfront owned by a middle-aged Creole called Da Silva. It was simple and clean, and the owner was prepared to rent them rooms for the night and a stable for the horse and mules. Leo thought the price he asked was extortionate and said so, but he agreed to pay when Pablo pointed out that such accommodation was hard to find, and the lady of the house was prepared to cook a meal for them.

'I only hope it's not chilli and beans,' Leo said, deciding to accept. 'I've had enough of those in the last two weeks to last a life time.'

'*Panuchos*, she say,' Pablo told him. 'Chicken *tortilla* with onions.'

Señor Da Silva called to his wife, who conducted Stella to a room where there was an iron bedstead, an unsteady table, a rickety chair, a hip-bath waiting to be filled and a cracked mirror. Compared to the wagon that had been her home for over two weeks, it was a palace. While she was inspecting it, Leo arrived with her basket.

'Is this enough?' he asked. 'Do you want your trunk brought in?'

'No, thank you, this is enough for one night.'

'I think we shall be here more than one night. We need to buy supplies, for the salt is damp, we're low on coffee and there are one or two other items we should have. Besides, you need to rest.'

'A few hours is all I need. I shall be ready to continue first thing tomorrow.'

'You are exhausted. Just look at you, almost asleep on your feet! You can't go on like that.'

'I can and I will. I must find Jimmy.'

His face was set in a mask of indifference, though his voice was cracked with suppressed emotion. 'It will get worse, you know.'

Yes, she thought, it will get worse; with every day that passed, the sweet agony of having him so near would get worse. And it *was* agony, and the only way she could bear it was to remind herself again and again of how she had felt when he abandoned her in Trieste. He had never mentioned that and she certainly had no intention of doing so, but it was there, an unspoken accusation between them, and that was the way it had to stay, because she was married to James Wainright. Leo Manfred had no place in her life.

'I won't change my mind, Leo, so please say no more about it.'

'We'll decide tomorrow.' There was no point in arguing with her. 'Now I have some business to attend to.'

'Business? Here?'

'Why not? You do want to find that husband of yours, I suppose?'

'Of course. I want nothing more.'

A shadow passed across his features and his blue eyes darkened, and she suddenly realised how tired he looked. He had said she needed sleep, but he needed it more. He had done the work of ten men to bring her this far, driving himself and the animals to the point of collapse, always watchful, night and day. She had been insensitive not to have noticed it.

'Then do as I say and rest,' he went on. 'Then pretty yourself up. I'll be back for supper.'

He left her, and mounted his horse to escort the wagon, driven by Pablo, down to the jetty, surrounded by laughing, chattering children who clung precariously to the back and sides of the vehicle. Her intention to follow later to see where he went was abandoned when she took off her dress and stretched out on the bed in her underclothes. It was soft and comfortable after the hard boards of the wagon, and the room was cool and quiet. In no time at all she dozed, to be wakened by a light tap on the door, and Señora Da Silva came in carrying a jug of warm water and towels, and told her it would soon be supper-time.

She washed and dressed carefully in a soft blue-grey silk trimmed with a darker shade of velvet ribbon at the throat and round the full skirt, which her grandmother had condemned as too plain when she had bought it. Today it suited her mood: she had no wish to try to impress Leo Manfred with her elegance. Her soft auburn hair she coiled and pinned at the nape of her neck.

In the dining-room, a table had been laid for two. Pablo would be eating with the family in the kitchen.

There was no sign of Leo, and she wandered to the window. She could see the sea, glinting like dark pewter in the half light between day and night, the tiny boats securely tied to the jetty, and, a little further out, a larger vessel, a paddle-steamer by the look of it, which had not been there when they arrived and which was now moving away towards the horizon. She supposed it had brought supplies and news from the outside world. Leo would tell her about that, if they could manage to stay on amicable terms long enough to converse civilly. But the trouble was that they never did; one moment he was considerate and caring, the next just the opposite. He was like two different people in the same body.

She moved away from the window when she saw him riding towards the house. A few minutes later she heard footsteps going upstairs, heavily, as if he were too tired to put one foot in front of the other, or perhaps because he did not want to join her for the meal. She moved to the door, intending to return to her room, but he suddenly reappeared at the top of the stairs and came towards her.

'I apologise for being late,' he said stiffly. 'I'll join you in five minutes, no more.'

She returned to the dining-room, and before the five minutes was up, he was with her, having washed, shaved and put on a clean white shirt, although he wore no cravat or jacket. Señora Da Silva brought in their meal and left them to serve themselves.

'Did you find any news of Jimmy?' she asked, putting food on his plate for him.

'I learned that there is a white man in one of the villages a few miles south of here, though no one seemed to know if he is still there.'

'Could it be Jimmy?'

'Perhaps.' He poured wine in her glass. 'I thought I would ride there tomorrow and find out, before we went any further.'

'You mean you intend to go without me?'

'It would be quicker, and if it turns out to be a false

report, we shall have lost nothing but a little time.'

'I want to come too.'

'No, you stay here and rest. It is cooler by the coast, and, besides, you could finish buying the supplies so that we are ready to proceed when I return.'

'And if you find Jimmy?'

He smiled lopsidedly. 'I shall bring him straight back to you, Mrs Wainright. That is, if he wants to come.'

'Wants to come?'

'Had it occurred to you that he might prefer to stay lost?'

'No, it hadn't,' she said sharply. 'How can you say such a thing?'

'Have you never wondered why he didn't answer your letters?'

'Yes, but that was because of the situation in Mexico and because he had left to come to Yucatan.'

'You are very sure of him,' he said wryly. 'It must be gratifying to be the object of such an unquestioning love.'

'I have no reason to question it, and I would prefer it if you would refrain from making unfounded accusations like that!'

'Very well, we shall assume that James Wainright loves his wife and wants nothing so much as to be with her again. But why did he stay here after Sir Peter died? Why did he not return to England to comfort you in your sad loss?'

He was only voicing doubts that had plagued her for some time, but she did not want him to see that. She looked down at her plate.

'I shall take Pablo with me,' he said. 'That is, if you have no objection. He speaks the Mayan language, and I might have need of that.'

'As you wish.' The atmosphere between them was thick with unspoken thoughts, half-remembered joy, unfulfilled promise, doubts and longing. It was unbearable, and she was so close to tears that she did not see the pain in his eyes, did not guess that it was the same for him.

He poured more wine in their glasses, swallowed his at a gulp and then reached for a bottle of tequila that Señora Da Silva had stood on the table. 'Do you like tequila, Mrs Wainright?' he asked.

'I don't drink spirits.'

He poured some into a clean glass for her. 'You should try it with fresh orange; it's very good.'

'No, thank you.'

'I insist you try it,' he said, adding a generous quantity of orange juice. 'It will help you to relax.'

'I am perfectly relaxed.'

'No, you're not. You're as stiff as a ramrod. Please drink.' He held the glass out.

She took it and stood it on the table at her elbow. He had a cold angry look in his eyes which frightened her, and she began to look wildly about for a way of escape.

'Are you afraid of me?' he asked suddenly.

'No.' She wished her voice held more conviction.

'Then you are afraid of yourself, afraid of your own emotions. You dare not drink in case you give yourself away.'

'I am not hiding anything.' She picked up the glass and sipped it gingerly, almost as though she expected it to explode in her face, and was surprised to find that it tasted very refreshing.

'That's better.' He smiled. 'Now we will have a normal conversation like two civilised people. We'll pretend James Wainright does not exist.'

'Oh, but we can't do that,' she said quickly. 'He is my husband, part of my life, and I need him desperately.'

'God, woman!' he shouted, getting up from the table. 'Can you think of nothing else? I'm sick of acting nursemaid to a child—yes, a child, because that's all you are! You have not matured since you left the school-room, you know nothing of life, or of love. And I'm sick of travelling the earth in search of your dream, because your dream is *my* nightmare.' He pushed his chair back so violently that it fell over with a crash, then he strode from the room, slamming the door.

The silence that followed his going hung in the air like a threat. It menaced her peace of mind, it stifled her, making her want to scream, to shout, anything to fill it with some sound. It was unbearable. She ran from the room.

He was standing outside the door, as if debating whether to return. 'Stella . . .' His voice held an anguish she was not disposed to hear, and she pushed past him to go up to her bed.

It was hours before she could sleep, and when she did, she dreamed. It was the nightmare she had had so often since coming to Mexico; there was always a forest, dark and foreboding. Leo Manfred and Redford Carson were there, sometimes as two separate people, sometimes in one body, and in the background, unseen, her father and Jimmy. She tried to turn and see them, but they were like wraiths, they always disappeared before her eyes.

When she awoke, it was day and the sun was shining into her room, making it hot and uncomfortable. She went downstairs to seek out another human being, some ordinary everyday contact to drive away that dream. In the dining-room, the breakfast was laid out on the table, and she saw immediately that Leo had had his meal and left. She was obliged to eat alone.

As soon as she had finished, she fetched her hat and went out into the village. It was very small, and had few houses apart from those along the waterfront. Obviously all the business of the village was transacted about the little harbour, and fishing was an important part of that. The little boats she had seen the previous evening had all put to sea in search of the day's catch.

She wandered along the beach, leaving footprints in the white sand, and gradually her spirits revived. The air was cool near the water and everywhere was quiet and peaceful. She doubted if the conflict in the rest of Mexico had reached here, and she hoped it never would. When she found Jimmy, they would leave for Europe at once, and she need concern herself no more with Maximilian and his crumbling Empire. Let Leo worry about that!

She supposed he had gone to the next village as he had said he would, but then the thought came to her that perhaps he had deserted her. He had certainly been angry enough to do so last night. She did not understand that outburst, it had been so unexpected and so violent. If he did, would she be able to find someone else to take her on? She doubted it.

She was approaching a little jetty and, moored to it, a small sailing-boat that had not gone out with the others. For no reason that she could think of, she stepped on board and then realised, to her horror, that it was not empty. She heard someone moving about in the tiny cabin. Before she could retreat, he had emerged on deck and she found herself looking into the smiling face of Redford Carson.

'Why, Stella, this is an unexpected pleasure. What are you doing here?'

'Looking for my husband, as you very well know.'

He spread his hands. 'As you see, he is not here.'

'I did not mean that he was with you,' she said. 'We are resting for a day or two before going on.'

'You intend to go on, then?'

'Of course. I shall continue until he is found.'

'Why are you so sure he is lost?'

He seemed to be saying the same thing as Leo had last night, or, at least, hinting at it, and it puzzled her. 'I didn't mean he was lost, just that I had not found him yet.'

'How did you get here, when I took the last boat?'

'We came through the jungle.'

'You did that? On foot?' There seemed to be a grudging admiration in his voice.

'We had the wagon and the mules, though, to tell the truth, we did walk most of the way.'

'The wagon, eh? I told you that would be a good buy, didn't I?'

'You were right.'

'Where is it now?'

'Behind the stables where we are staying with the Da Silvas.'

'And where, might I ask, is the estimable Captain Manfred this morning?'

'He went on to a village in the jungle where he heard there was a white man. If it's Jimmy, he'll bring him back.'

'Are you sure that's what he's about? You don't think he might have tired of the escort duty and left you to return to his beloved Emperor, who seems to have changed his mind about leaving and gone back to Mexico City?'

'No, why should he? He would not abandon a task half done.'

'All the same, I should make alternative arrangements, if I were you,' he said. 'And, since you are aboard, come into the cabin and let's talk about it.'

Half reluctant, half relieved to find a friendly face, she followed him down the half-dozen steps into a tiny cabin, which also served as a galley. There was a coffee-pot on the stove, and he poured two cups of coffee from it and handed one to her.

'Sit down, my dear. This cubby-hole is too small to stand on ceremony, and we are old friends, are we not?'

There was nowhere else to sit but on the bunk, which was rumpled as if he had just left it. He pulled the blankets straight, and she sat down on the edge, her nerves taut.

'What are you doing here in Yucatan?' she asked.

'I have business here.'

'Have you been following us?' she demanded suddenly.

He laughed. 'How can I have been following you when I have been here all of a week already? No, my dear, Mrs Wainright, if anything, you are following me.'

'That's nonsense!'

'Is it? I think not, I think that Captain Manfred is after my blood, and he is prepared to use you to get it.'

'Why should I believe that? You ran away, and left Leo to defend your house and look after me. That was a cowardly thing to do.'

He smiled easily. 'My dear, you should not judge by appearances. I had urgent business to attend to, and arguing my way out of that situation when the guerrillas over-ran the place was not part of my plan.'

She was not altogether convinced, though he did not seem like a cowardly man to her. 'And Jimmy? Are you saying that he is not in Yucatan, after all?'

'Oh, he's here, all right, but Leo Manfred has no great desire to find him. Just the opposite, in fact.'

'What do you mean?'

'Come now, ma'am, you must know that Leo Manfred harbours a lustful desire for you, and that finding your husband is not part of satisfying that desire.'

She stood up suddenly, almost banging her head on the timbers of the deck above her. 'That's a pre-posterous suggestion!'

'Is it?' His smile was maddeningly self-confident. 'Think about it. Do you really want to trust yourself to him? I told you before that I would not trust him with my dog, and that still holds good.'

'I think I should leave,' she said weakly. 'I have to arrange to buy some supplies.'

'I am going for a little trip into the jungle tomorrow,' he said. 'I could take you to your husband without all this pretence of having to search for him.'

'You know where he is?'

'Within a few miles.'

'How do you know?'

'Does that matter? Think about it, Stella. Think about it.' He took her hand and raised it to his lips, and she gasped, wondering what he would do next, but all he did was laugh at her discomfiture. 'I'll call this evening for your answer. We must make an early start in the morning.'

'I haven't agreed to come yet.'

'Oh, but you will,' he said confidently. 'I'll wager my last dollar on it.'

He was so arrogant that it was unbelievable, but if he really did know where Jimmy was, would it not be better to travel with him? It would also spare her the torment of fighting with Leo, when all she wanted was to be held in his arms. It was no good deceiving herself. Leo Manfred held her heart as securely as he always had, and she had been unbelievably cruel to Jimmy in marrying him. Was that why he had come to Mexico with her father and stayed on, when he could have come home, because he guessed something of the kind? Somehow she would have to put Leo Manfred from her mind for a second time and concentrate on making a success of her marriage; she owed it to Jimmy.

'And what do you hope to gain from it?' she asked abruptly.

'I assume you are prepared to pay me for my services? It would be a business arrangement, and your husband would wish it.'

'I'll think about it,' she said, feeling like a traitor, for no reason that she could understand.

'Good. I shall call for your answer tonight.'

'And if Captain Manfred has returned?'

'He won't have. It's all of a day each way to the nearest village.'

'Are you suggesting that I should leave before he comes back?'

'Why not? It will save his having to pretend he isn't pleased. You know he never wanted to bring you; he will be vastly relieved.'

She left him and went looking for the provisions they needed, hardly realising what she was buying or how much they cost. Her thoughts were on the conversation with Carson, and Leo's possible reaction when he heard. Anger or relief? Would he agree to let her go or try to persuade her to stay with him? If he did, it would only be because he could not go back to the Emperor with his mission unaccomplished. One thing she was determined on: she would not leave before he returned; she owed him a proper explanation.

Carson could hardly disguise his anger when she told him that evening. If Señora Da Silva was surprised that she was prepared to entertain a visitor when the Captain was away, she did not show it, putting out a carafe of wine and two glasses, with a plate of little honey cakes, before leaving them in the parlour alone.

'You're a little fool,' he said. 'Do you expect your husband to understand your reasons? In his shoes, I think I would put you over my knee and spank you!'

'Then I am very glad you are not my husband,' she said hotly. 'Jimmy would never dream of doing anything like that. He is very understanding.'

She looked on, puzzled, as he roared with laughter. 'You are unbelievable, Mrs Wainright! Your husband is a hot-blooded male, and he will stand no nonsense from Leo Manfred or anyone else. You think you know him, do you? How long had you been married before he came out here? Six months, wasn't it?'

'That has nothing to do with it. I merely said I would not go without speaking to Captain Manfred first and relieving him of the duty he finds so onerous.'

He rose and picked up his wide-brimmed felt hat. 'I shall leave at first light, whether you accompany me or not. And I shall tell James, when I see him, why you refused to come with me, why you preferred other company than mine.' He moved towards the door. 'Goodnight, Stella.' He paused to smile at her, and it was as if her very soul had been laid bare and he could see every thought and every emotion that lay there. 'Until tomorrow.'

As soon as he had gone, she went up to her room and lay on the bed in an agony of indecision, made none the easier by the knowledge that Redford Carson had guessed the truth. She loved Leo Manfred, and had loved him since the day they first met, and she always would. Nothing could alter that—not her marriage, not his cruel behaviour towards her now, not the memory of past hurt. The old ruse of reminding herself of what he had done to her in Trieste no longer worked. It made no difference, no difference at all.

CHAPTER EIGHT

THE DECISION was taken out of her hands, because when Stella rose next morning she found that Carson had already commandeered her wagon and mules and taken them to a building down by the harbour that was used as a warehouse. By the time she arrived, it was heavily loaded.

'What are you doing?' she asked. 'Don't you think you should have asked before taking my wagon?'

He smiled. 'You are coming, aren't you?'

'And if I said I had no intention of doing so?'

'Then I should call your bluff and set off without you.'

'With my wagon? That's stealing.'

'No, I am only borrowing it, but as you are coming too, the question does not arise.' He signalled to one of the Mexicans, who climbed aboard the driving-seat. 'Get up,' he commanded.

She put her basket under the seat and got up on the wagon, only to find herself sitting next to Miguel, the diligence-driver. She was more than ever doubtful that she had done the right thing, but it was too late to change her mind, as they were on the move and being escorted by half a dozen Mexican riders wearing ponchos and sombreros and carrying rifles.

The journey, most of it through heavily wooded country, was a silent one, broken only by Carson's sharp commands to the escort and Miguel's singing of 'La Cucuracha'. Stella spent the time wondering what Leo would do when he found the letter she had left for him. While thanking him courteously for bringing her thus far, she had been careful to keep its tone businesslike and to the point, but she had been weeping when she wrote it and its surface was stained by more than one tear. He would be angry that she had forced him into disobeying Maximilian's command, but she did not doubt, for one moment, that he would seize the opportunity to take the boat Carson had left for his use, and return to the Emperor. It was for the best. He had no place in her life, and it was foolish to entertain hopes to the contrary. Better to make a clean break before she gave herself away and let him see how much she cared.

Late in the afternoon, they entered Villa-Hermosa. Carson seemed to know exactly where to go, and led them to a square in front of the church. Here some of the inhabitants sat in the shade, gossiping and cooking over *al fresco* fires, while nearly naked children played in the dirt at their feet. They stopped whatever they were doing to watch the wagon until it halted outside a single-storey whitewashed house bigger than the rest and roofed with tiles. It even had glass in its windows and a pleasant enclosed garden.

They were greeted at the door by a strikingly handsome Creole in an embroidered shirt, jodhpurs and jackboots. '*Buenos días*, Redford, my son,' he said, then, bowing to Stella, '*Señora*, welcome.' He turned, waving his arms towards the cool interior. '*Mi casa es su casa.*'

She knew enough Spanish to know that this was the traditional welcome, 'My house is your house', and she smiled her acceptance as she passed through into a dim hall, whose tiled floor was dotted with colourful rugs. A Mexican-Indian woman came from one of the rooms and ran past her to embrace Redford. She was dressed very simply in a green *huipil* that emphasised her slim figure and enhanced the dark honey colour of her bare shoulders.

He laughed and kissed her. 'Manuela,' he said, turning to Stella, 'this is Mrs Wainright.' The introduction was followed by what seemed to be an explanation of Stella's presence there, but as it was in Spanish, she understood very little.

'These are Señor and Señora Gonzales,' Redford said, turning to Stella. 'And, in case you are wondering, they are Josefina's parents. Señor José Gonzales, as you can see, is a man of some substance; he had a position in the government before Maximilian arrived. Now he waits in retirement until he is needed again.'

'He is a *Juárista*?' she asked in alarm.

Carson laughed at the puzzled look on her face. 'You have nothing to fear from him. As you see, he is no bandit but a civilised man. He is also a friend of mine, and you'd oblige me by being polite and putting a cheerful face on things.'

'I do not need a lesson in how to behave from you!' she snapped. 'Nor do I care what activities you indulge in, so long as you take me to Jimmy.'

'Later, later,' he said. 'Now you can stay here for a while. Manuela will show you to your room.'

'My room?' She felt suddenly alarmed, as if she were losing control of the situation, as if fate or destiny, call it what you will, was pushing her in a way she did not want to go.

'Yes, my dear, this is the end of the trail for you.'

'You mean Jimmy is here?'

'I mean that Miguel and I will take the wagon and go on alone.'

She was taken completely by surprise, and then, recovering herself, said, 'You have used me for your own ends, and I want to know why!'

He smiled sardonically. 'Because, dear Mrs Wainright, you were travelling in the direction I wanted to go, and I had need of a wagon. Why do you suppose I persuaded you to buy it?'

'And I thought you were being helpful,' she said angrily. 'How wrong I was! It wouldn't surprise me to learn you have no idea where Jimmy is.'

'I know within a little, my dear, but are you sure you want to find him?'

'Of course I do! What a stupid question.'

'You may live to regret it.'

His words alarmed her, and she looked up to see him regarding her with his head on one side, as if deciding whether to tell her something. 'What do you mean by that remark? He is my husband and we love each other, so why should I regret it?' She was aware of the untruth as she said it, but that was a secret she would keep locked in her heart.

'How touching,' he said. 'If I did not know better, I could almost believe you meant that.'

'May I remind you that we have a business arrangement,' she said coldly. 'I would be obliged if you would keep your side of the bargain.'

He laughed. 'Stella, you are unique, one in a million, and in any other circumstances . . .'

'In any other circumstances,' she retorted quickly, 'I would have no necessity even to speak to you!'

'As it is, you need me, and will therefore do as I say.' His voice was cold.

'What are you going to do with me?'

'Do, dear lady? That rather depends on you. You can do as you are told and I will do my best to find your husband, *after* my business is done, or you can make a fuss . . .'

'And if I do?'

'You will be, shall we say, dealt with.'

'What does that mean?'

'Come, Stella, that is not a subject we should even be discussing, because you *are* going to be good, aren't you? You have nothing to gain by impeding me. Leo has gone—he can no longer help you—but your husband is still here. I reckon you understand me.'

She understood him perfectly and, angry though she was that she had been duped, she realised that to cross him now would land her in more trouble. While there was a chance he would do as he said and help her, she would do as she was told.

Before she could argue, he left and returned a few moments later with her basket, followed by Miguel with the trunk. 'Come, I'll show you your room.'

'You intended to come here all along, didn't you?' she

said, as she followed him unwillingly down the hall and into a plainly furnished bedroom. It was sparkling clean, and the bed looked inviting. She began to feel that perhaps, after all, she did need a little time to be by herself, if only to try to think clearly. 'They were expecting you, weren't they?' she said, as Miguel put the trunk down in the middle of the room and left. 'And Josefina is part of it all; she is a spy.'

Carson shrugged. 'What difference does it make to you?'

'You could have told me.'

'So that you could go and tell Leo Manfred? No, my dear, unlike you, he would soon have put two and two together.'

'Now that you have confessed you did not come here for my benefit,' she said angrily, 'why don't you tell me the whole truth?'

He reached out to touch her cheek. 'I don't think you are ready for that yet.'

'It's to do with the Liberals, isn't it? You are not as neutral as you pretend to be. That's why you and Leo dislike each other so much—he knows . . .'

'What does he know?' he asked sharply.

'You are helping the *Juáristas*,' she said, with sudden insight. 'You are one of those bandits who cause so much trouble to everyone.'

'The Confederates are with the Emperor,' he said evenly. 'That's common knowledge.'

'Yes, but you are not a true Confederate, are you? You don't even talk like a Southerner. You are a Yankee, and that makes a difference, though I'm not sure what.'

He put his hands on her shoulders and looked down at her. 'Stella, my dear, you would do best not to worry your pretty little head about things which do not concern you. We don't want to spoil a promising friendship, do we?'

'Friendship?' she repeated. 'Do you expect us to be friends after this?'

'Why not? Perhaps, one day, when you have learned to understand me better.'

'Understand treachery?' she demanded.

He smiled ruefully, dropping his hands. 'What is treachery? What is honour? It depends on which side of the fence you are standing, doesn't it? Don't let your misguided loyalty to Leo Manfred blind you to that fact. There are two sides to every conflict.'

'And Jimmy?' she cried, as another thought struck her bewildered brain like a thunderbolt. 'What has all this to do with my husband?'

'Nothing,' he said vaguely. 'He is not concerned with the rights and wrongs of the Liberal cause, nor has he any interest in the affairs of the United States. His loyalties, such as they are, lie elsewhere.' His tone was scathing, as though he were condemning Jimmy for his neutrality, but she was glad of it. For one terrible moment, she had thought Jimmy was involved with whatever Carson was up to.

'I know that,' she said hotly. 'He is like my father was, interested only in botanical things.'

He laughed with genuine amusement, opened his mouth to say something, and decided against it. Then, moving to the door, he turned and smiled. 'Now I have things to do, so I suggest you rest until supper-time, and I'll see you then.'

He left her and she took off her skirt and blouse and stretched out on the bed in her shift. She would rest, but there was too much whirling about in her brain to allow her to sleep. Had she been wrong to leave Leo? He had not wanted the job of accompanying her, but he saw it as a duty he could not shirk, whereas Redford Carson thought only of himself and would not hesitate to rid himself of her if it suited him. Could she have spent any more time in Leo's company now that she had admitted to herself how she felt about him? He must never know about that, must not know that he had such a hold over her that even after making it plain he did not want her, he could make her forget her marriage vows. He would gloat, and she could not bear that, so better to stay right away from him and put her trust in Carson.

The American had no reason to harm her, just so long as she did nothing to obstruct him, and he had said he knew where Jimmy might be found. Her life was with her husband, there was no room in it for anyone else, and if she told herself that often enough, it might become true. Besides, it was too late to change her mind now, the die had been cast when she left the Da Silva house.

The bed was soft and comfortable after the hard boards of the wagon, and, in spite of herself, she dozed. She was awakened by the sound of Redford returning, laughing with Miguel, and calling to Manuela that he was hungry enough to eat a horse. Stella, rising to wash and dress, realised suddenly that she, too, was hungry and the smell of food cooking increased her appetite.

The meal was extremely good—spiced pork baked in banana leaves, Manuela told her—and Redford was in a cheerful and relaxed mood, laughing and joking with their hosts and filling their glasses with the local red wine. It went to Stella's head in a surprisingly short time and she found it difficult to concentrate on the conversation, even though they were speaking in English. Their voices became a blurr of sound and the room unbearably hot, so that she had difficulty in keeping her eyes open. She fought it for some minutes, then her head began to feel so heavy that she could not hold it up, and her shoulders sagged.

'Bed, my little lady.' Redford's voice was right against her ear, though she had not seen him move from his seat.

Agreeing with him, she tried to stand, and fell against him. He picked her up and carried her back to her room, where he laid her on the bed and took off her shoes. 'There you are, my stubborn one,' he said. 'I didn't want to do it, believe me.' He bent his head, and through the mist of semi-consciousness, she felt his lips brush hers. 'Sleep well, my darling girl.'

She woke in the early hours of the next morning when

it was still not yet light, and lay for a moment wondering what had roused her from so deep a sleep of exhaustion. She recalled Carson's helping her from the dining-table to her room and she even had a faint memory of him kissing her, but nothing more until now, and she was still dressed in the lilac taffeta she had worn to supper. Alcohol had never affected her like that before, and she had had little more than one glass. Now she had a dreadful headache and her mouth was dry. She got up, picked up a glass of water from the bedside table and took it to the window to drink it and breathe the fresh air.

The sound of a horse neighing and a muffled command made her turn her attention to the rough road leading into the jungle, and what she saw stung her into action. The wagon—*her* wagon—was disappearing from sight, escorted by Carson's band of followers. She was sure now that she had been drugged and that José Gonzales had been told to keep her there. She ran to the door, afraid that it would be locked, but it opened silently, and she ran along the hall to the front door, carrying her shoes, half expecting someone to come rushing out to stop her. But they obviously expected the drug to keep her asleep for the rest of the night, and no one stirred. She slipped out, shut the door carefully behind her, and, stopping only to put on her shoes, hurried after the wagon.

It was day when she caught up with it, but by that time they were in the jungle again and the light was dim. She followed for some distance, moving in the cover of the trees and dodging out of sight when any of the outriders glanced back. She was angry, and curious too, and had little doubt that she would either be sent back or held prisoner once Carson realised she was there, and she meant to find out as much as she could before that happened.

The wagon was heavily laden and was causing more problems than it had before, sticking in the mud, falling into holes, catching its wheels on unseen roots. It was some consolation to know that it was moving in a southerly direction towards Palenche, still nearly ninety miles away. At noon, when she was almost too exhausted to stumble any further, the forest suddenly opened out into a clearing. Here was a collection of huts grouped around a square, on one side of which stood the *cabildo*, a long communal building of adobe, where the villagers congregated to see the party arrive.

Hidden on the edge of the clearing, Stella watched Carson jump down and greet one of the men, who appeared to be a village official. The outriders dismounted and dispersed among the villagers, chattering and laughing and slapping each other on the back, while the children scrambled all over the wagon.

Suddenly Carson turned and pointed straight at the spot where Stella was hiding and gave an order which resulted in two of the villagers rushing over and pulling her, struggling angrily, to where he stood. She knew, by the way he laughed, that he had known all along she had been following them.

He looked down at her now, mocking her. 'So, little lady, you couldn't bear to be parted from me. How touching!'

'Tell these brutes to let me go at once!'

He signalled to the men, and they released her, but remained close enough to grab her again if she made a move to run. She was so angry that she forgot how exhausted she was and stood before him with eyes blazing. 'You drugged me and stole my wagon! I insist on an explanation.'

'Insist all you like,' he said calmly. 'You will not get one, except that had you stayed with José Gonzales, I would have returned and taken you wherever you wanted to go, as I promised.'

'Now that you have apparently reached your destination,' she said with all the dignity she could muster, 'perhaps we can go on to wherever Jimmy is, which is, after all, what I have been paying you to do.'

'If you think I have reached my destination, you are wrong,' he said calmly. 'I have important tasks, so your petty little expedition will have to take second place.'

'You are despicable!' she said.

He laughed. 'But you need me, is that not so? As you have taken so much trouble to join us and I cannot spare anyone to take you back, you will have to stay. But, make no mistake, you will do exactly as I tell you. Today we rest, tomorrow we go on.' He shouted to Miguel, who returned to the driving-seat and drove the wagon behind the *cabildo*, where Stella guessed there were stables or storerooms. Turning to Stella, he said, 'Now please come inside, where a meal has been prepared for us. Then I will find somewhere for you to sleep. After all, you seem not to have had your full quota last night.'

'No thanks to you! You would have me still asleep now and in ignorance of what is going on.'

'Better to be ignorant,' he said. 'Better to be ignorant than dead, don't you think?'

Not until she sat down at the long table in the *cabildo*, surrounded by what appeared to be the whole population of the village, did she realise just what a precarious position she was in. Four dozen pairs of eyes watched her eat, four dozen tongues spoke a language she did not understand, and if she did anything to anger them, four dozen arms would be raised against her. Leo had told her not to trust Carson, and he had been right, but what good did it do to admit that now? If she had known what was in store for her, would she have continued? Yes, she decided, because it had not been in her power to turn back, any more than she could do so now. She was being drawn inexorably towards her destiny by the serpent of the forest, the one in her dream.

The natives were not hostile—she realised that when the meal was over and they went outside—but simply curious. The women wore white embroidered *huipils*, while the men were clad in the native tailored Mexican trousers and waistcoats; the children wore nothing at all. Some of the bolder ones reached out to touch her skirt, and she smiled readily at them, making them giggle and chatter among themselves.

'Come,' said Carson. 'The villagers have offered you a hut to yourself. I am assured that it is in good repair and completely secure. I'll show you.'

'We are going to stay here?'

'For a day or two.'

'But I have no clothes with me.'

He laughed. 'That comes with rushing off without stopping to think! One of the village women will give you a *huipil*.'

'I can't wear one of those.'

'Why not? I'm sure you will look very fetching in one.'

He escorted her to one of the roughly-plastered little huts, which was next to the one he had been allotted. She moved away from him to bend under the low lintel and go inside, but was detained by a hand on her arm. 'You may move freely about the village,' he said, 'but do not try to go any further, because escape is impossible.'

'Why should I want to escape?' she said coolly. 'I have not yet found my husband.'

'As you see, he is not here.'

'But has he been seen by anyone? Did you ask?'

He shrugged. 'There are reports . . .'

'Reports?' she put in quickly. 'What reports?'

'There is a white man in the jungle a few days' march from here.'

'Leo heard that, too. Oh, Colonel, if you have any pity at all, take me to him.'

'I'll repeat what I said before,' he said calmly. 'When my business is done, I'll attend to yours.'

'Is Jimmy well? He isn't hurt, or anything?'

'I know no more than I have told you.' He paused. 'If you want to find him, you will not hinder me in any way, do you understand? Now I must go.'

She stood and watched him cross the compound, wondering why she had ever thought him charming; he was very far from that. He was cruel and unfeeling, but if what he said about the white man in the jungle was true, she needed him as much as ever.

A young woman came over to her and shyly handed

her a flimsy blue garment, pointing at Stella's be-draggled dress. Stella smiled and thanked her, and went into the hut with it.

The tiny home had only one room with wooden furniture and no covering on the rough earth floor, but it was dry, and the colourful Mexican blanket on the simple bed was clean. There was a pitcher of water and a bowl on a table against the wall, and she stripped off her clothes and washed. It was obvious that she could not wear the *huipil* over her petticoats and she was half inclined to put her own clothes on again, however torn and grubby, but when she tried on the native garment, it was cool and comfortable and she realised why the women wore it.

Carson was waiting for her outside when she emerged, somewhat self-consciously. She halted, ready to retreat when she saw the look on his face—it was lustful, there was no other word for it.

'My, what a beauty!' he said. 'Hidden beneath all those petticoats was the body of a goddess. I guessed as much.'

She could back away into the hut and stay there, she thought, but she would have to come out sooner or later, and she had it in mind to explore her surroundings and perhaps find someone who could speak English or French. She wanted to know more about the reports of the white man in the jungle, so she faced him out.

'You know, Stella,' he said, reaching out to touch her cheek, 'you could make me forget who I am and what I am. You could make me throw my hand in. With you beside me . . .'

She gave a brittle laugh that betrayed how nervous she was feeling. 'I'm quite sure Jimmy would have some-thing to say on the subject!'

'I'm inclined to believe that your husband would be quite flexible on the matter.'

It was the second time he had hinted that Jimmy not the faithful husband she had believed him to be, but he was only saying that to get his own way with her.

'Take me to him,' she said, much more calmly than she felt. 'Then we shall see how flexible he is!'

'I can't do it, Stella, not yet, and if you value your life and his, you will not mention it again.'

'You are despicable!' she said, trying to pretend that there were no tears running down her cheeks.

He smiled suddenly. 'Come, dry those beautiful eyes. We shall find your husband, I promise, but now we'll take a stroll round the village arm in arm and I shall show you off to my friends.'

They remained in the village for two days, during which he seemed too busy to bother about her at all and she was grateful for that. Even if he had not intimated as much, she knew she was a prisoner because she was guarded, not particularly closely because she could not have gone far, but guarded none the less by two natives with rifles. And the rifles were not old, like the one the man had died for in Mexico City, but shining and new. She supposed she was lucky still to be alive because she had heard Carson and Miguel arguing heatedly about her, and though she did not understand the Spanish in which they spoke, she had picked up enough to realise that Miguel was in favour of shooting her on the spot and that Carson had vetoed the suggestion. He had some gentlemanly feelings, she decided—unless, of course, he had other plans for her. The thought was abhorrent; her only hope was that they would reach Jimmy soon.

On the third day, Carson came to her and told her to get ready to leave, and as she had only the *huipil* and the clothes she had been wearing when she arrived, it took her no more than five minutes. In no time at all they were on their way again. Stella had been through so much during the last few weeks that she was almost able to accept her destiny philosophically. When she told herself that every jolting uncomfortable mile on the front seat of the wagon was a mile nearer to Jimmy, there was a traitorous little voice deep inside her which kept telling her that it was also a mile further from Leo.

Miguel said that they were on the main highway from

the north coast to Guatemala, and if that were so, it was little wonder that communications were bad. Progress became even more difficult when, after two more days, they turned off it and moved deeper into the jungle, which hid a landscape of rivers and deep ravines, escarpments and pools, and the track twisted and turned to avoid them. Anyone deviating in the slightest from the marked path would have had to hack his way through dense undergrowth, and sending messages to the outside world would be almost impossible.

She could not understand why her husband had chosen to come to such a place: she would have expected him to return to Europe after her father died, not to hide himself away in this outlandish spot. 'Hide himself,' she found herself repeating. Was he hiding? If so, from whom? His own wife? No, that was too fanciful. She would not think such disloyal thoughts; he would tell her when she found him, and all would be well.

The armed escort remained with them, helping to push and pull the heavy wagon, until, five days after they set out, they arrived at another small village. Here, on three sides of a square, was a collection of roughly-plastered huts, and on the fourth, an unexpectedly enormous church, palm-thatched like the huts. It had plaster pillars and niches containing the carved figures of the saints, green as the forest. No bells hung in the tower, and the great iron cross atop it all was rusty and corroded. Jungle plants grew on its roof, where their seeds, blown by the wind, had fallen and germinated; the building was at one with the jungle that surrounded it.

Carson reined in, and Miguel pulled the wagon up beside him, as the inhabitants came crowding out from their houses and surrounded them, chattering excitedly. They all turned, and the chatter died as from the largest of the huts strolled a heavily built man wearing nothing but a white loincloth and a pair of enormous spurs on his bare feet, which jingled as he walked. Stella was hard put to it not to smile at this comical figure, but he was obviously a very important person in the village and his arrival was greeted with deference.

Carson addressed the crowd in Spanish, which was translated by Miguel into the Mayan language. They listened without interrupting, but what he said provoked a great deal of discussion and some quite heated argument. She could not understand, and her attention wandered to her surroundings. The village had evidently been hacked out of the jungle, as had the fields of sisal, used for making rope, which were laid out on one side and probably formed the villagers' main livelihood. The extraordinary church suggested that it had once been more prosperous, and several of the huts were collapsing.

The discussion ended abruptly, and Carson's men set about unhitching the wagon and looking after the animals, and the villagers dispersed, except the fat man with the spurs, who stood in the middle of the square, staring up at them.

'Why does he wear those ridiculous spurs?' Stella whispered to Carson. 'He makes me want to laugh.'

'It's just as well he doesn't understand English,' he said. 'He would not appreciate your remarks. In his book, the *gapuchines*—those who wear spurs—are the masters, and though he has no horse and no riding-boots, he does have the spurs as his symbol of authority.'

'He is the *alcalde*?'

'Yes.'

'And has he been convinced by your argument?'

'Argument?'

She laughed lightly. 'You were not having an idle conversation, were you? I have no doubt you wanted something from him. Did you promise him the horse and boots to go with the spurs?'

He laughed and dismounted. 'Something of the sort.'

'And in return?'

'Accommodation for you.'

'And your men and animals, not to mention the contents of the wagon.'

He looked up at her sharply. 'The contents of the wagon are no concern of yours.' He held out his hand to help her down, but she ignored it and jumped down unaided.

'Go with our friend here,' he added. 'He will show you to your hut. Then join us all for supper in the *cabildo*, you'll find it behind the church. The same rules apply as before: stay within the village boundary. They have a very secure prison here, and I shall have no compunction about locking you up if you become a nuisance.' He pointed to one of the huts set apart from the others. It was in good repair, with a stout wooden door with bolts on the outside and bars at its single window. 'You do understand me, I know.'

It seemed to Stella, as she made herself at home in a hut exactly like the one she had left five days before except that it was rather more dilapidated, that they were going round in circles. Whatever Carson's business was, and she was beginning to make a very good guess at it, her needs and wishes would not be considered. She wondered why he even bothered to maintain the fiction that he was taking her to Jimmy. If she could only find one friendly person, someone who spoke enough English to tell her how to find her way out of the jungle and back to civilisation, she could ask someone else to lead her expedition.

The next day Carson came to her in a very good humour, and suggested a short expedition into the jungle. 'I have something to show you,' he said.

Thinking that it might have some bearing on her search for Jimmy, she agreed, though she hardly supposed that she had a choice. They went on foot— Carson, Miguel, one of the villagers and Stella— hacking their way through thick, steamy jungle, swatting at the mosquitoes with their handkerchiefs while watching the ground for spiders and snakes. Above their heads, a bird with a spectacular voice filled the air with its song, while monkeys, using the stems of the liana as a trapeze, chuntered to huge-beaked toucans.

The air was so close and still that she could hardly breathe.

'Not far now,' Miguel said. 'Uphill another quarter of a mile, and then you'll see it.'

The jungle suddenly thinned, and there before them was an enormous pyramid with broken stone steps leading up to a temple on its summit. Down each side of the stairway slithered a huge stone serpent, brilliantly coloured. To one side were the tumbledown walls of a vast building, all covered in hieroglyphics and geometrical symbols, almost hidden by foliage. Huge carved figures of people, gods and animals were scattered as though a giant hand had tossed them up and let them fall. It seemed as though the jungle was growing out of the stone, and yet in some places the stones seemed to be a living part of the trees. Some monoliths still stood upright, their fronts and sides covered in glyphs, others were sculpted with symbolic human figures, richly dressed and ornamented. It was the place of the drawing she had found in her father's room, and suddenly she knew she was very near the end of her journey. Here the questions that had been plaguing her might be answered.

They moved slowly up the steps and explored the temple, which had lost its roof and was open to the sky; fruit-bats, disturbed by their coming, flew out and circled above their heads, squeaking their dismay at the intrusion. The air suddenly became eerily still and the jungle quiet, and then, just as suddenly, the wind began to howl, tearing at the tops of the trees and sending the monkeys scuttling to the ground, shrieking in fright. The bats dived for cover, and the toucans, protesting angrily, swooped among the stones looking for a place of safety. In seconds, rain was lashing down as if some giant sluice-gate had been opened above their heads.

'Come on!' shouted Miguel above the din, leading the way down. 'One of the lower chambers still has a roof.'

His voice was drowned by the noise of the storm, the battering wind, the howling of the frightened animals, the torrential rain, the crashing of ancient trees and reverberating cracks of thunder. In seconds the steps of the pyramid were more like a waterfall than a staircase, as Stella, slipping and sliding, followed the men to the ruined building at its foot, where they pushed their way through the undergrowth and climbed down a steep bank to a room with a solid roof. More bats flew out of their crevices at their coming.

The darkness in the chamber was pierced by the light from swarms of luminous fireflies, filling the air around them, but every now and again their light was eclipsed by a flash of lightning that lit up the jungle like day and allowed them to see each other very briefly. But they did not need to be able to see, to know that they were all soaked through to the skin, their hair and clothes were clinging to them and water squelched in their shoes.

'It won't last long,' Carson shouted. 'These storms never do.'

He began prowling round, examining the stonework of the chamber, feeling over it with his hands and going to the entrance to look upwards. 'It's a magnificent ruin,' Miguel said. 'The jungle has encroached so much that it's impossible to take it all in at once, but I'm sure it was once a sizeable city and very prosperous. The pyramid and temple suggest that it was quite an important centre.'

'Is this the only chamber with a roof?' asked Carson.

Miguel spoke to the villager in his own language, and translated the reply. 'He says he doesn't think there is another, but it would take years to uncover the whole site. They haven't the labour to do it.'

'It will serve our purpose very well,' Carson said. 'It's bone dry and safe from fire. I couldn't have found anywhere better if I'd searched a year. And we have James Wainright to thank for it.'

Stella twisted round in the darkness towards the sound of his voice. 'Did you say James?'

'I did.' There was amusement in his voice. 'He has been a great help to the Republican cause.'

'I don't believe you,' she said at once. 'Where is he? Is he here?'

'Patience, patience, my dear,' he chided. 'He was here, but he moved on.'

'But you do know where he is now?'

'Perhaps.'

She wished she could see the expression on his face; it might help her to decide if he were telling the truth. 'Take me to him.'

'Not yet.'

'You are lying,' she said suddenly. 'You have no idea where he is!'

The sound of Carson's laugh echoed eerily in the darkness, making her shiver with apprehension. He moved, and she saw his shape outlined against the entrance to the chamber, blocking what little light there was, but he spoke in a normal voice. 'The rain has stopped, and we have been away far too long.'

'Why the urgency?' she asked, as she followed him, then said boldly, in spite of her unease, 'Could it be that you are not as sure of your little band as you would have us believe? Loyalty that can be bought, can be bought again.'

'Nonsense. They are true Liberals.'

'And the villagers?'

'Those too.'

'But they have yet to be convinced?'

He did not reply, and a few moments later, they emerged from the trees into the village compound. Instead of escorting her to her own hut, he led her to one of the others, more dilapidated than the rest. 'Come, you haven't seen everything yet,' he said. 'I have something else to show you.'

Like the others, the hut consisted of only one room, and part of that was open to the sky. There was a table, a stool and some shelves, on which stood a variety of containers, some of which were beautifully decorated; she guessed they had come from the ruins. They held a variety of tiny plants such as a botanist might collect. But it was the microscope that caught her attention, because she recognised it as once having belonged to her father. Carson took a roll of paper from one of the shelves and spread it out on the table.

'Your husband discovered the ruins, and see, he made a plan of them.' He ran his fingers over it, then pointed, 'Here is the chamber. Now do you believe me?'

'Tell me where he is,' she pleaded. 'For the love of God, tell me.'

'Why so impatient?' he said calmly. 'What will you do when you find him?'

'Go home,' she said promptly. 'Leave this barbaric country and return to England.'

'Aren't you forgetting something? Aren't you forgetting that perhaps James won't want to return?'

'Why ever not?'

'Perhaps he can't.' Carson paused, and smiled down at her knowingly. 'You think that going back to Europe is going to solve your problem, don't you? It won't, you know. It will follow you, because it is deep inside you and you won't be able to break free of it. You can't hide it from yourself, and you will not be able to hide it from your husband.'

She ignored his innuendo, though it discomforted her by its unassailable truth. 'If you won't take me, I'll go alone.'

'Sometimes, Stella,' he said, as if talking to a recalcitrant child. 'You try my patience sorely. Go, if you want to. Try and beat the jungle. How long would it be before you were hopelessly lost, or attacked by animals, not to mention shot by *Juáristas*?'

She knew he was right. She needed him as much as ever, and now that they seemed to be close to the end of her search, it was important not to antagonise him. She would make herself as agreeable as possible, and bide her time.

CHAPTER NINE

DURING THE next few days, Carson hardly left her side. At night he escorted her to her door, where a guard took over, pacing up and down outside until it grew light and the Colonel returned. In spite of that, she felt he was becoming less secretive and more inclined to be friendly, and that was something she felt it was in her best interest to foster. She showed a passing interest in what he was doing without being over-curious and arousing his suspicions, but her head was becoming stuffed with facts and figures, place-names, people's names, and any information she thought might be useful, if the opportunity ever arose to go on alone. Besides, it helped to pass the time, and she needed that to stop her from thinking too deeply. Thinking hurt her head and did no good.

'I'm going to the ruins,' Carson said, about a week after they arrived. 'Do you want to come?'

He rarely gave her any choice about what she did and where she went, and she supposed the question was not one that required an answer, but the diversion was welcome, and she readily agreed. It became obvious, before they had gone very far, that the track to the ruins had been widened and the ground levelled; it was quite a respectable path now, and she wondered why he had taken the trouble to construct a road that went nowhere when he seemed to have more than enough to do to organise his little army.

The pyramid seemed no less spectacular on the second viewing than on the first, and she spent some time wandering round looking at the carvings, wondering what the strange symbols meant. 'This is an extraordinary place,' she said. 'It's a great pity Papa did not live to see it.'

'Yes.'

'He knew about it, didn't he?'

'Yes. He met an explorer, who described it to him and gave him the drawing. He and James were planning the expedition when he died so tragically.' He continued, more slowly, 'James decided to continue alone.'

'That's what I find so surprising. I would have expected him to come home.'

'No doubt he thought the work they had both been engaged in was too important to abandon, and that Sir Peter would have wished him to continue.' His voice was casual, as though he were just making polite conversation, but she wished, as she had done ever since she came to Mexico, that she knew more about what had happened when her father died.

'Yes, I expect so.'

He tucked his hand under her elbow to guide her along the edge of a huge chunk of fallen masonry towards the chamber where they had sheltered from the storm. The undergrowth round the entrance had been uprooted, the ground trampled and the opening itself widened.

'What have you been doing here?' she asked. 'It looks as though a herd of elephants has been through.'

'It has made a very good storehouse.'

'For what?' She peered into the gloom, and knew the answer. It was stacked from floor to ceiling with guns and ammunition.

'How did it all get here?' she asked, and then, 'Oh, that's why you wanted my wagon!'

'Yes, it came in very useful.'

'Why didn't you just buy one for yourself. Why did you need me?'

'It might have aroused suspicion, especially in the mind of a certain Hussar Captain, who was already becoming too curious. And my need of you has nothing to do with any of that.'

'Why didn't you tell me the truth?'

'As I said, you were not ready for it.'

'But I am now?'

'Now it is too late for you to do anything about it. You have been branded a *Juárista*.'

'I am nothing of the sort!'

'Try convincing the royalists of that.' He paused, smiling. 'Just think. You changed carriages to save yourself from the ambush of the diligence, you defended Liberal supporters and attacked a French officer, and you went to prison for your beliefs.'

'That was all coincidence.'

'Tell that to Leo Manfred, and see if he believes you. Now you are with me, helping to arm the people, preparing them to rise against their oppressors. He will draw his own conclusions.'

'I believe he knows me better than that.'

He laughed. 'Do you? My dear Mrs Wainright, he will believe his eyes and ears.'

'It's of no consequence what he believes,' she said, trying to convince herself as much as him. 'I am not involved in the affairs of Mexico any more than Jimmy is. I want to join my husband; that is all.'

'And if joining your husband forces you into making a choice, what then? Martha was right, you know. No one is allowed to stay neutral.'

'But you said that Jimmy had no loyalty to the Republican cause.'

'So I did.'

'Then please explain.'

'He will explain himself when we catch up with him.' His voice held a grim note, almost a threat. It was as if he suspected Jimmy of running away, and, to tell the truth, she had wondered why the reports and rumours they had heard of a white man were always one village away, that every time they moved, so had he—or so it seemed.

'When will that be?' she asked evenly.

'Soon.'

'Does that mean that your business is nearly concluded and that you can attend to mine?'

'Very nearly.'

'When can we go?'

'Perhaps tomorrow. If the villagers are ready.'

'Ready for what?'

He smiled enigmatically. 'For the struggle to come.'

'And have you promised them money if they take up arms and follow you?'

'More or less.'

'Do they know they might have to kill to get it?'

'Yes, I reckon so.'

'And are they also prepared to die?'

'If necessary.'

She looked at the weapons, and shuddered. Each had the power to inflict death; together they could wipe out a whole village. 'There is more than one wagonload here,' she said.

'Miguel has been going backwards and forwards for several days now,' he said, 'but he had to stop because the wheel-shaft broke on the last trip. The rest will have to stay with Señor Gonzales until we can repair the wagon.'

'Who is paying for it all?' she asked. 'Not the villagers, I know.'

'The Liberals . . . Juárez.'

'And what do you gain from it?'

'The satisfaction of duty done,' he said evasively.

She looked up into his face, trying to guess what was going on in his head, but his expression told her nothing. She shivered suddenly. 'Can we go back now, Colonel?'

While he made a final inspection of the site and stopped to speak to one of Miguel's men who stood guard, she turned to take a last look at the pyramid, walking slowly up its steps and admiring the grandeur of it. She wondered what those ancient people had been like. They had lived and loved and given birth and died, just as everyone did, but what sudden catastrophe had wiped them out? A great war? People on two sides, determined to kill each other, just as the Liberals and Conservatives were doing now? Had there been men like Leo and the Colonel then, fanatical men who would stop at nothing to win?

The recent rain on the fallen leaves and the droppings of the birds and animals had made the stone slimy; Stella, obeying Carson's call to rejoin him, slipped and fell, twisting her ankle beneath her. Her cry of pain brought him to her side immediately. He carried her the rest of the way down the steps and sat her on one of the overturned obelisks, then pulled a large handkerchief from his pocket, stooped to soak it in a puddle and, taking off her shoe, bound her ankle very efficiently. 'There, how's that?'

'Better, thank you.' She took her shoe from him.

'Can you walk?'

She stood on one leg and gingerly put the injured foot to the ground, wincing. 'With a little help.'

He put his hand under her elbow. 'Lean on me.' He smiled suddenly. 'I wish you would always lean on me. I would prove a far greater support than either James or Manfred, neither of whom deserves you.'

She stopped her painful hobbling. 'Redford, if you continue in that vein, I shall sit down here and refuse to go any further.'

'No time for that,' he said, sweeping her up into his arms to carry her. 'We have to get back.'

Stella, looking over his shoulder, saw a movement in the undergrowth and tensed, fearing another snake, but it wasn't a snake, it was a young boy who had evidently followed them from the village, and now scampered away. He had been extraordinarily like Pablo, and the thought of the little Mexican reminded her of Leo. Did he really believe she was siding with the *Juáristas*? And did it matter what he thought? It did, she admitted. It mattered dreadfully. She did not want to be a party to arming innocent villagers who did not understand what the struggle for power was about; their way of life would continue whichever party held the reins of government. Carson was cruel to involve them. As soon as she had been reunited with Jimmy, she would alert the authorities to what was going on.

The thought made her begin thinking about Jimmy in

a way she had not been doing for several weeks; it was as if the search for him had become an end in itself and the outcome unimportant. She tried to picture his face, and failed dismally; she tried to imagine his arms round her and his lips on hers, but what she saw and what she felt was Leo Manfred. It frightened her and made her feel guilty at the same time.

Carson turned his head to look down at her, clinging to him with her arms round his neck, and chuckled.

'Why are you laughing?' she demanded.

'I just thought that if Captain Leo Manfred were to see us now, what a cosy picture we would make. It might convince him whose side you are on.' And he lowered his head to brush his lips across her hair.

It was as much as Leo could do to stop himself from breaking cover and giving away his carefully laid plans. His personal enmity must take second place to the need to bring the Emperor the proof he had asked for, and that meant capturing the whole band, including Stella and James Wainright. To show himself now would ruin his chances of doing that, and they were slim enough as it was. He backed away carefully, silently, like the lion of his namesake, until he was far enough from the newly-made path to stand upright without being seen by the American or his guards.

Pablo was at his side almost at once, and they walked together to a small clearing, where a band of Mexicans waited with the *alcalde*.

'Well?' the *alcalde* asked.

'The ruin is guarded, but not very carefully. Most of the armed men seem to be in the village.'

'*Señor*, please do not destroy my village.' He was looking decidedly worried. 'We are loyal Mexicans, and we will do all you ask, but I beg you to avoid bloodshed and damage to our homes.'

'*Señor*, I will try, but it depends on the resistance I meet.'

'There will be none from my people.'

'But from the armed *Juáristas* there will be a great deal, unless we can take them by surprise. We need to disarm the American first.'

'And the *señora*?'

'Leave her to me.' Leo spoke flatly, though he had no idea what he was going to do about Stella, if his plan succeeded. He cursed the day he had ever met her, but then his honesty made him admit that he would not want to forgo the memory of Trieste, however painful, or the journey through the jungle, even though at the end of it she had done what she had before, left him for someone else. She was an incredibly beautiful woman, but, more than that, she was spirited and fearless. She was, in his opinion, also fickle.

He told himself that it was not so much the fact that she had left him which hurt—she was, after all, a married woman—but that she had turned to Redford Carson, who stood for everything that was cruel and treacherous. The most charitable thing he could say about her was that she did not know what she was doing, and that her anxiety for her husband was over-riding her common sense. Did she love James Wainright? For a moment, when he had kissed her on the beach and he had thought she responded to him, he had been foolish enough to hope. He cursed himself for his folly and turned his mind to more practical things, one of which was to decide how to overcome the ex-Confederate without causing too many casualties, and with only the help of a few trusted villagers.

Stella was woken in the middle of that night by the wind rattling the shutter, and, for a moment, thought it was part of her dream, the one she had had so many times recently. It was always Redford Carson drawing her away from Leo, and in the background was an unseen, shapeless shadow, like a storm-cloud, which was identified as Jimmy. Each time, there was a snake or serpent coiled ready to strike. She lay in the dark trying to shake it off, and it was a moment or so before she realised where she was.

Once fully awake, she went to the window and flung the shutter open, standing for a moment to look out on the quiet, deserted compound, its collection of huts, its *cabildo*, and the huge church that looked eerie, silhouetted against the sky with the moon shining through the foliage that sprouted from its thatch. The heat was more oppressive than ever; the wind that had woken her became still, as if there might be another storm. Unable to settle, she paced the tiny room.

Suddenly the ground rocked beneath her feet, and the sound of an enormous explosion burst on the silent night, shaking the hut and sending trickles of soft adobe dust down the walls. She ran to open the door wide. A column of smoke and long tongues of flame shot skywards from the direction of the ruins, and she knew that the Colonel's arsenal had been blown up. The square was suddenly teeming with people, old and young, streaming from their homes, shouting and calling excitedly and pointing at the sky, which was shot with red and blue and yellow like a particularly colourful dawn. From the direction of the jungle, the screeching of terrified animals and squawking of birds reached their ears. One or two trees caught alight and crashed, and smoke drifted on the wind to hang over the village.

Carson ran out of his hut, tucking his shirt into his trousers, but paused when he saw her. He stood for a moment to look at her standing in the doorway, wearing nothing but a chemise and petticoat, lifted his hands towards her, then dropped them to his sides and ran off across the compound.

A voice called loudly through the darkness from the vicinity of the church. 'Colonel Carson, sir, over here! I've found something.'

He changed direction and made for the church, where someone was standing in the shadows holding a lantern. It was almost like a beckoning finger, and Stella slipped on her dress and followed. The figure with the light had disappeared, and Carson stood there, undecided. His men had all scattered, some to investigate the explosion, others to see to the frightened animals, still more to take shelter in case there was more to come. He was about to turn away, when he saw Stella.

'What do you think you are doing? Get back to bed unless you want to be killed!' He walked over and stood beside her, as another thought came to him. 'Do you know anything about this?' He jerked his head in the direction of the explosion.

'Of course not! But I won't say I'm not pleased. At least the guns and ammunition can't be used now. The destruction of an ancient ruin is nothing compared to the saving of a living village and its inhabitants, and perhaps others in other villages.'

'Go back to your hut. I haven't time to stand arguing with you.' There was a tiny sound from inside the church, and he turned his head to listen. Someone was moving about in there, and, through the half-open door, they could see the flickering light weaving its way, seemingly without human aid, down the aisle.

'Colonel Carson, sir.' The voice was hoarse, anxious. 'There's a body here. It's . . .' The voice faded.

Carson seized Stella by the arm and flung the creaking door wide open. 'On second thoughts,' he said, pushing her inside in front of him, 'you can come with me.'

After the heat of the tropical night, it was cold and dank, and their footsteps echoed on the stone floor as they approached the altar. She was trembling with a mixture of cold and fear, and kept her eyes straight ahead, because she sensed, rather than saw, a movement in the shadows. Carson held her arm in a grip that hurt, and she knew that he, too, was afraid, and it gave her a great sense of satisfaction. Suddenly what little light there was went out, and he was wrenched from her. She was pushed away so violently that she stumbled and almost fell. She regained her balance and turned in the darkness, realising that Carson was grappling with an assailant, but unable to see who it was. The noise of blows, fists on flesh, grunts and heavy breathing came from the floor at her feet, and she dared not move for fear of becoming entangled with them. There was a sickening thud, then silence, and then the lantern was uncovered, throwing huge, long shadows across the floor and over the Colonel's postrate form. Leo, dressed in Mexican clothes, was standing over him, and Pablo was dancing excitedly from one foot to the other a few yards away. Behind them stood the *alcalde*.

Leo was not back in Mexico City, he was here, not two yards away, and the boy in the jungle that afternoon *had* been Pablo! Stella's mind whirled with questions, but it was a moment or two before she could find the voice to speak.

'Leo, tell me I'm not dreaming again! You are here, you are not a ghost?'

'I'm no ghost,' he said with a wry smile. 'And you are not dreaming.'

Reluctantly she dragged her eyes from him to look down at Carson's still form. 'You haven't—haven't killed him, have you?' she whispered.

'I am not an executioner,' Leo said, and his voice was as cold as the church. 'I leave that to others.' He turned from her and spoke to the *alcalde*. 'Take the prisoner and lock him in the gaol. Pablo, you come with me. I want you to go on an errand to Villa-Hermosa. Stella, go back to bed.'

'Back to bed!' she exclaimed.

'Yes.' His voice was firm. 'Back to your hut, and stay there. I could lock you up, too, but I won't, if you promise to stay inside and keep out of mischief.'

'Lock me up? Why? What have I done?'

'Do you need me to tell you that? Now do as I say, before I hand you over to the villagers, who will not feel obliged, as I am, to remember that you are a woman, and a European at that.'

'But I have done nothing wrong? You surely don't believe I am one of the bandits?'

'What I believe is of no consequence. My duty is clear, and I would be failing in it if I did not point out that you are under the gravest suspicion.'

Carson had warned her that she might be branded a Liberal, but until now she had not believed him. But if Leo thought so, what hope had she of convincing anyone else? 'I never heard so much nonsense in my life!' she said angrily. 'I thought you knew me better than that. I thought you understood why it was so important for me to make this trip.'

'I don't know you at all,' he said. 'You are a stranger to me, a meddler in what does not concern you. Somehow you have to be taught not to interfere in the affairs of Mexico.'

'This has nothing to do with the affairs of Mexico, and I am sick and tired of having to repeat it. Once I am reunited with my husband, then I will leave. And I shan't be sorry to go!'

'Stella, go back to your hut and wait until I have decided what to do with you,' he said wearily. 'I have too much to do to argue with you now.'

'But I won't be treated like a common criminal,' she said. 'It was bad enough being held prisoner by the Colonel, but to be mistrusted in this way by you is just too much.'

'You have never given me any reason to trust you,' he said, 'though the Lord knows I tried. As for being held prisoner, if my memory serves me, you went of your own accord, and what I have seen since has not made me change my mind.'

'I can explain.'

'You will have an opportunity to do that later. Now I must finish what I started.'

What he was saying was inexplicable, and she took a step towards him. 'Leo, I . . .' She stopped when she saw his expression by the light of the lantern the *alcalde* was carrying; it was hard and unyielding. Smothering a sob of anguish, she turned to leave. It was then she realised that the church was no longer empty: several armed men were standing in the shadows. She stopped, and cried out.

'They won't hurt you.' She heard Leo's voice behind her. 'So long as you do as you are told.'

She went to her hut and shut the door, but there was no question of going back to sleep. What was Leo going to do? Would there be a fight? She did not want that to happen; it meant people might die, and not just soldiers, but innocent villagers. Or Leo himself. Was he concerned for her safety, or was he simply afraid she would get in the way or do something to frustrate him? He could not believe she was in league with the *Juáristas*, could he? If only he had managed one soft word to her, just one word.

Daylight came as she stood at the window. She could see Carson standing at the bars of the prison window, gazing at the plume of smoke, now being rapidly dispersed by the wind, and she wondered what he was thinking. He would be angry, there was no doubt of that, and he might even blame her for his capture. She caught a glimpse of Leo hurrying across the compound, issuing orders and directing the repair of her wagon, one side of which was propped on stones. The takeover of the village appeared to have been bloodless, and she was thankful. Having dressed, she walked across the square to Leo, passing the prison hut on her way.

'Stella!' She heard the Colonel call her, and paused, half turning towards him, then gathered herself and moved on.

She stopped beside Leo, who was again in uniform and squatting down to examine the underside of the wagon. Moving his head to one side, he caught sight of Stella's skirt billowing slightly in the breeze, remained still for a moment, then slowly looked up over her waist and gently heaving breasts to her face. He looked exhausted, she noticed, and there were deep lines etched around his eyes, but his voice, when he spoke, was impersonal, almost impatient. 'Hallo, Stella.'

'Why are you avoiding me?' she asked bluntly. 'Have

you nothing to say to me?'

'I'm not avoiding you, but I'm extremely busy.' He stood, so that he was looking down on her. 'And what do you suggest I should say?'

'An apology wouldn't come amiss.'

'Great heavens, what for?'

'For the dreadful accusations you made last night. I can only assume that you were tired and anxious and not quite yourself.'

He laughed, but there was no humour in his voice, and his eyes held the shadow of a pain. 'Go away, Mrs Wainright. Go away.'

'Aren't you in the least bit interested in what has been happening to me, or how I have been used?'

'Carson has been looking after you, hasn't he?'

'If you call being watched night and day, and guarded by men with rifles, being looked after, then I suppose he has.'

'That was your choice, Stella. You always wanted him to lead the expedition and not me, didn't you? Did he tell you he knew where your husband was before we left Cordoba?'

'No, he said he did not know exactly, but Jimmy is very near, I know it. The Colonel had promised to take me to him tomorrow.'

'You don't still believe that?'

'Yes, I do. That hut over there is full of my husband's things. There are labelled plants and a plan of the ruins, and Papa's microscope. Jimmy was here not so very long ago.'

'Stella, we'll talk about it later, but now I have no time. The weather is changing, can't you feel it? We must leave as soon as we possibly can, if we are not to be bogged down by rain and mud.'

'I will not leave without Jimmy. I've come too far to turn back now.'

'You have no choice.'

'I am your prisoner, is that it?'

'For your own protection.'

'And because you do not trust me,' she said bitterly.

He moved past her to go over to one of the villagers, who was helping him on the other side of the wagon. 'Stella, please go back to your hut.'

'What will happen to Colonel Carson?'

He smiled slowly. 'I was wondering when you would come to that.'

'In spite of everything, I cannot find it in my heart to hate him, and I'm sorry to see him going back a prisoner.'

He smiled lopsidedly. 'Colonel Redford Carson is an enemy of Mexico, believe me. He has provided the *Juáristas* with guns and money; he was responsible for the attack on the diligence and the loss of the lives of people you had met and travelled with. Don't forget, Stella, that you were the one who wanted the perpetrators of that outrage caught and punished, or so you told the Emperor.'

'How do you know the Colonel did that?' she demanded.

'Because he had your portrait. I saw it on his coach.'

'So did I, but as you said you might sell it or give it away, I thought that was what you had done.'

'To Redford *Carson*?' His voice betrayed his surprise. 'You thought *that*?'

'Or Josefina.'

'I left it on the diligence, Stella. Carson stole it the night before it was attacked, the same night he delivered two boxes of rifles and ammunition to the ambushers.'

'Stole it? Why?'

'You don't know why? Do you mean to tell me he has not been making advances to you?'

'Yes, but I'm sure he didn't mean anything by it. And he knows I would not dream of betraying my husband.'

'Of course not,' he said flatly.

She looked up at him, wondering if she had imagined the note of sarcasm in his voice, but he appeared to be busy inspecting the newly repaired wheel-shaft. 'What are you going to do with him?'

'Take him back to Mexico City to stand trial along with Miguel and his men.'

'Then what?'

He shrugged. 'It will be out of our hands, Stella. Others will judge them; it is not our place to do so.'

'Will they get a fair trial?'

He looked at her keenly. 'I have no reason to think otherwise. And before you start pleading on the Colonel's behalf, I must tell you that I cannot let him go. In fact, I ought to send you back to stand trial with him.' His voice held a note of bitterness.

'Leo, I didn't know he was a Liberal. All I knew was that he wanted to bring me to Yucatan and you did not.'

He straightened up from his inspection of the wheel and turned slowly to face her. 'Don't you know why I didn't want to escort you? Don't you understand?' He was scanning her face in a way which was making her shaky and nervous, as if he were trying to read what was in her heart through her eyes. He laughed suddenly. 'You must have a very short memory.'

'I don't know what you mean. There is nothing wrong with my memory.'

'No? Well, we won't go into that now.' He turned, as one of his men approached to speak to him, almost as if he were glad of the interruption. Annoyed that he could upset her so, she walked away.

'Stella!' he called softly. She stopped, but did not turn round. 'I'll see you at supper.'

She nodded, choking back angry tears, and continued walking, passing the prison hut where Carson stood at the window, as he had stood most of the time he had been held there, staring across the square, watching the comings and goings with impassive features. A certain contrariness in her nature made her go across to him.

'I'm sorry, Colonel.'

He smiled. 'The fortunes of war, I suppose.'

'You will have a fair trial. Leo has promised it.'

He laughed suddenly, and she wondered how he could be amused by the situation. 'He has no power to make such promises. If he succeeds in taking me back, I shall die the day he hands me over, probably the same hour. Do you really want that for me?'

'But you're American, not Mexican.'

'Do you think that will make any difference?' He smiled wryly. 'On the other hand, he might find that there is no Empire left to try me and that the Liberals are in control. Has he considered that? I wonder. I might just be in a position to reverse our roles and send him to his death. Stella, think of that, will you?'

'You'd do it, too, wouldn't you?' she retorted.

'It depends on you, my dear.' He paused, watching her face. 'I need my freedom and I need you.'

'Me?'

'Didn't you know that? Hadn't you guessed?'

'No,' she said, wondering how it was that Leo could have noticed something that she had not.

'Stella, let me out of here.'

'I can't possibly do that.'

'Yes, you can.' He looked intently at her. 'I know where your husband is, and Manfred does not. I can still take you to him.'

She turned to walk away, but he reached through the bars and put a hand on her arm to detain her. 'Think about it, Stella. You can let me out. Do it tonight. We'll be long gone before we're missed.'

She wrenched herself away and almost ran to her hut.

The rest of the day was spent on practical tasks which left her mind free to wander, but again and again she came back to Carson's offer to take her to Jimmy. Nothing had changed: all the old arguments were still valid.

Her dilemma was no nearer being solved when she joined everyone for supper. The villagers were cheerful and noisy and looking forward to returning to a normal life once more, although some of the men had volunteered to help escort the prisoners as far as Villa-Hermosa. Leo, sitting on a bench a little apart, seemed deep in thought. Beside him, on a rough wooden table, stood a pitcher of the local wine and a glass. His blue eyes were dark-shadowed, etched by fine lines as though he had done a great deal of frowning of late. But he was still the handsome lion of her dreams, and nothing could alter that. Realising that made it more important than ever to find her husband.

She went to sit beside him, determined to make him listen to her. 'Leo, I am sorry if I displeased you. I should never have left you in order to come with the Colonel. It was a mistake, but I truly believed I was doing the right thing. I knew I had been wrong almost at once, but it was too late to turn back. I thought you had taken the boat and returned to the Emperor.'

'I would not have left my mission unaccomplished.'

'But I relieved you of it.'

'I was not referring to your expedition, but to my orders to prove that Redford Carson was helping the Liberals.'

She looked at him in surprise. Had Carson been right? Had Leo made use of her, too? 'Leo, I swear I did not know that before we arrived here and I saw all those guns. He was using me, just as you used me.'

'I?'

'Yes, you! You wanted to catch Colonel Carson, and now you've done it, you should be pleased. For someone who has just had a bloodless victory, you are extraordinarily morose.'

'I am not morose, I have a great deal to think about.'

'I know,' she said, with some asperity, 'and I am loath to add to your problems, but I need to know where my husband is. It seems that everywhere I've been, I have just missed him.'

'Stella,' he said, turning towards her and looking into her eyes for the first time that evening, 'had you thought there might be a reason for that?'

'Yes,' she said slowly, 'I've been thinking of nothing else for weeks now. He is running away. I can only think he no longer loves me and doesn't want to face me. If that's true, I want to know.'

He turned towards her, and his eyes, so hard before, had softened and his expression was gentle. It tore at her heart. 'Would you be very hurt if that were so?'

'I can't tell,' she said honestly. 'Until I meet him face to face, I won't know.'

He stood up suddenly and held out his hand. 'Come, it has been a tiring day and tomorrow we have a long way to go.'

She stood beside him, eyes flashing angrily. 'You have not listened to a word I've said, have you? Nothing has changed.'

He took her arm. 'Let me take you to your hut. We'll talk about it again tomorrow.'

She walked beside him, conscious of the pressure of his hand on her arm. Was it the hand of a friendly escort or a gaoler taking her back to prison? And though she was all too aware of his physical presence beside her and her desperate need of him, her thoughts were in a turmoil. Surely, surely, he would not make her leave without Jimmy?

It was a fine night, but the wind was strengthening and a few clouds drifted across the sky, obliterating the stars. The rainy season was threatening to begin early, and if that happened, travel through the jungle would become well-nigh impossible, especially with a wagon, and she could understand Leo's haste. Suddenly it all became too much to bear, and she cried out, 'Oh, Leo, what am I to do?'

'Trust me,' he said quietly.

The gentleness in his voice took her completely by surprise, and she turned to look up at him. 'I did that once before, and you failed me.'

'I did? *I* failed *you*?' The emphasis was unmistakable. 'When am I supposed to have done that?'

'You are the one with the short memory,' she said, deciding to have it out with him, to clear the air once and for all; then perhaps she could put him from her mind. 'In Trieste. You promised to call at our villa, and I believed you. I trusted you then, but you never came.'

'But I explained why in my letter. Surely it was not too much to ask that you meet me at the waterfront instead?'

'Letter? You mean you wrote to me?'

He stopped and turned to face her, seizing her shoulders and looking deep into her eyes glistening with tears. 'You didn't receive a letter from me?'

It seemed as if her heart had stopped beating, that her feet had left the ground; she hardly dared to breathe, to hope. 'I received nothing, nothing at all. It was as if you had never come into my life. I had only memories, and they turned sour.'

'Stella, oh Stella, my darling.' He was gripping her shoulders so tightly it was hurting. 'Do you mean that all this time you thought I had deserted you?'

'What else was I to think?'

'But I could never do that. I thought you had rejected me.' His voice had suddenly become light, almost boyish.

'Leo, I don't understand. How could I reject you when I was never given the opportunity to do so?'

He cupped her upturned face in his hands and bent his head to brush her lips very gently with his. 'Stella, my darling, my own love, I would never have willingly left you at all. I loved you then and I love you now, you must know that.'

Her senses were reeling: he loved her, just as she loved him! She clung to him, while their surroundings, the mud-baked square, the tumbledown huts, the extraordinary church, faded away, and all that was left were two people so much in love that nothing existed for them but each other. It had all been a terrible, terrible mistake, but whatever he did in the future, she would never doubt him again. It was several minutes before he allowed her to speak, but there were still some questions on her mind, and she had to ask them. 'But why did you leave so suddenly? Why didn't you tell me you were part of Maximilian's household?'

'I wasn't at the time. What I told you was true—I was visiting the castle. Maximilian did not tell me he wanted

me to come to Mexico with him until very late on the
evening of his departure.'

'And you could not refuse?'

'No. My mother had already agreed to come as lady-
in-waiting to Carlota, and as I had misgivings about the
whole thing, I had to come to look after them both. My
first thought was for you; I could not go without telling
you how much I loved you, that I would be leaving my
heart behind and had every intention of returning to
claim it, so I wrote asking you to meet me. The young
pageboy I entrusted with the letter assured me that he
had given it to you personally.'

'I never saw him.'

He held her closely in his arms, laying his cheek
against her soft hair. 'I realise that now, but at the
time . . .' He paused to kiss her again. 'And even
though you did not come to meet me in Trieste, the hope
that you might write buoyed me up for weeks after I
arrived in Mexico City. But when no news came . . .'

'Oh, Leo, I'm sorry, truly sorry I had so little faith in
you.'

He drew away to hold her at arm's length and look
down into her eyes. 'And I in you, but when your father
arrived with your husband, what was I to think? I
concluded that you had never felt about me the way I did
about you. You had forgotten my existence.'

'I tried,' she said. 'Until a few weeks ago, I thought I
had succeeded.'

They stood looking at each other without speaking.
The moon came out from behind a cloud, throwing the
shadow of the church across their path, its cross outlined
on the bare earth of the compound in front of them. An
animal howled from the jungle, a loud gust of laughter
came from the direction of the *cabildo*, a horse neighed.
The air was close and still.

He reached out and took her in his arms again, and she
buried her face in his broad chest and allowed the tears
to run unchecked, while her thoughts whirled. He loved
her and she loved him, and what she wanted was to stay

in his arms for ever. But it was impossible, and they both knew it. It was too late, much too late.

'Please, Stella.' His voice was cracked with strain. 'Please don't cry.' He wiped away the tears with a gentle finger, then bent to kiss each cheek in turn.

She drew herself away from him at last and looked up into his face. 'Josefina,' she said. 'I thought you and Carson were both in love with her.'

'We are both in love with you. Didn't that occur to you?'

'No, it never crossed my mind.' Then, as she remembered something else. 'Josefina is a spy. Her father is a leading *Juárista*; he lives in Villa-Hermosa.'

'I know, I found that out a few days ago. It is the answer to several mysteries about how the Liberals always know our movements, how they manage to be in the right place at the right time to attack us. We have got to get back as soon as possible to warn the Emperor.'

'Oh, Leo,' she said, 'how can people behave like that towards each other?'

'They become wedded to a cause, and the cause is the most important thing in their lives; more powerful than love or mercy.'

'Stronger than a man's love for a woman?' she asked softly.

'If the two are in conflict, then, yes, I believe so.'

'And are you wedded to Maximilian's cause in that way?'

'Maximilian is my friend as well as my Emperor.' He smiled down at her. 'And, like you, I had something I wanted to forget.'

'Oh, Leo.' She dropped her head on his chest again and he held her, gently stroking her hair. 'I have been a fool, a headstrong untrusting fool! Now I must suffer for my folly.'

'Things will seem different in the morning,' he said.

'In the morning,' she repeated. 'And what of all the other mornings, one after another, for the rest of our lives? I have a husband and I have done him a terrible wrong. That has not changed.'

'You should not feel guilty,' he said, wishing he dared tell her the truth about James Wainright, but he knew it would serve no purpose and would make her more unhappy than ever. He turned with her to continue walking to her hut. At the door, he stopped and took her hands in his, turning them palm uppermost and lifting each in turn to his lips. 'Goodnight, my lovely star. Try to sleep.'

Sleep! It was impossible, there was too much going on in her head, memories of Leo in Trieste, thoughts of her parents, and Jimmy. Oh, what was she going to do about Jimmy? She went to the window to watch Leo stride away across the square, and was surprised to see him go over to where the animals were tethered and saddle a horse. He glanced briefly towards her hut as he mounted and then rode out alone.

Restlessly she paced the tiny room, but it was too confining, almost claustrophobic, she needed to be out in the air. On impulse, she went out and crossed the compound to the church, pausing at the creaking door before entering and making her way to the altar. It was cold, and she shivered as she knelt and covered her face with her hands, trying to bring peace to her troubled mind. But it was no use, the church reminded her of the events of the night before, events that had changed everything and then left them exactly as they were before. She rose with a heavy heart and made her way across the village square.

There were a few people about, but no one paid her any attention. The prison hut was dark, and she wondered what the Colonel was thinking. Did he really know where Jimmy was? And was finding Jimmy the answer to her dilemma? Would her path become clear when she saw him again? A man was walking across the compound towards the hut, carrying a covered tray. On an impulse, she hurried to catch him.

'I'll take that,' she said, reaching out to take the tray.

He paused, reluctant to part with it, and she realised that he did not understand. After a moment or two of sign language, understanding, or rather misunderstanding, dawned and, grinning, he gave her the tray, turned to unbolt the door and stood to one side so that she could enter.

'Colonel,' she called into the darkness of the room. 'I've brought your supper.'

He emerged from the shadows, smiling. 'What a pleasant change from the surly Injun who came before! I couldn't make him understand a word of what I want.'

'What do you want, Colonel? Perhaps I can ask for it for you.'

He seized her shoulders, and the tray she held clattered to the floor. She expected the guard to come running in to see what had happened, but no one came. 'This is what I want,' he said, pulling her roughly towards him and bringing his mouth down on hers in a bruising kiss that took her breath away. Shocked by the violence of it, she struggled helplessly, realising, too late, how rash she had been. Suddenly he drew back. 'I'm sorry, Stella,' he said softly. 'Sorry it has to be like this.'

She saw his clenched fist raised inches from her chin, and then nothing but darkness as she slid to the floor.

CHAPTER TEN

IT WAS FOOLHARDY to ride through the jungle at night, but Carson's comings and goings over the last few days had made a well-defined path, and as long as Leo followed that, he could be reasonably sure of his way. With luck he would be in Villa-Hermosa by daylight.

Liberal sympathiser or not, Stella must be allowed to leave Mexico without hindrance; he could not stand by and see her imprisoned and tried for spying and subversion, or whatever else the American was accused of. If only she had not spoken of Trieste tonight, he could have gone on thinking she was fickle; it would have been much easier for them both. Tonight's revelations had changed everything and she had to be protected at all costs, and the cost was likely to be high. It meant that she would leave Mexico with her husband, who would have to be allowed to go, and he would never see her again, *must* never see her again.

There was little doubt that Wainright was in league with Carson, which was why he had been so reluctant to be found. If he were taken back to stand trial with the other prisoners, he would be condemned to death and Stella would be free. Leo cursed aloud, and the horse laid back its ears at the sudden sound, but continued its steady walk. He could not do that, not now; it would kill their rediscovered love stone dead; and she would not turn to him for consolation in such circumstances. Like it or not, he would have to be the instrument for reuniting husband and wife and sending them safely on their way out of Mexico—and out of his life. And the sooner the better. He urged his horse into a canter, praying that it was sure-footed enough not to stumble.

Dawn was in the sky as he rode into Villa-Hermosa and made for the single-storey house where he had sent

Pablo to meet Ramón. The shutters were closed, but Pablo must have been awake and heard the horse, because the door was flung open and he ran out, all smiles.

'*Señor*, you come early!' He looked behind Leo, as though expecting others. 'Ramón still sleeps in the back room.'

Leo dismounted and handed over the reins. 'Look after my horse, Pablo, he's had a long ride.' He paused to ruffle the boy's hair. 'See if you can find me a fresh one, I have to go back.'

'*Si, Señor.*'

Leo watched him lead the horse away to a livery stable, then turned and went into the house, walking purposefully through to the room where his lieutenant was sleeping. He took hold of the bare foot poking out from under the blanket, and pulled. 'Wake up, lazy-bones!'

Ramón stirred and opened his eyes slowly, one by one, blinking as Leo flung back the shutters and let in the morning sun. 'Go away! I want to sleep.' He shut his eyes again and turned over, intending to do just that. Leo bent to grip the side of the bed and tipped it up, depositing his protesting friend on the floor.

'Forgive me! I know that you, like I, have had a long ride, but we must start work. Later you can go back to the dream that put such a smile on your face.'

Ramón struggled to his feet, pulled on his trousers and shrugged himself into his shirt. 'Will you allow me to breakfast first?'

Leo laughed. 'Yes, and I'll join you.' He turned to leave the room. 'I'll wait in the kitchen.'

The woman of the house was up and about, stirring the fire and setting a pan on the flames to begin cooking breakfast. She greeted Leo cordially in Spanish and poured him a cup of the local coffee. It was black and strong and revived his flagging energy, so that when Ramón arrived, he was ready to make plans.

'Pablo told you what happened when he caught up with Carson?' he asked.

'Yes, but why didn't you wait for me?'

'There wasn't time, and besides, the *alcalde* turned out to be friendly. He lent me some of his men. Once I had blown up the ammunition store, it was easy.'

'And Mrs Wainright?'

Leo paused, wondering how much to tell him, and then related everything except the personal details that he hugged to himself as a precious memory. 'She has convinced me that she is innocent,' he said. 'I must let her go.'

'And Wainright?'

'Him, too.'

'But he's a villain of the first order! He is worse than a traitorous Mexican, because he did it for money, not out of conviction. He and that dog of an ex-Confederate should be hanged and their bodies thrown to the jungle beasts, or, better still, given to them alive!'

Leo laughed, tucking into his food. 'You Mexicans are a bloodthirsty lot, I must say.'

'It's no more than they deserve.'

'Redford Carson must be taken back for trial. I want everyone to know what he's done, because it will prove what I have been saying all along—that the Liberals are being supported by the American government.'

'And you are going to let Wainright go free?'

'I have no choice. For Stella's sake, I must.'

'Forgive me for saying so, my friend, but your reasoning is a little back to front. With James Wainright gone, your way will be clear.'

'Not clear, Ramón, not clear at all. The way to Stella would be blocked by Wainright's dead body; it would always be between us.'

'Then let me be the one to condemn him. I will gladly do it.'

Leo said slowly, 'No, that won't work either. Where is he, by the way?'

'Tied to the bedpost in the next room. He appears to

have an easy conscience, because he went to sleep much sooner than I did after I brought him here.'

'He didn't have your journey. When did you arrive?'

'Just after midnight.'

'Did he give any trouble?'

'No, not when I made it plain what would happen to him if he resisted.' He paused. 'How did you know where he would be?'

Leo laughed. 'It's more difficult for a European to hide in this part of the country than in Mexico City, and asking questions soon produced answers. Carson has been leading poor Stella round in circles for days, pretending that her husband was just a few miles ahead of them. What she didn't know was that he was here, hiding in Villa-Hermosa, all the time.'

'Does she know you know where he is?'

'Not yet. I was going to tell her last night, but then other things intervened and I found I couldn't. I want to talk to him first.'

'I don't agree with what you're planning to do, Captain,' Ramón said. 'If the Emperor should hear of it . . .'

'As far as Maximilian is concerned, Mr Wainright is an innocent explorer, looking for exhibits for the National Museum, who accidentally stumbled on evidence that will convict Colonel Carson and prove my point about the Americans. No one will tell him any differently, will they?'

'I'll say nothing, but I'm not so sure about Carson. Won't he drag him down with him?'

'The Emperor will not believe it because of his high regard for Sir Peter Gardiner, and because he appointed them both.'

'I would sooner you took that gamble than I,' Ramón said. 'And I give you fair warning, if Wainright makes one wrong move while he is still on Mexican soil, I shall take the matter into my own hands and chance your wrath.'

Leo smiled as he left the room. 'Understood, my friend, understood.'

He went to the room next door, and flung back the shutters so that the full light of day flooded over the sleeping form in the bed. The young man stirred and tried to sit up, falling back on the pillow when he realised he was still securely tied. His hair was tousled and he had a half-grown beard, but he was handsome in a rather flabby way. He would be middle-aged before his time, Leo thought, as he sat on the end of the bed, struggling with an almost overpowering desire to vent his frustration on the helpless prisoner and lash out with fist and foot.

'I hope you have your wits about you,' Leo said calmly, 'because we have a great deal to talk about.'

'I'd as lief have breakfast first,' the young man said. 'Talking on an empty stomach always upsets me.'

'Pablo will bring you something in a minute, when we have reached an agreement.'

'Agreement? Do you need my agreement to put an end to my life?'

'I have no wish to put an end to your life, only to your nefarious activities.'

'Oh, then it's blackmail. I should have known you would be no different from Carson!' He sighed heavily. 'What is it you want? If it's money, I'm afraid you'll be unlucky. I have none.'

'I want a full written confession. I want to know exactly what Carson and Josefina have been up to —times, dates, everything—and I want you to confirm this to the Emperor when I take you to him.'

'And suppose I know nothing?'

'Oh, but you do, though why you should choose to help the Emperor's enemies, I have no idea.'

'Of course you haven't,' the younger man said bitterly. 'You don't know what it's like to be penniless, to have to depend for every mouthful on a senile old man whose head is so far in the clouds or, to be more accurate, in the branches of trees that he can't think of earthly things like wanting to eat and drink and make love.'

'I take it you are referring to Sir Peter?'

'Who else?'

'And he stopped you from doing those things so dear to your heart?' Leo looked at the young man with contempt. This was the man who had taken Stella from him, an immature puppy of a boy who had no idea how a woman like Stella should be treated. 'Tell me about it.'

'What does it matter to you?'

'It matters a great deal. Your life depends on your answers, so they had better be truthful. How did you become involved with Redford Carson?'

'He was well known in Mexico City, and we met from time to time to drink together and play a hand of cards. He was a good companion and generous to his friends. Sir Peter disapproved, but I didn't see why he should dictate my life for me simply because I was married to his daughter. She was thousands of miles away and, to tell the truth, I found it difficult to remember her. I didn't see why I should lead the life of a monk.'

Leo was keeping a very tight rein on his temper, but he did not let it show, as he said, 'Go on.'

'Carson had lent me money some months previously, and was pressing for payment. Old skinflint would not cough it up, and things went from bad to worse. Then Sir Peter died, so there was no more help to be had from that quarter. In the end, Carson promised to write off the debt, if I helped him.' He stopped suddenly and looked up into Leo's eyes. 'That's all there is to it. I ran a few messages, transported a few guns, nothing more.'

'And Stella?'

'What about Stella?'

'Do you love her?'

'God, Manfred, you ask the craziest questions! How do I know whether I love her or not? I haven't seen her in over a year, and we were married only six months before I left England.'

'I can't understand how she ever came to marry you.'

'Oh, I can be very charming and persuasive when I choose, and I had a good ally in her grandmother, who was afraid that her grand-daughter would be left a spinster.'

'Why did you leave her?'

'For the same reason as I got involved with the Liberals—money. I had debts in London, and I paid some of them off with Stella's dowry, but that was all used up in no time.' He laughed harshly. 'I made the mistake of confiding in my father-in-law, and his answer was to offer to bring me out here. He said I could pay off my debts with my wages, and he would stand surety until I did. I suppose he imagined that he was protecting his darling daughter from a feckless husband!'

'Did Stella know anything of this?'

'No, that was part of the bargain: she was never to know.'

'And she still must not know, do you hear? Neither must she learn about your guerrilla activities, because she thinks you came to Yucatan to continue Sir Peter's work. I don't want her to be disillusioned. If I let you go, I want your solemn oath you will be a model husband.'

Puzzled by this unexpected leniency, James looked at Leo, and suddenly understood. 'Oh, that's the way the wind lies, is it? And if I don't?'

'I shall personally put an end to your wretched life.'

'Where is she?'

'A few hours' ride away. I'm going back to fetch her now. I shall tell her I found you in the jungle; it won't do for her to know you were hiding in Señor Gonzales' house.'

James chuckled suddenly. 'It was ironic that we should be under the same roof when she was searching so diligently for me! If she hadn't run off after the wagon, we would have met at breakfast the next morning.' He paused, then added, 'How are you going to explain the sudden reappearance of her trunk and basket along with her husband?'

'I found them put up for sale on the market, and recognised them.'

'Not very convincing, but my dear wife was always

very gullible. She believes everything she is told.'

'I don't enjoy lying to her, but it is for her own sake.'

'What will happen to Carson? That little Mexican beggar you keep took great glee in telling me that you had captured him and his followers.'

'That Mexican beggar is more man than you'll ever be!'

'You say that, but you are prepared to trust Stella to me.'

'I have no choice.' He paused. 'But others have. *I* may say you can go, but that does not hold good for any of my men, so be glad of my protection.'

'I shall need it, but not necessarily from your men. If Carson ever gets free, he'll want revenge for my turning informer. I'll be a marked man.'

Leo stood up to leave. 'Have I your word that you will leave Mexico and look after Stella properly?'

'You would have it, my gallant friend, if I had the means to leave! Crossing the Atlantic costs money.'

'You shall have enough for that.'

James gave an inclination of his head, meant to be a mock bow. 'Very generous of you, Manfred. But why not just pay me off and keep my wife?'

The temptation was there, almost overwhelming. Leo turned and left the room, slamming the door so that the noise reverberated through the house and brought Pablo running from the kitchen. He put his hand on the boy's shoulder and went with him to where he had left the fresh horse. Ramón came out of the back door as he was mounting.

'I have his word,' he said, 'but watch him. And make sure he is presentable and sober when I come back.'

He was in a grim mood as he rode away to tell the woman he loved that he had found her husband for her.

Stella's jaw hurt, and she had a raging headache that would not allow her to think clearly. Redford Carson had gone, and though some of the men had searched the jungle for a time, it seemed he had got clear away. She dreaded to think what Leo would say when he returned. He might even think she had let the American out on purpose, even though she had a bruise on her chin, and a lump the size of a hen's egg on the back of her head where she had hit the floor. She had been pleading on Carson's behalf the night before, and Leo would see that as evidence.

She was quite sure she had dreamed their reconciliation: it was all too remote, too far away to have any reality. She went about the village the whole day in a trance-like state, hardly hearing or seeing what was going on about her. But even that did not blind her to the fact that the men who were going to escort the prisoners were preparing to leave. She would be glad of that if she knew where Jimmy was. But Carson had taken that secret with him.

Leo returned at dusk, almost falling from his horse with exhaustion, and walked across the compound to talk to the *alcalde*. Stella, wearing the blue *huipil*, stood in the doorway of her hut and watched the two men talking, and she knew Leo was receiving a report of her folly. In her usual fashion of going to meet trouble halfway, she walked across to join him.

He looked at her, moving his gaze slowly up from her bare feet and over her slim hips and tiny waist to her bare shoulders and auburn head, and she realised that it was the first time he had seen her in the native garment, and he might think it was too daring. But he reached out and took her hand with a gentle pressure that belied his grim expression.

'Well, Stella?' he asked, wanting more than anything to take her in his arms again, but knowing that to do so would only prolong their agony. He had to be strong, to behave as if the previous night had not happened. But it had, and he could not forget it; he could only curse the trust he had put in that pageboy at Miramar. 'What madness possessed you to unbolt the door of the prison? Surely you knew what would happen, or did you intend to set Carson free?'

He looked at her closely, and she wondered if he still

had doubts about her involvement with the American. 'I don't know,' she said. 'The last thing I remember is being in the church, kneeling at the altar, and then nothing until I came to my senses on the floor of the prison and the *alcalde* was bending over me.' She paused to search his face, looking for reassurance. 'If I did, it was only so that he could take me to Jimmy.'

'He had no intention of doing that,' he said. 'Surely you realise that now?'

She sighed. 'I suppose you are right. I was a fool to expect him to take me; I would only have slowed him up. Now . . .' She stopped and looked towards the preparations for leaving going on around the wagon.

He smiled wearily, unable to condemn her. 'Is it so very important to you to find your husband, now after . . .?' He did not finish.

She looked up at him, trying to convey her dilemma in her eyes. 'Leo, he is still my husband.'

'Then I have good news for you.'

'You've found him!' she said at once.

Her apparent pleasure turned the knife in his wounded heart, and he almost winced. 'Yes, he's waiting for you at Villa-Hermosa.'

'But we've been there! That's where Josefina's parents live. Did Carson know he was there?'

He shrugged. 'Since you let him go, we can't ask him. We'll set out first thing in the morning, and we should be there by nightfall if we make good time.'

'Only a day? But it took a week to get here.'

'You didn't exactly come by the most direct route.'

'I knew we were going round in circles,' she said suddenly. 'Carson was recruiting all round the area, talking of a free Mexico, a strong Mexico, where poverty is unheard of and Jack is as good as his master. But why did he take me with him?'

'Oh, Stella, my love,' he said, smiling, 'he didn't, did he? You ran after him.'

There was no denying the truth of that. 'But he could have told me!'

'He had his reasons for not doing so, no doubt.'

'I don't understand.'

'No, I don't suppose you do. Are you ready to leave?'

'Yes.'

'I shall need the wagon to transport the prisoners. Do you think you can ride?'

'Of course.'

'We haven't a side-saddle.'

'I can ride astride.'

He looked down at the *huipil*, and laughed. 'I advise you to change your clothes first, or you'll have the whole male population of the village with their eyes popping out of their heads!'

She smiled back at him, but when she looked into his eyes she could see no joy there, and her own eyes clouded. He was being strong and practical and she was grateful for that, because, level-headed as she normally was, she knew that inside she was like jelly. If he weakened, she would be lost. It would have been better if they were still at loggerheads, still blaming each other for the past. No, not that, she thought, as she turned from him to obey. Whatever the future held, she would have the knowledge that once she had had the love of a wonderful man.

Leo's estimate of the time it would take to reach Villa-Hermosa was wide of the mark. Almost as soon as they started, it began to rain, and the downpour continued unabated the whole day. Although, like Leo, she was mounted, Stella had to walk when the going became too rough. The wagon was bogged down so frequently that it had to be abandoned and their supplies strapped to the mules taken from the shafts. The prisoners were made to walk, roped together in a kind of chain-gang. During a brief stop to rest, Miguel and one other managed to escape, and disappeared into the dense undergrowth. An hour was spent searching, but in the end Leo gave up and ordered everyone back to the march. They were still short of their destination when night fell and forced them to make an overnight stop.

Leo had become more and more silent as the day progressed. Stella could guess the reason and knew how he felt, because it was the same for her. Very soon he would hand her over to her husband, and she would be lost to him and he to her. In spite of all she had been through, the discomfort, the danger and the despair, she found herself dreading the moment when she would be once more face to face with the man she had travelled halfway round the world to find. Memories of their life in London had already become difficult to recall, even before she found herself in Leo's arms in the middle of a moonlit Mexican village square. Now she had to force herself to think about the reason why she had made the journey, because very soon she would have to put it into words.

The next morning they reached the so-called highway, and their speed increased marginally so that by early afternoon they emerged from the jungle into bright sunlight and found themselves on the outskirts of Villa-Hermosa. They plodded through the town, past the Gonzales' house, past curious townspeople, who stopped what they were doing to watch the strange cavalcade, until they drew up outside a single-storey house at one end of a palm-fringed square.

Leo reached across in the saddle to take Stella's reins. 'You go in alone,' he said quietly. 'I'm going to take the prisoners to the town gaol and see to the animals.'

He did not want to be present at the reunion, she realised that, and who could blame him? Slowly she dismounted, and stood, with thumping heart, looking at the closed door of the villa, afraid of what lay beyond it. Behind her, she heard Leo order the men forward, and she was tempted to turn and run after him, to tell him that she would not, could not, give him up. But that was a coward's way, and it would solve nothing. She took a deep breath and walked purposefully forward.

The door opened, and Jimmy stood silently watching her and then grinned and held out his arms. He was still the handsome man she had married, a little thicker about the waist perhaps, but his easy smile was the same, and the dark eyes searching her face were the same. He came forward to meet her. She stopped, unable to go on because her legs had turned to jelly.

He had had time to prepare for this meeting, and his greeting was ready on his lips. 'Stella, is it really you? Here was I, thinking you were far away in England and longing to have you at my side, and in reality . . .' He took her hands in his, holding them wide so that he could look at her, then he bent his head to kiss her lips.

His breath smelled of alcohol and suddenly she wanted to push him away, to ask him to give her time to come to terms with the conflicting emotions that chased each other through her tired brain: relief that her search was finally over, despair because the reunion had not driven Leo from her mind, and she knew it never would. She slid towards the ground, and he picked her up and carried her into the house and along a corridor to a small sitting-room. Setting her down on a sofa, he called to the woman of the house to bring a carafe of wine and two glasses.

'Poor Stella, what you must have been through!' he said. 'A glass of wine will revive you, and then you can tell me all about it.'

She was so nervous that she could not keep her hands still; she clasped them tightly together, and forced a weak smile. 'That's all behind me now, and I have found you.'

The woman came in with the wine and a little plate of cakes, set them down without speaking, and shut the door behind her as she left.

'Tell me all about it,' he said, seating himself beside her. 'Manfred won't interrupt us for ages yet.' He seemed to take great pleasure in telling her that, and she looked at him sharply. Her nerves were on a knife-edge; she was keyed up with apprehension, fear, almost. It was like being locked in a room with a strange man, because this man was a stranger. It was guilt on her part, she decided, nothing more. She had loved him once, and she must try to recapture that feeling and do her best to make amends without arousing his suspicions that she was less than overjoyed.

'How long have you been here?' she asked, as he poured the wine. 'Are you alone?'

'Yes. I had a couple of bearers, but they went off to join the army. Now tell me how you came to be here, when I thought you were six thousand miles away! What your mother was thinking of to allow you to come, I can't imagine.'

'She is dead, Jimmy.' There was a catch in her voice as she said it. 'She died nearly six months ago. I think Papa's death broke her heart. She couldn't really accept it. I wrote to tell you, asking you to come home, but when there was no reply I became very worried about you. I began to think something dreadful had happened, especially after Papa's death.'

'I received no letter, my darling,' he said, looking at her over the rim of his glass. 'I would have come back at once, had I known. And since Sir Peter's death was a pure accident, it was unlikely to happen to me, was it?'

'In England, we heard all kinds of rumours.'

'What about?' he asked sharply. 'About Sir Peter?'

'No.' She was puzzled by his reaction, almost as if she had put him on the defensive. 'I meant about bandits and the dangers of travelling.'

'Oh, that! Greatly exaggerated, I should say. I've had no trouble on that score; the only difficulties are the climate and the state of the roads. I expect that's why your letters never reached me.' He paused to drain his glass and immediately filled it again, smiling easily at her. 'So you decided to come and see for yourself?'

'I had to, Jimmy. It was only when Mama died that I was told about the state of our financial affairs. By the time I had paid everyone, there was only enough left to finance this expedition.'

He reached for the carafe and emptied it into his glass. 'You mean that you did not know?'

Were they really having this conversation, or was she dreaming it? Nowadays it was so difficult to tell dreams from reality. She stood up and walked over to the window to look out on the busy square, trying to compose herself. After all, she had come to Mexico to find him and the answers to just such questions. 'No, I want you to explain. Our lawyer told me that Papa had mortgaged his house to stand surety for your debts. But surely they were not so great as to take all he had?'

'No, of course not; he made some bad investments, too.' Jimmy went to the door with the empty carafe, and shouted towards the kitchen for someone to take it and refill it, then he turned back towards her. 'Come and sit down beside me. After all this time, I want to be able to see your face and touch you, not look at the back of your head. What is out there that you find so interesting?'

She returned to sit beside him. 'Nothing. What investments, Jimmy?'

He took her hand and, turning it over, put the palm to his lips. She felt nothing, she told herself, nothing at all. Had it always been like that? 'He wanted to show his faith in the future of Mexico,' he went on. 'He invested heavily in its railways, and he persuaded me to do the same, telling me he would stand surety for me because I had no capital of my own. He was thinking of our future, Stella—yours and mine. Unfortunately, we lost it all because of the state of affairs in Mexico. When he died, I had no choice but to continue with his work and hope to recoup some of it.'

It all sounded so plausible. 'Is that why you came to Yucatan?'

There was only the slightest pause before he said, 'Yes. What other reason would I have for coming to this godforsaken place when I would much rather have come home to you?'

A young Mexican girl brought in a fresh carafe of wine, and Jimmy immediately filled his glass again. 'Drink up, my darling, we have a lot of celebrating to do.'

'How long have you been here?' she asked, leaving the wine untouched.

'In Villa-Hermosa? A day or two.'

'Before that, you were in the jungle?'

'Yes, I've been moving all over the province. It's full of interesting places hidden away. I found a magnificent ruin, one previously undiscovered.'

'I know,' she said. 'I saw it. Unfortunately, Leo had to blow it up.'

'Blow it up!' His indignant exclamation was a little too forced. 'That's sacrilege!'

'It was necessary,' she said, 'because of what Colonel Carson was doing.'

'What was he doing?'

'You don't know?'

'I haven't seen Redford Carson since I left Mexico City,' he said carefully. 'How should I know what he's been doing?'

'He implied that you were in league with him, that you were helping him.'

His eyes narrowed as he picked up his glass and drained it yet again. 'Helping him to do what, Stella? You are not making sense.'

'How long have you been in the jungle?' she countered. 'How long since you had news of the outside world?'

'Two or three months, I suppose. Why, what has been happening?'

'Mexico is on the brink of civil war, and the Liberals have been attacking towns and cities all over the country. Colonel Carson has been going from village to village recruiting the natives. He has been telling them that Porfirio Díaz is sweeping up from the south, capturing every town in his path, and Juárez's troops are marching down from the north. He has been inciting them to join a force he is gathering to move west against the Conservative flank. He told them that there would be little resistance because the Emperor has no troops, though why he should interest himself in Mexican affairs, I don't know. He tried to implicate you.'

'Redford Carson is interested in only one thing—power—and he will stop at nothing to get it! The Emperor cannot fight America as well as Juárez.' Jimmy laughed suddenly. 'As it is, not even Juárez on his own; that much is plain. But what has that to do with me?'

'Nothing,' she said. 'I told everyone you were a naturalist and interested only in your work. If Carson used your discovery, it was without your knowledge.'

'Oh, what a champion I have in you, my sweet Stella!' he exclaimed. 'You are right, of course. But what did he do?'

'He made the chamber you found into an arsenal and filled it with guns and ammunition. That's why Leo blew it up and took Carson prisoner.'

'What is he going to do with him?'

'He intended to take him back for trial, but unfortunately I allowed him to escape.'

'You did what?' There was no mistaking the alarm in his voice.

'I unlocked the door of his prison, and he hit me, knocked me clean out of my senses, and got away.'

'Didn't Manfred go after him?'

'No, it happened while he was away, and though the other men looked for some time, he couldn't be found —not easily, anyway.' She paused. 'To tell the truth, I'm almost glad. I hate to see anyone locked up, and I'd feel even worse if I thought that anything I had said was instrumental in having him executed, and I fear that was what would have happened.'

'Stella, you must have been out of your senses! The man is dangerous. What did Manfred say when he came back?'

'What could he say? It was done and couldn't be undone, but I'm not sure he doesn't think I'm a *Juárista*.' She tried to laugh, but it sounded unnatural. 'Do you know, I spent three days in prison in Mexico City for intervening in Mexican affairs?'

He looked up from pouring more wine. 'Great

heavens, Stella, what did you do to deserve that?'

'It's a long story.'

'We have plenty of time.'

She realised that he was becoming more and more drunk, and wondered what would happen when he tired of talking; it was something she wanted to stave off for as long as possible. It was foolish, because she could not deny him his rights as a husband for ever; sooner or later she was going to have to come to terms with that. But not yet, she told herself, not yet, not while her reconciliation with Leo was so new, so fresh in her memory. She needed time, and if telling him the story of her imprisonment gave her a little respite, then she would talk and go on talking.

He listened without interrupting, stroking her bare arm with the backs of his fingers in an absent-minded way, and smiling to himself.

'That's all?' he asked, when she had finished.

'Goodness, isn't it enough?'

He put her hand to his lips. 'Stella, my dear, you have given me a history lesson on the affairs of Mexico, and very succinctly put, too, but not one word to say you are pleased to see me.'

'Of course I'm pleased! That was the whole reason for my journey—to be with you.'

'You might show a little more enthusiasm. A tear or two glistening in those beautiful eyes might be more convincing.' He sighed. 'But then you were never prone to weeping, were you?'

'Why weep? This is supposed to be a happy occasion. I am smiling, am I not?'

'And now you are with me, what are we going to do?'

'I want us to go home. I have had enough of Mexico, and now there is no reason to stay, I want to leave as soon as possible.' The words she spoke aloud gave the lie to her innermost thoughts. She had a very good reason to want to stay, but she could not acknowledge it, even to herself.

'Of course, my dear, and you shall have your wish just

as soon as I have cleared up one or two matters in
Mexico City.'

'What matters?'

'Business matters, nothing you need concern your
lovely head about. And I should make a report to the
Emperor. He is, after all, my employer.' He paused to
try and pour more wine from the empty carafe, but only
a few drops trickled down into his glass. 'But why are we
talking about such things when we have only just been
reunited? I can think of better things to do.' He reached
across and drew her to him. 'You are like a breath of cool
fresh air in the hellish heat of this place.' He crushed her
mouth with his, holding her against him and pulling her
dress from her shoulders, to cup his hand round her
breast.

His breath reeked of stale wine and his fumbling with
her clothes had no finesse, but in spite of his drunken-
ness, he was very strong and held her firmly. She
squirmed, and managed to free her mouth from his so
that she could speak. 'Jimmy, not here! Someone will
come in.'

'Then they will have to go away again. You are my
wife, and I want you. Now.' He grabbed her again, and
lowered his face into her neck. 'Why the reluctance, my
sweet? If it's Leo Manfred you are thinking of, you had
better make up your mind to forget him.' He chuckled
suddenly. 'He has been paid off.'

She could not believe what he was saying and opened
her mouth to protest, but he covered it with his own,
stifling her.

Behind them, the door opened and a voice muttered,
'Oh, I beg your pardon', before it shut again, but she had
recognised Leo's voice and wanted to tear herself away,
to cry out to make him come back and save her from her
own drunken husband.

Jimmy drew away from her, and laughed. 'That will
give him something to think about, won't it?'

CHAPTER ELEVEN

THE NATIVES who had accompanied them as prison guards left to go back to their village, and Ramón and Pablo had been sent on ahead to hire a boat, leaving Leo to escort the half-dozen prisoners with only the help of Stella and a very reluctant Jimmy. But Stella was glad to be on the move again; it meant that she did not have to be alone with her husband for any length of time, and during the overnight stops, she slept in the wagon while the men slept under the stars.

The journey was only a little easier than the one to Villa-Hermosa. When two more of the prisoners managed to escape, time was wasted searching for them, but five days later, weary, footsore and bedraggled, they emerged from the trees into bright sunlight. Ahead of them, set against the sparkling sea and a cloudless sky, was San Josef.

A small brown figure waiting on the side of the road ran towards them as they approached. He wore tailored white trousers, tucked into glossy black boots and decorated in the traditional way with silver coins down the outside seams, a white shirt, bright red embroidered waistcoat and an enormous sombrero. But for his broad smile, he was almost unrecognisable.

'Well, my friend, you seem to have put the money I gave you to good use!' Leo, who was leading his horse, tipped Pablo's new sombrero over his face, then laughed as the boy solemnly settled it back on his head. 'Quite the young beau, aren't you?'

'*Señor?*'

'Never mind. What news of the outside world? Where is the Emperor?'

'Gone back to Mexico City.'

'And Juárez and Díaz, where are they?'

The boy shrugged. 'Some say one place, some say another . . .'

'In other words, nothing has changed.' He paused and looked down at the boy who gazed up at him with a look of adoration that Stella found touching. 'And have you done the other things I asked?'

'*Si, Señor*, Ramón and me, we hire boat like you say. We tell captain you come in two, maybe three, days and take boat to Vera Cruz.'

'And?'

'We buy flour and coffee and sugar and chickens, all you say, then we wait. We wait, and you no come.' It was almost an accusation.

'We were slower than expected,' Leo said, 'but we're here now, and the sooner we set sail, the better.' He put his hand lightly on the boy's shoulder. 'But first, my friend, we need to lock up our prisoners safely, so show us the way to the town gaol. Then we will go to Señor Da Silva and see if he has a bed, a bath and a meal for Señor and Señora Wainright.'

Stella laughed. 'Not necessarily in that order.'

They went first to the town prison, where the gaoler was obliged to turn out two drunks and a prostitute to make room in the cells for the four prisoners Leo handed over, and though he protested, money, threats and Leo's uniform prevailed.

Once the prisoners were safely installed, Leo relaxed a little, and they all went to the house on the waterfront where they had stayed before. Jimmy and Stella were conducted to a room where there was a large fourposter bed with grubby hangings which, so Jimmy told her, was the Da Silvas' own room. 'They think we are newly married and must have the best,' he said, laughing.

Stella smiled wanly without speaking. She could not remember what it had been like in the early days of their marriage, but she was quite sure it was better than being mauled by a drunken, clumsy man whose impatience made him brutal and insensitive. The most charitable thing she could think of was that it was because he loved her and had not seen her for so long, and that he would soon return to being the man she had married.

She moved round the room, which was a larger version of the one she had occupied before, with the same kind of old, unstable furniture, a similar wash-stand and jug and cracked mirror. What she saw in that both amused and horrified her. She was filthy, her clothes hung in grubby creases, her stockings were torn. Several of the tiny buttons were missing from her blouse, so that she was hardly decently covered. Her hair had escaped its pins and hung about her cheeks in wet wisps. She was giggling aloud when Leo knocked on the door. She went to open it, and he handed her her basket.

'You'll need this,' he said, without looking into her eyes. It was always like that these days: they could not look at each other because of the pain it caused.

He was gone again before she could thank him, and when she turned back into the room, Jimmy was grinning at her in a way which made her want to slap his face. She controlled herself with an effort, and spoke cheerfully. 'I knew I must be dishevelled, but I didn't realise what a dreadful state I was in until I looked in that mirror. I look worse than a street beggar!'

He took her hands and leaned back to survey her at arm's length. 'You look wonderful.'

'Oh, don't be ridiculous! Compliments when they are deserved are one thing, downright untruths another. I'd thank you to be honest with me.'

'I am honest.' He reached out, and opened the edges of her blouse where the buttons were missing. 'Even if you do look like a woman of the streets, you're still my wife.' He pulled her to him and crushed her lips with his, making her heart sink and her body tense for the onslaught she knew was coming. She was beginning to run out of excuses to hold him off and before long he would realise the reason, if he had not already done so. She was still puzzling over the remark he had made, the day they were reunited, about forgetting Leo because he had been paid off. She did not, would not, believe that, but why had Jimmy said it?

'Relax, my dear,' he said. 'You are with me now, your very own Jimmy.'

'*Perdón, Señor, Señora.*'

Taken by surprise, they sprang apart to allow their hostess to pass with a jug of hot water and a towel.

He laughed. 'You have been saved by the timely intervention of the *señora*, and you must be grateful! Now, turn yourself once more into the very respectable, very proper, Mrs Wainright, while I take a turn along the waterfront. I need a breath of fresh air.'

It was a tense evening, although the food was good and their host and hostess friendly and anxious to please. To Stella, the conversation seemed forced and unnatural, as though the two men had things on their minds they did not want to talk about. As usual, Jimmy was drinking too much, and the more of the local wine he swallowed, the more argumentative he became.

Leo, ignoring Jimmy, teased Pablo about his new clothes and told him exaggerated tales of what it was like to go to school in Europe and serve in the Austrian army, and Stella guessed that he had offered to adopt him. He talked of his work as an official artist, illustrating the events of history, and how that was being changed by the advent of the camera. After the meal, he sat down with paper and charcoal and began a sketch of the boy.

'I began some drawings of the ruins,' Jimmy said sullenly. 'If you hadn't been so quick to destroy priceless national treasures, I would have finished them and had some recognition for their discovery, and I needed that. Now no one will believe me, because, by all accounts, there is nothing left but a heap of rubble.'

'It had to be done,' Leo said, without looking up from his sketch. 'I couldn't risk the guns being used. As it is, I'm not sure there aren't more such places. I would have liked to get at the truth from Carson, but there, it's no good crying over spilt milk; the fellow is gone, though I find myself wondering where.'

'Back to Washington,' Stella said.

'Is that what he told you?'

'Not exactly, but when we were in Cordoba, he hinted he might be recalled.'

'I wish I could feel confident about that,' he said. 'It's much more likely that he is still in Mexico, still pursuing his original intention—the destruction of the Empire. I'll wager we haven't seen the last of him.'

'I don't understand him at all,' Stella said. 'What is he? Is he a man dedicated to a cause, or someone using the unrest in Mexico for his own ends? An idealist or a mercenary? One day I think one thing, the next another.'

'Whatever he is, he persuaded you into having some sympathy for what he was doing,' Jimmy said. 'You are half a Liberal yourself, even though you won't admit it.'

'I am no such thing!' she protested quickly. 'You should know better than to suggest it.'

'You let Carson out of prison. That was not the act of a loyal Conservative!'

Stella was aware that Leo was staring at Jimmy with an expression she could only describe as threatening, and yet she could see no reason why he should react in that way: Jimmy was only repeating what many people believed to be true. 'I am not a Conservative, either,' she said firmly. 'And I did not free him; he escaped.'

'I think this conversation has gone on long enough,' Leo said quietly. 'If we are to make an early start tomorrow, I, for one, intend to retire early and I suggest you do the same.' He stood up and thanked their hostess for a delicious meal, then turned to Pablo. 'Come, my son, it's time for bed.' He inclined his head towards Stella, bade her goodnight and left her once more alone with her husband.

Jimmy stood up and reached for his coat, which hung untidily over the back of a chair. 'I'm going to take a turn outside. No need to wait up for me.'

She had her suspicions of where he was going and

why, but it no longer mattered that he was seeking a more willing love; she was simply grateful to be left alone. Would it always be like that? Would they ever be able to rebuild their marriage? Would it become better or worse? She refused to answer herself.

It was dawn when he returned, and she was already up and preparing to leave. They ate breakfast in silence and then went down to the harbour to board the *Santa María*. It was an extremely old and decrepit small steamer, and she found herself wondering how they would all crowd on to it and if it were seaworthy. But Leo had inspected it, and he would not commit them to a voyage, however short, in a vessel that leaked.

He had gone to the gaol to fetch the remaining prisoners, but Pablo was on hand to show her to her quarters, a tiny cabin that he assured her was the Captain's cabin, requisitioned for her use. The prisoners would be kept in the hold, and Jimmy and Leo would probably sleep on deck with the crew.

'Better on deck,' Pablo assured them. 'It no rain.'

She laughed. 'I hope you are right. When do we start?'

'When Señor Leo come back.'

Her luggage had already arrived, and she had hardly settled her belongings in the tiny cabin before Leo returned and all was bustle as they prepared to set sail. She decided she would be in the way if she went on deck, so she stayed where she was, looking out of the small porthole at the palm-fringed beach where some fishermen worked on their boats, women sat mending nets and children ran about shrieking in play. It was a peaceful scene: these people, while hearing news of the troubles in the rest of Mexico, seemed not to be affected by them. But that was a false picture, she knew, because of what Carson had been doing, making them discontented and urging them to take up arms against oppressors they hardly knew.

One of the boats was being pushed out into the sea by half a dozen men, who scrambled aboard as soon as it was afloat. She watched idly as they began to row towards the *Santa María*, but then something caught her attention and she moved closer to the porthole and peered out with narrowed eyes. The men in the boat were armed with rifles, and one of them was Miguel!

She ran out of the cabin and scrambled up the companionway to the deck, stumbling over the sleeping form of her husband, who was leaning against the wheelhouse with his legs stretched out in front of him. He stirred, but did not get up.

'Jimmy, Carson's men are coming! Where is Captain Manfred?' She did not wait for his reply, but ran along the deck looking for Leo.

He was standing facing the jetty, supervising the casting off of the mooring-rope and did not immediately turn round, but she pulled on his arm and made him face the seaward side. 'Look!'

He saw the boat at the same time as Miguel fired, hitting the wooden superstructure just above Stella's head. Leo pushed her to the deck, grabbed a rifle from one of his men and levelled it at the boat.

'Turn round and go back!' he yelled. 'Go back, or I'll fire!'

'Not without our comrades.' Miguel's voice carried clearly over the water. 'We want the prisoners, and we want that snake Wainright and his wife. Hand them over, and you may proceed.'

'What did he say?' Stella asked, lifting her head. 'Did I hear him say Wainright?'

'Get down!' Leo, concerned for her safety, spoke more sharply than he intended; he softened his voice to add, 'Go back to your cabin, Stella, and stay until I tell you to come out.'

More shots were fired, both from the rowing-boat and the steamer, but this time they were well aimed and one of the rowers collapsed over his oar. Miguel, incensed, directed a hail of bullets at the steamer which, without its mooring-rope, had drifted out into the bay. Stella moved on hands and knees towards an injured man, not only to help him, if she could, but to take over his rifle.

Leo saw her, and shouted angrily, 'Stella! I said go below!' He turned and yelled over his shoulder to Pablo, and the boy appeared immediately. 'Take Mrs Wainright back to her cabin, and keep her there.'

'Si, Señor.'

'But I can fire a rifle,' Stella said.

'And who would you be shooting at?' he asked with a smile. 'Go on, Pablo, take her away and keep her safe. I've enough on my hands, as it is.'

As if to demonstrate this, a shot whined so close to his head and into the side of the wheelhouse behind him that it was a miracle he was unhurt.

Pablo took Stella's arm and pushed her in front of him down to the little cabin. 'You stay here,' he said, stationing himself in front of the door to bar her exit. 'You do what Señor Leo say!'

She could hear firing and shouting and running feet above her head, but it was impossible to tell what was going on, and she fidgeted impatiently, pacing the half-dozen steps it took from door to porthole and back, while the boy looked on impassively. From the porthole she could see nothing of the fight, which had moved round to the other side of the boat, there was only a calm ocean and a beach, although the townsfolk were now standing in a line at the water's edge, watching the fray with a great deal of interest. She turned away to try to persuade Pablo to let her pass, but he had his orders and was immovable.

Suddenly she saw his eyes widen and his mouth drop open as he caught sight of something behind her. She whipped round. There was a rope dangling over the porthole, and as they watched, almost mesmerised, hands appeared climbing it and then a head and shoulders. She still held the rifle and, without thinking, lifted it and fired. The man fell; they heard his body splash as it hit the water.

'Go and tell Leo!' she gasped, pushing him towards

the door. 'They're climbing up behind them.'

He disappeared, and she sank on to the bunk, horrified by what she had done. The noise above her head increased as the defenders raced to face the new threat. There were yells and screams, crashing and banging, rifle-fire, as some of the attackers succeeded in boarding the boat. In a lull in the noise she heard Carson's voice quite clearly. 'So, my friend, we meet again, but under very different circumstances. I'll thank you to hand over your prisoners and Mr and Mrs Wainright.' She did not hear Leo's reply, and the American went on, 'I haven't time to stand here all day! Fetch the little lady, and dig her husband out of whatever rat-hole he's hiding in.'

'No.' Leo's voice was steady.

Stella picked up the rifle, which she had thrown on the bunk, and then crept to the door and up the companionway, step by step, slowly and silently, until her head and shoulders emerged into the strong light of day.

Leo, who had his back to her, was standing between her and the American and she had no clear target; not that she wanted to kill the man, her intention was to regain the initiative for Leo, nothing more. Carefully she moved up another two steps, and saw Jimmy creeping round the wheelhouse to come out behind Carson.

Leo, too, must have seen him, because both men seemed to move together at the same instant as Miguel shouted a warning to Carson from somewhere to her left. Then she was thrust to one side as the prisoners freed themselves from the hold and clambered up the companionway behind her. She fell on the lower deck, partially stunned, while pandemonium broke out above her head. It was a minute or two before she realised that the vessel was listing alarmingly.

She started to her feet as Pablo's head appeared at the head of the steps. 'What's happening?' she asked. 'Are we sinking?'

'Señor Leo say wait here, he come soon,' he said, then added, 'He say you very brave girl.'

'No, Pablo I'm not brave, I reacted without thinking. I killed that man, didn't I?'

'Si, Señora.' He was grinning broadly. 'You not miss that close.'

'No, I suppose not.' She shuddered. 'I saw his face, Pablo. I saw his face and fired right at it. I'll never forget it, not if I live to be a hundred.'

'He want to kill Señor Leo,' he said. 'He bad man.'

'Who are we to judge good and bad?' she said wearily. 'We have no right to decide that.'

He looked puzzled, but said nothing, and then his head disappeared and Leo jumped down beside her. 'Are you hurt?'

'No, just shaken.'

'Good. Come on, then.' He took her hand and pulled her after him up to the deck.

'Where are we going?'

'On shore, before this old tub sinks beneath us!' He turned to the boy. 'Pablo, bring Señor Wainright to the starboard rail.'

'Si, Señor.'

Pablo scuttled away and Leo ran back up on deck, pulling Stella behind him. He seemed to have a sixth sense that detected danger before there was any evidence of it. Twice he pushed her to the floor as bullets whistled overhead and once he almost threw her behind the wheelhouse when a knife flew through the air and splintered the woodwork. He ran to the gate in the rail and opened it.

'You'll have to jump, Stella, but it's not as far as it looks. Can you swim?'

'Of course.'

'Go on, then.'

'Where is Jimmy?'

'Behind you, Stella.' Jimmy's voice was right against her ear.

She hesitated only a split second before she stepped out over the water. Even before she surfaced, Leo was beside her, putting his hands under her arms to help her to the shore.

He did not let her go until her feet touched the ground, and she struggled up the beach with her clothes clinging to her figure and weighing her down. One of the women who had been working on the fishing-nets ran to throw a cloak about her; it reminded her of the day, not so long before, when she and Leo had bathed in the sea together. That was before she had found Jimmy, before Leo had explained about Trieste, before she had admitted she loved him still, before her heart had been broken for a second time. Now everything was different, and she did not know how she was going to bear it. Leo left her abruptly to go in search of Ramón, almost as if he could read her thoughts.

She stood beside Jimmy, clutching the cloak about her, and watched the *Santa María* go down. The water was too shallow to submerge it completely but it looked a sorry sight, tip-tilted and wedged on the sandy bottom of the bay, making it a hazard for the fishing-boats that would soon be returning with their morning's catch.

'Are there many casualties?' she asked, turning to watch the men straggling up the beach. Wet and bedraggled as they were, it was difficult to tell victor from vanquished.

'I don't know. Leo got one with his first shot, and I bagged another and you another. I would never have dreamed you were capable of it!'

'It was a subconscious reaction, I wouldn't have done it if I could have stopped to think.'

'At least two of the prisoners escaped, and so did Carson, blast him, but at least he left without dragging us with him.'

'Jimmy,' she ventured, 'why did he want you so especially?'

'No idea.' His laughter sounded forced. 'But perhaps it was you he really wanted.'

'That's silly!'

'No, it isn't.' He turned from watching the beach to

smile down at her. 'Oh, Stella, don't be such a simple-ton! That's what this war between Carson and Leo is all about, haven't you realised? It has nothing to do with Liberals and Conservatives; it's a personal thing. Both men are set on making you a widow.'

'I don't believe it! Are you sure you don't know more about Carson's activities than you have admitted?'

'Not you, too,' he said angrily. 'If my own wife will not believe me, how can I convince other people I am an innocent bystander? I am less involved than you are.'

Before she could question him further, Leo returned to them, his face set in a cold white mask of fury, but behind it, his blue eyes were shot with misery. 'Ramón is dead,' he said flatly.

'Dead?' she repeated. 'Oh, Leo, I am so sorry.'

'If only you hadn't allowed that snake to escape . . .' He stopped when he saw the stricken look on her face. 'I'm sorry, Stella, I'm not blaming you, but Ramón was a good soldier and the best friend a man could have. And he had to die defending that no-good husband of yours. If I ever come face to face with that American again . . .' He stopped speaking suddenly and turned to scan the beach and the sea, and then the road behind them. 'Where is Pablo?'

'I don't know,' she said. 'He jumped with us, didn't he?'

'Yes, he went before me.' He paused to look back at the wreck. 'He can't have drowned. He can't! He can swim like a fish.'

She turned to look up and down the beach and out to sea, as Leo dashed up and down, asking after the boy, but no one had noticed him on the beach.

'I refuse to believe he drowned,' Leo said, returning to them when it was obvious that the boy was nowhere on the beach. 'If the little devil is hiding . . .'

'You don't think he could have been taken prisoner?'

'There's no way of knowing,' he said. 'The *Juáristas* were on the other side when we jumped.'

He moved away, then paused and turned back. 'You

and James had better go back to the Da Silvas and wait there until I decide what is to be done.'

'Where are you going?'

'To look for Pablo, and see what I can salvage from this sorry mess.'

She turned away from him with tears running down her cheeks, not so much because he was angry, that was understandable, but because he was probably right. How gullible she had been to think that Carson would be grateful for his freedom and leave the country! And the worst thing of all was Pablo's disappearance—Pablo, who had wormed his way into both their hearts, Pablo, the common denominator of their lives. A picture of the boy standing on the road waiting for them in all his new finery, smiling and showing big white teeth, came to her with such clarity that she cried out and her shoulders were racked by sobs. The war was becoming very real, very close, and death never very far away. Who would be next, she wondered, who would be next to be sacrificed to man's unhumanity to man, to greed and the struggle for power?

'Come. We had better do as he says,' Jimmy said, taking her arm to lead her away. Behind them, work had already begun on towing the *Santa María* up on the beach and retrieving as much of the baggage and stores as possible.

The boat had been holed by the prisoners themselves in an effort to help their liberators. While Miguel rowed round the vessel to the seaward side, a second force led by Carson had clambered aboard from the other; it was one of these Stella had seen at the cabin window, and her shot had alerted the defenders to the danger. Leo spent all the daylight hours on the beach supervising the repairs, recruiting labour from the local people and making them work long and arduous hours, joining in and labouring with them as though a frenzy of activity would lift his burden.

Jimmy had given up his nightly excursions into the

town and never left the house, not even to help Leo, who returned each night when darkness fell and joined them for the evening meal. It was usually a silent affair, punctuated only by terse comments about the progress of the repairs and the state of the weather, no more. Afterwards he sat in a corner of the room that had been given over to them as a sitting-room, and continued the portrait of Pablo he had begun the night before the raid, using oils to transfer it to canvas. He worked with the utmost concentration, swiftly and deftly, like a man possessed by a devil who could be expelled only through paint. It was the same every night until the picture was finished, and then he withdrew even more into himself. Stella knew he was grieving for the little Mexican.

On Christmas morning they went to church, and afterwards Señora Da Silva cooked them a special meal, but no one felt like being festive. Leo spent some time with the boat, but he could get no one else to work with him and returned to the house to sit and drink tequila in an effort to drown his anxious thoughts.

Stella, hiding behind a book, watched him become more and more drunk and longed to tell him to stop, but she knew that would not be wise and instead went to fetch the drawing of the ruins, which, in spite of all her adventures, had remained in her luggage.

'Leo, Jimmy wanted a drawing of the ruins. Would you finish this one for him, please?' She held it out. 'Let him have something to take back to show for all his work.'

'I'm in no mood for drawing.'

'I'd appreciate it if you would,' Jimmy said placatingly. 'You do that, and I'll begin on the report you want.' He stood up and went over to a table in front of the window, where he sat down and drew a piece of paper towards him. 'In writing, you said?'

Leo took the sketch from her and went to the corner where he habitually sat to paint, and taking out a selection of coloured crayons, began to work, his half-empty glass of tequila forgotten. Stella smiled, and went back to her book.

There was silence for hours, except for the scratching of Jimmy's quill, the turning of the pages of Stella's book and the squeaking of the crayon. At dusk Señora Da Silva came in with the lamps, and when she had gone, Leo flung his work on the table.

Stella put down her book and went over to it, trying not to appear too eager. It was a picture of the ruins, very detailed and very accurate, but the stone serpent that slid down the staircase had Carson's head, and a carrion crow perched on a treetop in a corner held something in its talons which dripped blood. Hidden in the foliage of the trees, seen only when the picture was held sideways or upside-down, were rifles; they were dotted everywhere. In one of the bottom corners sat Pablo, cross-legged and smiling up at a girl who stood on the bottom step of the stone staircase with her hand on the head of the serpent and the other holding a rifle. At her feet lay a fallen star. The girl was easily recognisable as Stella. It was a work of great quality, there was no doubt of that, but it was also the work of a troubled mind. It looked as though Leo saw her as the ally of the serpent, and Pablo—innocent, trusting Pablo—as her victim.

She stared at it for a long time, trying to gather herself to speak calmly. 'It may be very good,' she said at last, 'but it's not exactly what I had in mind.'

Her voice brought Jimmy to stand beside her. He looked at it for some time, then he laughed aloud. 'Oh, it's good, my dear Manfred, very good, but why have you found no place for me?'

Leo pointed to a tiny monkey. 'That's you.'

'Why have you done this?' Stella asked.

He shrugged. 'The devil in me, I suppose.'

'It ought to be destroyed.'

'Do as you please. It belongs to you.'

'I think I'll keep it,' Jimmy said. 'One day I might want to prove that you are out of your mind.'

The next day Leo went back to work on the boat. But it was as if the act of drawing had driven out the devil and softened the harshness in him. Two weeks later, he arrived back at the house to say that the repairs were finished and the *Santa María* was once again moored to the jetty. They could leave on the next tide.

They arrived back in Mexico City at the end of January, to find the situation there very little changed from what it had been three months before except that Maximilian's Empire had contracted still further and he no longer lived at Chapultepec Castle but at the Hacienda de la Teja, just outside the city.

There were few Europeans in the Emperor's entourage now, and he seemed more than ever dominated by the sinister Father Fischer and General Marquez, both of whom were present when, after two days of waiting at the Iturbide Hotel, they were summoned to the Hacienda. Josefina was nowhere to be seen; Stella guessed she had realised that it would be dangerous to stay at court, and had left.

Once she had been presented, Stella retreated to sit by the window and listen to the men talking. It was soon made plain that, beneath the show of normality, the situation was desperate, and that nearly all the European troops would be leaving when the French left.

'I intend to honour my oath of allegiance to your Majesty,' Leo said quietly, looking across at Stella, as though willing her to understand.

'We did not doubt you would, Leo, my friend,' Maximilian said. 'Now we want to hear about your adventures.'

Leo gave a very succinct account of their journey through Yucatan, Carson's involvement with the Liberals, and the blowing-up of the ammunition store.

'That proves nothing,' the priest interrupted. 'Just because one Yankee mercenary has joined the *Juáristas*, it does not mean that he has his government behind him. Juárez is financed and armed from raiding our coffers and our stores, from theft and extortion; when the French go, the people will no longer be afraid and they will rally to the Emperor.'

'And how will you arm them, these people who are going to flock to the banner?' Leo asked. 'The French are too worried about an attack on their rear to leave anything behind for us to use. We have been hearing explosions all over the city ever since we returned.'

'Leo,' the Emperor said, 'we do not wish to hear defeatist talk. Now leave us and return to your post.'

Leo, dismissed, dared not argue. He bowed to the Emperor and, studiously ignoring the other men, went over to Stella and took her hand. Bending low to kiss it, he whispered, 'Goodbye, my darling, darling star. God keep you safe.' His eyes searched her face as though trying to burn it into his memory, then he turned abruptly on his heel.

Stella did not hear the remainder of the conversation between her husband and Maximilian, or Jimmy's very full account of how, in his own words, he had been duped into helping the Liberals. She heard nothing and saw nothing, because her whole body was crying out to follow Leo, to be with him wherever he went, to share his life and, if need be, his death. She remained in her seat, turned to stone, except that stone eyes do not produce real tears.

CHAPTER TWELVE

STELLA STOOD with her husband on the morning of the 5th of February, crammed together with thousands of others, to watch the departure of the *pantalons rouges*. The troops formed up in front of the National Palace and the cathedral, waiting for the arrival of Marshal Bazaine to lead them away. He came out from his headquarters and, while the troops saluted, the Mexican onlookers slowly removed their sombreros. There was complete silence as the Marshal turned and saluted the crowd, then mounted his horse, which was saddled and waiting in front of the first contingent of Spahis. At his signal, the drums began to roll, French trumpets sounded for the last time in the city, and the march began.

Apart from the music of the military band and the sound of marching feet, there was silence as the column passed James and Stella and continued down the Calle de San Francisco, past the Iturbide, whose balconies were crowded with hotel guests, out through San Antonio Gate and past the French military cemetery, where the men removed their headgear and dipped colours in salute, then on into the countryside.

When they had gone, Stella glanced up at the roof of the National Palace, where a lonely figure in a long grey cloak stood looking down on the square. There had been no official leave-taking, no special ceremony, but Maximilian was watching the last of the French leave his Empire. As he turned to go, another figure moved forward to take his arm and guide him away, a man in the uniform of an Austrian Hussar, a man with a mane of dark curls. Stella felt her heart lurch, realising that that brief glimpse of him might be the last she would ever have; she would carry it in her heart for ever.

The next day their boxes, trunks and baggage were

loaded on the coach provided by Maximilian, and they set off at a leisurely pace, knowing that it would not be long before they caught up with the rear of the French army.

It was only six months since Stella had first come to Mexico but it seemed like a lifetime, a lifetime in which she had known hope and despair, had endured hardship and hate, shot and killed one man, had helped to condemn others to prison and possible execution, found a husband she could not love, and loved a man who was not her husband. In that time she had learned a great deal about herself, her strengths and weaknesses. And her greatest weakness was that she needed Leo so desperately that she did not know how she was going to go on living without him, how she was going to face her husband at breakfast every morning for the rest of her life and know that another day was beginning, another long, empty, loveless day, loveless in more ways than one, because Jimmy did not love her and had never really loved her, she knew that now.

She began to laugh, silently at first, but then aloud, hollow, bitter, hysterical laughter, until Jimmy leaned across and took her hand, slapping the back of it to bring her to her senses. 'Stella, stop it. Stop that at once!' He took her shoulders in his hands and shook her. 'Stella, are you laughing or crying?'

'I don't know,' she sobbed. 'I don't know. You tell me, am I laughing or crying?'

He changed seats to sit beside her and put his arm about her shoulders. 'Stella, hush! Don't think I don't know what's going on in that head of yours, because I do. You'll get over it.'

Startled, she looked up into his face, but she could not fathom his expression; it was as if he were a long way off, in a different place, a different time.

'You have got to face life as it is and not dwell on what you would have liked it to be,' he went on. 'You are my wife, for better for worse, for richer for poorer, and just now things could hardly be worse and we are as poor as church mice. Let's be thankful that we are being allowed to leave this godforsaken place.'

Her sobs subsided a little. 'I suppose you are right.'

'Cheer up! I don't want to spend the rest of my life looking at a wife with a long face.'

She smiled wanly, ashamed of betraying herself, and mopped up the tears with the handkerchief he had handed her. She had given way to her misery for the first and last time; from now on she was determined to be calm and practical.

'You are not the only one to have to make adjustments,' he said suddenly. 'I have my heartbreaks, too.'

'You?'

'Why not? Did you suppose you were the only one capable of falling in love? It happens all the time for all sorts of reasons.'

'Who is she?'

'That's my secret. There's nothing to be gained by telling you her name.'

'Is she Mexican?'

'Yes, and very devout.' He moved back to the opposite seat, leaned against the squabs and shut his eyes, effectively shutting her out. 'The subject is closed, Stella, and we shall never speak of it again.'

The coach swayed on its way, and slowly she began to feel calmer. She dozed a little, and when she woke it was dark. Peering out of the window, she wondered where they were and how soon it would be before they stopped for the night. In the distance she could see camp-fires, and guessed they would soon join the coaches, wagons and carts that made up the rear of the marching French army.

'That's funny,' Jimmy said. 'I would have expected them to have got a little further than this.'

He had hardly uttered the words when they heard rifle-fire very near at hand, and then the coach gave a sudden lurch as the driver brought the horses to a halt.

'Get down!' Jimmy yelled. 'On the floor.'

It was only then that she realised that the firing was being directed at them. A bullet hit the coach, splintering the woodwork, and then she heard Jimmy cry out. He was clutching at a wound in his shoulder. The blood spread through his fingers and dripped on her skirts as she went to help him.

'Jimmy!' she shrieked, as the vehicle was surrounded by horsemen and the door was wrenched open behind her. She turned to find herself looking into the dark eyes of Redford Carson.

'*Juáristas!*' Jimmy gasped. 'I'm done for.'

Carson reached in to help Stella out, but she shrank from him. 'Don't you touch me! Don't you dare!'

He called for the lantern from the front of the coach, and leaned across to look at Jimmy, who sat slumped in the corner, deathly white and breathing irregularly. 'He's wounded,' he said to someone behind him.

'Not seriously, I hope.' It was Miguel's voice. 'We don't want him to die just yet, do we?'

'Tell the driver to go on,' Stella demanded angrily. 'The French are over there, and they will have a surgeon with them.'

'Those aren't the French,' Carson said. 'They passed through yesterday. Those lights are the camp-fires of the Liberal army.'

He held out his hand to help her down, but she ignored it. 'I hate you!' she said, and watched him wince at her words. 'I hate you, and everything you stand for.'

He smiled thinly. 'Hate is akin to love in many ways; it arouses the same strong passions.' He called to one of his men to lead his horse, climbed in beside Stella and ordered the driver to move on.

They lurched forward, swaying from side to side, while the stain on Jimmy's coat grew larger and his face paler. She tore at her petticoat to make a pad to staunch the bleeding.

'I shall do my best to persuade Díaz to let you go,' Carson said. 'He is not a monster. He might allow you to leave, just as he allowed the whole French army to pass unmolested—twenty-three thousand men, and not a single casualty.'

'Except Jimmy,' she said dully.

'Except your husband,' he agreed. 'But don't be deceived by all that blood; he is very far from dying of his wounds. He will live to stand trial.'

'Trial? What has he done?'

'He betrayed his trust. He told the Emperor all he knew to save his own rotten hide.'

She could not believe that he was serious, but he was far from smiling. 'That's outrageous! He's an English citizen; they have no power to try him.'

He smiled. 'You don't think so? Jimmy believes it. Don't you, my friend? You knew what you were risking.'

Jimmy did not answer, but his eyes betrayed him.

They were stopped by a guard on the perimeter of the Liberal camp. Carson looked out and spoke briefly to the soldier on duty, and they were allowed to pass. A few minutes later they stopped again and he left her, returning almost immediately with two men carrying a litter. Numbly she allowed him to help her down, so that the men could put James on the stretcher and carry him away. Before she could collect herself to follow, she became aware of a woman coming out of the shadows and running to the stretcher to take Jimmy's hand, and walk beside it. She stared, unable to believe her eyes because the woman was Josefina Gonzales.

The Liberal camp was centred on a small village and they were taken to the villa of the local *alcalde*, where Jimmy was carried to a room that had become the field hospital to have his wound dressed. Carson conducted Stella upstairs to a large bedroom that looked out on a pleasant courtyard.

The shock of finding Josefina in the Liberal camp and discovering that she and Jimmy were lovers was soon submerged by the greater worry over what their captors meant to do with them. But when she thought of the harm the lovely Mexican had done with her spying, her blood boiled. Josefina had been a witness to all the comings and goings at Maximilian's court, had often sat near him during meetings and discussions, where no one questioned her presence. To everyone, she was simply the Emperor's plaything, a silent and beautiful ornament. Silent she may have been, but she had seen and heard a great deal. And she had been the one to recruit Jimmy to the Liberal cause.

The implications of that slowly seeped into Stella's numbed brain. It meant that Jimmy, far from being duped, was a willing accomplice in Carson's activities in Yucatan and elsewhere, and her arrival in Mexico had certainly upset their plans. Even then, all might have been well for him had Carson not stolen Stella's portrait and Leo caught up with Jimmy at Villa-Hermosa. In a cleft stick, her husband had agreed to Leo's terms and revealed all he knew. It was for this that he was to be put on trial.

'You can make yourself comfortable here for the time being,' said Carson. 'I'll have some of your things sent up.'

'Time being?' she asked. 'Colonel, tell me what is going to happen to us?'

'You will both be put on trial, but I shall do what I can to have you released.' He paused. 'But that does not include your husband. As soon as he is fit enough, he will stand trial and I can do nothing to influence the outcome of that, even if I wanted to.'

'You don't have to give evidence against him.'

'My evidence is not crucial. Miguel's alone will condemn him.'

'Condemn him . . .?' She could not voice the terrible thought that had occurred to her.

'My dear Stella, Jimmy will die. Make up your mind to that.'

'But why? The Liberals are winning this dreadful war, so what can they, what can you, hope to gain by murdering him?'

He smiled slowly and reached to take her hand. 'You,

my dear, you! But my friends don't call it murder, they call it justice.'

She pulled her hand from his. 'Never! Never in a thousand years!'

'You are distraught,' he said calmly. 'Little wonder. You need rest. We'll talk again later.' He began to walk to the door.

'When is this—this trial to take place?'

'The court will be convened as soon as Wainright's wound permits. Possibly tomorrow.'

'As soon as that?'

'We have a war to win, and it cannot wait on protocol. In the meantime, you will stay in this room.'

'Jimmy must have a good defence. If you need money . . .'

'He will be allocated a defending lawyer. Now have some rest; I'll be back tomorrow.' He left her, and she heard the key turn in the lock.

As soon as he had gone, she went to the window, but the courtyard was a long way down, and it was enclosed on all sides by buildings. They were taking no risks. Did they suppose she would try to escape, try to spirit Jimmy away? Even if she could think of some way of doing it, he was too weak from loss of blood to be able to go far. She returned to the bed, where she lay awake the whole night. When Carson unlocked the door next morning, her face was grey and her eyes red-rimmed with exhaustion and worry, but she had washed and tidied herself as best she could and faced him squarely.

'Come, my dear, they are waiting for you.'

She followed him downstairs without speaking, and into one of the larger rooms of the house. The *alcalde* sat at a table, flanked by two uniformed Liberal officers.

She paused a moment, then walked firmly forward and halted in front of them, holding her back straight and her head up, facing them with eyes that did not betray her fear.

'Señora Wainright,' the *alcalde* began, and then looked down to read from a paper in Spanish. She could not understand the charges, but it did not seem to matter, and she knew it would do no good to protest. The man's voice droned on and then her three judges conferred for a few minutes, and she suddenly found herself being waved away. As a trial, it was a travesty. She turned to Carson, who escorted her from the room, smiling encouragingly.

'What did they say?' she asked. 'Surely I should have been offered an interpreter?' She managed a hollow laugh. 'But I don't suppose it would have made any difference.'

'No, but don't worry. They have sentenced you to be banished from Mexico.'

She let out a peal of hysterical laughter; it went on and on and she could not stop. As a punishment, it was as ludicrous as the trial.

He took her shoulders and shook her, gently at first and then with more force until her head rocked. 'Stella, stop it! Stop it, do you hear? It's all over, and you can leave.'

She was suddenly serious. 'And Jimmy? Am I supposed gaily to wave goodbye and leave him behind?'

'Why not? You have no love for him, I know that, and so does he.'

'Well, I won't go.'

'Then stay. Stay until we can leave together. I want you and need you, I told you that before. We could have a good life together, you and I. We could go to Washington; you'd like it there.'

She looked at him in stony silence, unable to express her abhorrence of the idea, and he grinned suddenly. 'Perhaps it isn't the best time to mention it.'

'It certainly is not!' She walked ahead of him up the stairs to her room. When he made to follow her in, she closed the door in his face. She heard the door being locked again, and him calling to a guard to stay outside it.

The long day dragged on. People arrived and shouted commands, and once she heard a woman's scream. It sounded like Josefina. Her midday meal was brought to her by a Mexican woman who did not speak English or French and who was obviously terrified of the guard; she learned nothing from her. At dusk, Carson unlocked the door and threw it open wide.

'Come, Stella,' he said gently. 'Your husband wishes to see you.'

'It's over?'

'Yes.' His voice was low.

'Sentenced to death?' She sounded calm, but inside she was screaming.

'Yes.'

'When?'

'Tomorrow at dawn. They were going to hang him, but I persuaded them that he should die by the firing-squad. It's quicker, and more dignified. It was his last request to me.' He paused. 'You don't have to see him if you don't want to.'

'Of course I'll see him!'

He took her arm to steady her as they went downstairs, along a corridor and down more steps to a cellar. Here he unlocked a door and stood aside for her to enter, retreating and relocking the door as soon as she had done so.

Jimmy, whose shoulder was heavily bandaged, was sitting on a rough wooden bench with his hands cupped round a steaming cup of coffee, staring at the floor between his feet. He was pale, but surprisingly composed. She sat down beside him, and for several minutes neither spoke.

'Thank you for coming,' he said at last. 'You know the verdict.'

'Yes.' It was barely a whisper.

'I have to tell you something—something for which I need your forgiveness.'

'For what? For falling in love with someone else? I am guilty of that, too. In fact, I think I knew I still loved Leo when I married you. I did you a grave wrong.'

'It's worse than that.' She waited, saying nothing.

'I . . .' He stopped, then went on in a rush. 'I killed your father.'

She stared at him. What he was saying was just unbelievable; the day's events must have turned his mind. 'Jimmy, please don't say things like that. It can't be true!'

'It is.' His voice was stronger now, as though, having taken the first step, he had somehow found the courage to go on. 'He found out about . . . Josefina and me. We quarrelled. He threatened me.'

She remained silent, simply because she could not take in what he was saying.

'I didn't mean to kill him. He was working with a scalpel, dissecting a leaf. I took hold of his arm and shook him, then I tried to grab the knife.' He paused to take a deep breath. 'It slipped.' When she still did not reply, he went on, 'Josefina came into the room while I was standing over him. I was too shocked to move. It was she who suggested that we should pretend we'd found him like that. The trip to Yucatan had already been arranged, and I had to get away. Carson was blackmailing me to help the *Juáristas*.'

'How did he find out?'

'Josefina told him. She went to him for help.'

He put the coffee-cup down on the floor and turned to take her hand. 'Say something, Stella. Say something!'

'Why are you telling me this now?' she asked in anguish. 'Couldn't you have let me go on thinking it was an accident?'

'I need your forgiveness before I go to my Maker.'

He seemed resigned to his fate and uncaring about the effect his revelations were having on her. 'It would be more to the point if you repented,' she said.

'I do. Of course I do, and I shall see a priest, but I need to hear from you.'

She could not let him go to his death without giving him what he asked. 'I'll try,' she said in a flat voice.

His body sagged as if he had been drained of all strength. 'Go now,' he said.

'You don't want me to stay with you?'

'No.'

Now that he had what he wanted, she was being dismissed. She got up, and called to the turnkey to let her out. As the door was unlocked and she passed into the corridor, a distraught Josefina pushed past her and went into the cell. To Stella, that seemed fitting: the Mexican woman had more right to be with him, to comfort and sustain him, than she had; to have pretended otherwise would have been hypocritical.

She returned to her room, but there was no question of going to bed. She spent some time on her knees, praying, though what she prayed for she could not afterwards recall, her brain was so numb. Then she went to stand at the open window and look out on the moon-bathed, silent courtyard. How long she stood there she did not know, but when she began to shiver uncontrollably she went to the bed, lay down and covered herself with a blanket, to toss and turn for the remainder of the night.

It must have been some hours, though it seemed like minutes, later when the sound of marching feet and shouted orders roused her, and she realised that day had dawned. She forced herself to go to the window and watch as the firing-squad was lined up and Jimmy, wearing only trousers and a shirt, was brought out between two guards, with his hands tied behind his back. He paused to look back before obeying their instructions to stand against the wall, and Stella knew he was looking at Josefina. She was filled with pity for them both, in spite of what they had done. When the firing-squad raised their rifles and the order was given, she turned away, unable to watch. Josefina's shrill scream filled the empty air after the sound of the shots had died away, and Stella sank slowly on to the bed and covered her face with her hands.

'God have mercy on his soul,' she whispered.

*   *   *

Stella was forced to leave with the Liberal forces simply because, according to Carson, there was no other safe way to travel. But, too numb to think or feel, she remembered nothing of the march, nothing of the people who surrounded her, or where they stayed each night. When they arrived in the hills above the city of Queretaro, however, her awareness of her surroundings began to return and she began to live again. One of the first things she noticed was that they appeared to be going to stop there, and that a vast army was gathering and preparing itself for battle. They were given quarters in a small cottage tucked away in a fold of the hills, with the tents of the Liberals all around.

Carson, noticing the change in her, suggested a walk, saying that she needed fresh air and something to think about beside James. They went to a vantage-point on a rocky outcrop, and he stood beside her as she looked down. Many of the city's buildings were in ruins, its streets were dotted with craters, and even as she watched, there were more explosions and more walls crumbled. The Liberal forces had been ordered forward, and they spilled out of their hiding-places in the hills to attack through the cemetery. Down in the city, she could see soldiers running out from their quarters, putting on their jackets and snatching up weapons as they ran; horses being mounted, ammunition distributed, field-pieces hauled into position, and even from that distance she could hear orders being shouted.

'Maximilian and the whole of his pitiful little army are down there,' Carson said.

'Leo?' she whispered.

'Unless he has been a casualty. He certainly left Mexico City with the army, I saw him myself.'

'You did?' She could not conceal her eagerness for news.

'It was the day after the—the execution, when I had gone to reconnoitre. He was sitting his horse at the northern gate of the capital watching the Mexican army, a mere nine thousand men, marching out. He should

have been at the head of the column, but I reckon he is
out of favour, or someone is afraid of his influence with
the Emperor, because he was sent back to take his place
between the infantry and the artillery. Maximilian was
riding a piebald horse with a Mexican saddle, and wearing the uniform of a Mexican general without its epaul-
ettes. He was armed with a sabre and two revolvers. Three
generals rode beside him. Behind them marched a raggle-
taggle army carrying battered muskets, old Enfield
rifles, Austrian pistols, French sabres, rusty old Spanish
swords, hatchets and pikes, and flanked by women and
children and stray dogs. The artillery was lumbering
along at the rear, drawn by an assortment of horses,
ponies and mules.'

'You saw all that, and you let them go?'

'Yes. The Liberals choose the ground on which they
fight.'

'Queretaro?'

'Yes. It's about the only city in Mexico still loyal to the
monarchy. The people demonstrated their support by
garlanding the arches of the aqueduct with banners and
ribbons and ringing the church bells. They are mostly
Mexican-Indian, and they ran from their homes and
threw flowers in welcome. But their joy was short lived.
We blew up the aqueduct, and now they are without
water.'

'And Leo is with them? You don't think he has
become a casualty, do you?'

He smiled. 'Our intelligence tells us not. In fact, he
has been one of the main impediments to our advance.
Wherever the fighting is at its thickest, wherever the
danger is greatest, there he is. One would almost think he
did not want to live. But he seems to lead a charmed life.'
He watched her face for tell-tale signs of hope, a lifting
of her mouth, a widening of her eyes, and he was not
disappointed. 'But it won't last, you know. He'll tempt
fate just once too often!'

She wanted to turn away, but she could not because
she knew that, somewhere down there, Leo was in the

thick of it, fighting for the Emperor to whom he owed allegiance and to whom he gave unfailing loyalty even in this impossible position. And she could see it was impossible, even though the defenders were contesting every inch of the way. She pointed to a huge plume of black smoke spiralling skywards, carrying with it the stench of death. 'What are they doing there?'

'Burning bodies,' he said, heedless of whether he shocked her. 'There have been over a thousand casualties, and they have neither the time nor the men to bury them properly.'

Sickened, she turned away at last. 'Can't you negotiate a peace? Surely, if Maximilian agreed to leave Mexico, the carnage could stop?'

'It's much too late for that now. Maximilian should have recognised the futility of fighting on after the French left. When the Liberals take Queretaro, and take it they will, very soon now, Maximilian will be tried before a military court and condemned to death.'

'But surely they can't do that to an emperor?'

'As far as the *Juáristas* are concerned, he is not an emperor but an Austrian archduke who has had the temerity to intervene in their affairs. His followers will share his fate, and that goes for Captain Leo Manfred too.'

'They are still fighting.'

'But not for much longer. General Marquez has broken out of the town with a thousand horsemen to go to Mexico City for reinforcements.' He smiled sardonically as her eyes lit up with renewed hope. 'We let him leave, because his going has reduced Maximilian's force to less than seven thousand men, and we have forty thousand surrounding the town. Time is on our side, we have food and water and ammunition in plenty; we have only to sit up here and wait until they die of hunger and thirst, or surrender. Marquez will not return.'

'You enjoyed telling me that, didn't you?'

'On the contrary, Stella, my dear, I enjoy nothing so much as harmony, but you needed to be shown the true situation. You have to come to terms with it. I am a patient man, and time is on my side, too.'

'Colonel, let me go, please?'

'Where would you go? Down there?' he asked, guessing what was in her mind. 'No, my dear, that would be condemning you to certain death. Even if you managed to reach the city safely, the Emperor and all his followers are doomed. There is no escape.'

'Oh, why did you have to help the rebels?' she cried out in despair. 'If you hadn't armed the *Juáristas* with rifles and ammunition, this wouldn't be happening now and untold lives would not have been lost. Why did you have to become involved?'

'I serve my country,' he said. 'I have to obey orders, even when they go against my own inclinations. You know, there was a time I considered abandoning everything for you. I think, if Manfred had not turned up at the ruins when he did, I would have done.'

'I would never have agreed! And aren't you forgetting that Jimmy was alive then?'

'No, but once you knew the truth about your father's death, not even you would have stayed with him. It would have made no difference to me whether you were widowed or divorced.'

'Jimmy once said that you and Leo were both intent on making a widow of me.'

'Leo, ah, Leo,' he said sarcastically. 'We mustn't forget him, must we?' He turned to her suddenly. 'Come, let's go back. I want to show you something.'

He took her arm, but she pulled herself away. 'I want to leave. I want to go to my friends. You have no right to keep me here . . .'

'It is for your own safety.'

'I care nothing for safety, nothing for you. Don't you understand that?'

He grabbed her hand and, though she struggled, he held it fast and forced her to go back to the cottage with him. In the little front parlour he went to a cupboard and produced a piece of rolled-up paper. Spreading it out, he held it for her to see. It was the drawing of the ruins she had taken from her father's room, the one Leo had embellished. 'I found this in the coach with Jimmy's belongings,' he said. 'It's good, but more than that, it tells me a great deal—a very great deal—about Leo Manfred. It's plain that he was jealous of me then, I wonder if he still is?'

'Not for one minute. He has no cause to be.'

'No?' He smiled and rolled it up again, wrote something on the outside, called an orderly and handed it over, giving him an order in Spanish. 'We shall see. I'm going to send it to him, with my compliments.'

'Colonel, I beg you, let me go to him.'

'And do you think he would want you now?' He sat down opposite her, regarding her intently. She had become very thin in the last few weeks and her cheeks were pale, but her eyes had lost none of their fire and she was still very beautiful. 'If he learns you are up here with his enemies, he will brand you a traitor. He's almost ready to believe it now; you know that.' He continued to stare at her, tilting his head to one side and smiling a secret smile of triumph.

She sat facing him with an air of quiet courage. He would not intimidate her, he would not keep her against her will, he would not subdue her. She was made of sterner stuff than that!

CHAPTER THIRTEEN

LEO WATCHED the black, acrid smoke of the massive funeral pyre drifting up towards the Liberal lines and wondered what they would do next. 'The Imperial army mourns its dead,' he said aloud to no one in particular, wishing he still had Ramón to talk to. The loss of his Mexican lieutenant still grieved him, and the tears in his eyes were not wholly caused by the stinging smoke.

The tumultuous greeting Maximilian's small force had received on their arrival at Queretaro had not masked the fact that this would be their last stand. Not even Maximilian, ever the optimist, could disguise the seriousness of the situation; they had not been there long before it had been forcefully brought home to them. General Miramón, urging the Emperor to take the initiative before it was too late, had set off to try to scatter the Liberal army. He had been driven back into the city with heavy losses, and they had known then that it would be a long and bitter siege. The Liberals fired at anything that moved, no supplies were able to get through, and very soon the Emperor's men were hungry and forced to scavenge for food.

But worse was to come when the *Juáristas* succeeded in blowing up the aqueduct, and the city's clean water supply was cut off. The river that ran down the mountain to the valley might have provided water but for the fact that it had been contaminated by the bodies of dead soldiers and ran red with their blood. Hardened though he was, Leo had been sickened by the sight of them being fished out of the water and piled up with those who had died in the city. Knowing that they constituted a hazard to the health of the living, he had ordered them to be burned. Now he waited for the enemy's next move and made what preparations he could for defending the stricken city.

In spite of everything, life in Queretaro continued and its citizens went on living, loving, giving birth, playing and dying, preserving their sanity with a kind of self-deception that all was well and that the Liberals, who also lived and loved and died on the other side of the defences, would suddenly tire of the cat-and-mouse game, and leave. 'Marquez will come,' they told each other. 'Tomorrow we shall hear the sound of bands playing and marching feet, and we shall be liberated!' A runner was sent out through the lines in the dead of a moonless night to urge him to hurry, but the poor man's body was seen next day, hung high on a post, with a placard round his neck proclaiming, 'The Emperor's Mail'.

It was no more than Leo expected and, in truth, Maximilian himself seemed to be resigning himself to the fact that the General would not be returning. His appearance, gaunt and shabby, resembled more and more that of the men among whom he lived, and yet he seemed content, as if he had found something more valuable than the Empire he had lost.

Every evening he walked round the square in front of the convent, talking to the people, ignoring or laughing at the artillery fire that often came dangerously close. He worried about the women and children, about the beggars, about his troops who were becoming increasingly ragged and hungry, sharing their meals of horsemeat and oxen, which, even steeped in vinegar, were so unpalatable that few could swallow more than a mouthful or two. Sometimes he joined the soldiers who manned the defences and, wrapping himself in a blanket, slept beside them on the hard ground. He was always bright and cheerful and Leo tried to emulate him, but he could not stop thinking about Stella.

She had escaped this terrible slaughter and would be on her way home to England by now, and he was grateful. He told himself so a thousand times a day, and again and again as he lay sleepless every night. But it did not stop him from wanting her and envying James Wainright, envying him from the bottom of his heart—a heart in chains. He cursed the cruel fate that had separated them, then reunited them, only to part them again for ever. And it was for ever, because even if he himself survived the siege, Stella would not leave her husband. Leo left the gruesome fire and returned to the barricades at the limits of the defence perimeter. He must not dwell on what might have been; he must concentrate on the present and his duty as a soldier and a faithful recorder of the events that made history, however painful.

The arrival of the picture, sent through the lines attached to the collar of a stray dog, was a devastating shock. Clearly addressed to Captain Leo Manfred, it was brought to him by the sentry who had caught the animal, intending to make a meal of it. On the back of the drawing, Carson had written: 'Now that I have the reality, you may have the likeness, with my compliments.'

Leo had always been ashamed of making that drawing. It had been done in anger, and revealed too much of his frustration and misery at that time, and now he swore and tore it into shreds, scattering the pieces about his room, and stamping up and down in a helpless rage. Then, just as suddenly, he flung himself across the bed and groaned aloud, 'Oh, Stella, Stella, my love, so near and yet still out of reach. Why is this happening to us?'

How long he lay there he was never sure, but he suddenly became aware of an increased artillery barrage, and the knowledge that the woman he loved was up in the hills at the source of the destruction drove him to a frenzy. He rushed out and ordered his men to counter-attack. They looked at him strangely, wondering if he had lost his reason; such a move was certain suicide. It was only General Miramón, taking his arm and drawing him to one side, who saved them. Leo shrugged him off and turned to survey the hills as though expecting to see an apparition of Stella, but instead he saw the white uniforms of the Liberals spread out on the hills to dry. It was a sure sign that there was a fresh attack on its way, because they always liked to fight in clean clothes.

Miramón, too, saw them. 'You will have your chance to be a hero later, my friend. Now I suggest you go and make ready.'

Recognising the wisdom of this, Leo inspected his men, their arms and the tiny amount of ammunition they still had, and then turned to go back to his room. He was crossing the courtyard of the Convent of the Cross, which they had made their headquarters, when he suddenly stopped and stared at a small figure making his way towards him. His eyes lit up with pleasure, and the mouth which had found so little to smile at recently broke into a wide grin. Pablo's beautiful new clothes were in tatters and he was filthy, but there was no mistaking the broad, white-toothed smile. Leo strode over and stopped in front of him, feet apart, hands on hips, and he laughed aloud.

'Well, what have you to say for yourself, young shaver? You let us think you'd drowned. Damned inconsiderate of you, d'you know that?' He stretched out a hand and ruffled the boy's hair.

'*Si, Señor.*'

'Where have you been?'

'*Señor*, I escape from *Juáristas*, I been in Mexico City. I look for you.'

Although Leo was anxious to hear the boy's story, he was, at that moment, more interested in the possibility of relief than how Pablo had come to be in the capital. 'Did you see General Marquez there?'

'*Si, Señor.* He bad man! He take gold and jewels and clothes, he take everything. He say *Emperador* send him.'

'That's true,' Leo said. 'He was sent to bring money and men.'

'He frighten people,' Pablo insisted. 'He take all, and

load it on wagons. He take picture of *señora* from your room.'

'Never mind that,' Leo said impatiently. 'What happened then?'

'He go to sea. He no come to help *Emperador*.'

'Deserted!' Leo said flatly. 'I'm not altogether surprised. What else happened?'

Pablo's English proved unequal to the narrative, and he lapsed into voluble Spanish so that it was all Leo could do to follow, but it seemed that Marquez, coming up against Díaz's advancing troops, had scattered the gold and valuables in the road to delay them, and had fled back to the capital. 'He no come,' Pablo finished happily. 'But I come. I fight with Señor Leo against bandits with rifles that go bang bang many times!'

'American repeating rifles—Carson's rifles,' Leo said, as General Miramón joined them. 'The Colonel will have the blood of a city on his hands!'

Their conversation was brought to an abrupt halt by an artillery shell that landed close to the convent and showered them with adobe dust. Leo pulled the boy into the shelter of a doorway. 'I'm going to see the Emperor,' he said. 'Something has to be done.'

There was very little ceremony left in court life, and Leo had only to make his way to the Emperor's quarters and request the guard on the door to knock and ask if he might enter. Maximilian's high-ceilinged room was so simply furnished as to be spartan, with no floor-covering and hard wooden furniture, but he did not complain; it was all part of his wish to be at one with subjects, to share their difficulties and their grief. He looked gaunt and drawn, but his eyes, fever-bright because he was suffering terribly from dysentery, lit up when he saw his visitor.

'What can I do for you, my friend?' he asked, waving Leo to a seat.

'Your Majesty, Pablo has brought news from Mexico City. Marquez has deserted, and will not be coming to our aid.'

The Emperor was silent for a long time, and then said 'Can you be sure that the boy is telling the truth?'

'I'd stake my life on it, your Majesty. He also said that the troops surrounding us are armed with American repeating rifles.'

'You were right about the ex-Confederate, then,' the Emperor said quietly.

'It gives me no pleasure to hear you say that, your Majesty.' He paused, then, emboldened by the urgency of his self-imposed errand, went on, 'Your Majesty, we cannot hold out much longer. The enemy has the upper hand, and he knows it. I beg your Majesty to try to break out. Pablo will guide you by the way he came in. If you take only a small escort, it can be managed. I shall stay with my men and draw the Liberal fire.'

'That would be suicide, Leo.' Leo shrugged, as if that were of no importance. 'And if I did break out, where would I go?'

'Back to Europe, your Majesty.'

'I do not wish to return to Europe; to do that would be to admit failure. Besides, what would happen to all the people I leave behind—the innocent citizens, the sick and wounded?'

'After you have safely left, we'll negotiate a peace, and the Liberals will look after them.'

'Negotiate with the enemy? I won't hear of it! No, if I die here in Mexico, at the head of my army, my death will be an honourable one. We fight on.'

Frustrated, Leo returned to his men manning the defensive positions. Deep in thought, he did not notice that he had walked into the enemy's line of fire, and only his instinct preserved him when he flung himself to the ground. The assault had begun.

Advancing behind an almost ceaseless artillery barrage, the Liberals sent in sharpshooters to rake the streets and prevent any organised defence from being mounted. Leo, in the thick of the fighting himself, was appalled to see the Emperor in the middle of the action with a drawn sword, advancing beside General Mira-món, while his troops dashed past him in the opposite direction. The General was obviously remonstrating with him, and a minute or two later Leo saw that wiser counsel had prevailed and that Maximilian had withdrawn. The Liberal cavalry rode on, and the Imperial forces, outnumbered and outgunned, fled back to safety in the centre of the city.

Stella, determined to join Leo in the beleaguered city even if she had to die there with him, chose the night before the assault for her escape attempt. Leaving the Liberal camp was not as difficult as she had feared, for the men were all busy preparing themselves and their arms for the battle ahead, and she was able to creep past a sentry who, secure in the knowledge that there were no Imperial forces in the vicinity, was half asleep.

She made her way slowly down the hillside towards the city without meeting anyone, and was on the outskirts when the barrage began. The noise was deafening, and the dust was making her choke. Unable to go on, she crouched behind a broken wall for some minutes until she realised that it was not going to stop, and if she wanted to find Leo, she had better be brave and make a move. She ran from cover to cover, from one doorway to the next, sheltering behind walls and abandoned vehicles, terrified that the next shell would demolish her shelter and her along with it. To have come so far and then to fail would be more than she could bear.

Soldiers ran past her, turned, and crouched to return the fire of the advancing troops, then retreated again. Officers on skeletal horses directed the defence, and no one paid her any attention. If a woman was foolish enough to be out in the middle of a battle, she would have to take the consequences. Once she thought she saw Leo in the middle of the mêlée of men and horses of both sides, but there was so much smoke and dust that she could not be sure, and when it cleared momentarily, he had disappeared. A shell burst beside her and she felt herself being flung up and forward, then darkness enveloped her and she knew no more of the fighting.

She awoke to an eerie silence. Lying in the bottom of a crater, half covered in rubble, she did not dare to move for several minutes, then she carefully sat up and was astonished to find that, apart from cuts and bruises, she was not hurt. The battle was over for the moment, but who the victor was, she could not tell. If the Liberals had taken the city, she would have expected to hear bands playing and the sound of cheering. She stood up and looked about her. The place was devastated; there was hardly a building which had not been damaged, and dead horses had been left where they had fallen. She knew that, if she looked longer, she would probably also see human bodies. She prayed that Leo had survived, because without him she might as well be dead herself.

Slowly she crept from her hiding-place and picked her way over broken masonry and uprooted trees to the centre of the city. There were civilians here, as well as soldiers, making their way towards the Convent. It was then that she realised that there *was* a band playing, people *were* cheering, and there was not a single Liberal uniform in sight! It was impossible to believe that they had been driven back. With her heart in her mouth, she pushed her way through until she found herself in the front of a thin line of spectators watching a military parade.

The Emperor's raggle-taggle army of starving troops, in tattered uniforms and carrying arms for which they had no ammunition, was drawn up in regimental lines, being reviewed by Maximilian himself with as much pomp and ceremony as could be mustered. Her heart swelled with pride as she picked Leo out, tall and upright and leading his own hand-picked men. Afterwards, Maximilian decorated several, Leo among them, with medals for bravery, and was himself decorated by General Miramón.

As soon as the parade had been dismissed and the men

began to disperse, Stella hurried over to where Leo was about to mount his horse. 'Leo! Wait!'

He turned sharply to face her, startled by the sound of her voice, then stood and stared as though he could not believe what he saw. He looked grey and exhausted, and his blue eyes, once so lively and full of humour, had lost their sparkle; it was as though he were already meeting death half-way. When he spoke, his voice was husky. 'Stella, my darling, what are you doing here?'

'Looking for you.'

'You shouldn't have come,' he said, thinking only of her safety. 'You would have done better to stay where you were.'

'Oh, Leo, you don't know how much I longed to come to you! Say that you are pleased to see me!'

'Pleased! Oh, my darling!' He held out his arms, and she ran into them, to be held close against his rapidly beating heart. 'I thought you had got safely away, and then I had a message from Carson to say that you were with him. It tore me apart.'

'That drawing! Yes, I think it was meant to. He imagined he could hold me after Jimmy was executed, and he wanted to gloat.'

'Oh, my love,' he murmured into her hair, 'I thought I'd never see you again, and then when Carson sent that damned drawing, I didn't know what to think. Forgive me, I was tired and confused.' He moved back a pace to hold her at arm's length so that he could look at her properly. She was dirty and bedraggled and covered in scratches and bruises, but her lovely grey eyes were alight with joy and relief.

'Did you say that James was dead?' he asked suddenly. 'How did that happen?'

'Carson and his men ambushed our coach. Jimmy was wounded, and they took us to the Liberal camp. They tried and executed him.' It seemed an age since that had happened, and she could not, in all honesty, grieve for him as a widow should. 'They tried me, too, but I was only sentenced to leave Mexico. There was no one to escort me and make sure I went, so the Colonel took me with him when he joined the Liberals up there.' She pointed to the hills above the city. 'But, in any case, I had no intention of going without you!'

He smiled, and kissed her. 'How did you get here?'

'I walked down last night . . . At least, I think it was last night. I was thrown unconscious into a crater by a shell-blast, and I don't know how long I was there.'

'Oh, my darling, you might have been killed! What a foolish thing to do.'

'It's the wisest thing I ever did,' she said, then looked at him defiantly. 'And it's no use your sending me away again, for I won't go!'

'I can't, my love,' he said. 'Even if I wanted to, there is nowhere I can send you.' He looked down at her, noting how pale she was, with dark circles under eyes she could hardly keep open, and his heart was full to bursting. She had courage, this star of his, and he hoped and prayed that they would both come safely out of the ordeal ahead. 'Oh, my poor sweet,' he said. 'How did I manage to get you into all this?'

'You didn't get me into it. I did it all by myself!' Now that Leo was beside her to take over the ordering of her life, she allowed herself to relax, and in so doing, all the tension of the past few weeks, which she had been valiantly holding in check, spilled over. She began to shake uncontrollably, and tears ran down her cheeks.

He took her in his arms again to comfort her, stroking her hair and wiping the tears from her cheeks with a gentle finger. 'Don't cry, my dearest girl. Don't be afraid.'

'I'm not,' she said. 'Not now that I'm with you.'

'Come, you need to rest.' He smiled, and she saw the humour of the old Leo breaking through. 'You also need to bath and change. You look like a beggar!'

'I *am* a beggar, for I have nothing but the clothes I stand up in! No luggage, nothing.'

'Pablo!' he called to the boy, who was hovering near

by, grinning widely. 'See what you can find for Mrs Wainright to wear. Bring it to the convent.'

Pablo ran off to obey, and Leo put his arm round her shoulders to guide her. 'The enemy has withdrawn for now, but I'm terribly afraid there is worse to come,' he said. 'If I can find some way of getting you safely out . . .'

'I won't go. There is nothing for me anywhere else. My destiny is here, with you.'

Because he could think of no way to send her away with any degree of safety, he did not argue, and Stella became a part of the life of Queretaro. Day after day the defenders fought off Liberal charges, using unexploded shells retrieved from the débris and ammunition taken from dead Liberals. She learned to live with constant fear, to ignore hunger pangs, the shortage of water to wash either herself or her clothes, the never-ending noise of gunfire.

Leo began sketching again, taking crayons and paper out into the city and drawing whatever he saw; the horror and the heroism, the fear and the dignity. He worked between his own spells of duty at the barricades, and later, watched by Stella, would take a table and chair into the cloisters and complete the pictures, faithful records of that terrible time.

Stella, as thin and hungry as everyone else, endured it stoically, with a smile for Leo's benefit, and went out to do her share of the scavenging for food, the nursing of the sick and wounded. She lived in perpetual fear that Leo would be brought back to her on a stretcher, dead or dying, but she was happier than she had ever been before and would not have changed places with anyone. Occasionally she would look up at the heights towards the enemy positions, reminded of Carson's taunt that the Liberals had time on their side, and she knew that that time was fast running out for those still alive in the city.

Almost as if to confirm this, Leo came to her room one night in May, something he had never done before, and being admitted by its occupant in a borrowed nightgown and with her hair falling about her shoulders, stood drinking in the sight of her before taking her in his arms and holding her so tightly that she could hardly breathe. Then slowly, very slowly, he let her go and stood back to look at her puzzled face.

'Stella, I'm sorry . . .'

'What for?'

'For what I am doing to you, making you endure this.' He jerked his head towards the window and what lay beyond it. 'I should not have come.'

He turned to leave, but she took his hand and drew him further into the room. 'Leo, don't you think it's the same for me?'

'Oh, Stella, my darling, I need you so.'

'I know,' she said softly.

'I have no right . . .'

She reached up to put her arms about his neck, and whispered, 'No one has a better right.'

'Oh, Stella!' He carried her to the bed and put her gently down, sitting on the edge of it beside her, leaning over to scan her face, imprinting every tiny feature of it on his memory. 'I love you more than I can put into words. You have made my miserable life worthwhile, and if I die tomorrow . . .'

She put her fingers over his lips to silence him. 'We shall not talk of dying!'

'No, of course not,' he said cheerfully. 'We're not done for yet! I, for one, have a very special reason for wanting to live, and I won't give up my life—or yours —easily.'

His lovemaking had a special quality, a tenderness mixed with urgency, which aroused Stella to the height of ecstasy, and she clung to him as though their union would make them one body and they need never draw apart again. Afterwards, they lay in each other's arms, not sleeping, because to sleep would cut short the time they had together, and both knew that the end was very near. They could pretend no longer.

'Sweetheart,' he murmured, stroking her hair, 'I want you to do something for me.'

'Anything.'

He smiled. 'You won't like it, I know.' He raised himself on his elbow to look down at her. The moon was shining in at the window, throwing a shaft of light across the bed. She was incredibly beautiful, with her auburn hair spread across the pillow and a sleepy, contented look on her face. He groaned as he bent to set a kiss on her forehead. 'After a great deal of persuasion, the Emperor has agreed to try to break through the cordon . . .'

'When?'

'Tomorrow night, the fourteenth.'

'Are we going with him?'

'You will, but I have to stay.'

His meaning was immediately obvious to Stella. That was why he had come to her room—to say goodbye.

'Leo, I will not leave without you. If it means that I die here, with you, I am content.'

'Please, Stella,' he begged, tracing the outline of her face, with his forefinger, 'do as I ask. I need to know you will be safe . . .'

'Supposing we can't get through the lines?'

'Pablo knows a way.' He smiled suddenly. 'He could squeeze through the eye of a needle.' He kissed her tenderly. 'Now go to sleep, love of my life, my guiding star. You will need to be strong tomorrow.'

She had no intention of leaving with the Emperor, but she did not argue; there would be time enough for that on the morrow, and if she could not get Leo to agree, she would defy him.

He waited until she was asleep, then gently eased himself away from her. Almost blinded by tears he could not hold back, he fumbled for his clothes and put them on, then stopped a moment to gaze down on the sleeping form before creeping from the room to complete the preparations for the Emperor's departure. When all was ready, he paced the corridors of the convent and was still there at dawn, fully dressed and armed, when Colonel Lopez came running towards him, shouting, 'Quick! Save the Emperor! The enemy is here in the convent!'

Leo's first thought was for Stella, and he ran to the tiny cell where Pablo slept, and waking him, gave him money and instructions to find Stella and guide her through the enemy lines to safety. Then he returned to Maximilian.

The Emperor, roused from a fitful sleep, had dressed hurriedly, flung a greatcoat over his shoulders and, taking up his sabre, joined Leo and a few of his retinue in the corridor outside his room. He was deathly pale, but completely calm. 'Get everyone up to the Hill of Bells,' he ordered. 'We'll make a stand there.' Then he led the way down a twisting stone staircase that led to the square outside the convent, determined to fight to the last.

Someone ran up leading a saddled horse, but the Emperor declined it, saying that if his loyal followers had to walk, so would he. Behind them they heard the bells of the convent ringing and the bugles of the Liberals sounding the Diana of victory, while all around their own troops were flinging down their rifles and surrendering.

Leo tried to rally them, to make them turn and fight, but they were deaf to his orders and he had no heart to force them. He followed his monarch with leaden feet. On the hill, they stood surrounded by a handful of Imperial soldiers to take stock of the situation. White flags could be seen fluttering on buildings all over the city, but even then Maximilian was not ready to give up: he asked if they could somehow pass through the enemy lines and escape.

'To pass is impossible,' he was told bluntly. 'But if your Majesty orders it, I am ready to die.'

Silently, Leo agreed. He would welcome an honourable death, if only Stella were safe. He wished he had been able to say goodbye to her, but realised it would have been impossibly painful and he would have had to harden his heart to her entreaties to stay. Better like this.

But Maximilian would not ask that final sacrifice. He took a white handkerchief from his pocket and tied it to a stick he had picked up, then he flung back his greatcoat to reveal his uniform and medals, and walked forward. His little band followed him to the bottom of the hill, where a Liberal officer stepped forward and stopped them. 'Your Majesty is my prisoner.'

A General rode up and, dismounting, walked towards the Emperor, who unbuckled his sword and handed it over. Leo's own weapons were taken from him, and choking, he turned away. Had it all been for nothing? No, he decided, holding his head up proudly, his honour and integrity were still intact; he would keep faith with that, as Maximilian had. He was hardly aware that Pablo and Stella had come to stand beside him until he turned to follow Maximilian, who was passing between the lines of Liberal troops and the decimated ranks of disarmed Imperial soldiers, to return a prisoner to the room he had so recently left as an Emperor.

'I told you to take Mrs Wainright to safety!' he said to the boy, half angry, half pleased.

'Did you think I would go without you?' she asked, linking her arm in his. 'I would never willingly leave you, and Pablo could not persuade me.'

He smiled wryly. It was too late to send her away now, and she knew it.

Life in Queretaro took on an unreal quality: a silence descended, as the dead were buried and the inhabitants came out of the holes and cellars in which they had been hiding and tried to return to normal, to rebuild their homes, to go about their daily business, to adjust to an unaccustomed peace.

The captured monarch, who was allowed to receive visitors and still held a kind of court, seemed almost content, believing, in his usual optimistic fashion, that he would meet and talk to Benito Juárez and that all would be well. 'We raised the white flag of surrender,' he said complacently. 'He will not shoot a prisoner who has surrendered.'

He was encouraged in this belief by the news that scores of his captured troops were being released to return to their homes. This did not include the few Europeans who had remained, although they were allowed a certain amount of freedom within the city until Juárez had decided what was to be done with them.

Neither Leo nor Stella shared Maximilian's optimism as they, too, tried to come to terms with the surrender and the uncertainty of their future.

'Leo,' said Stella, one day as he was sketching a Liberal parade passing against a backdrop of a ruined building, 'I want to ask you something.'

'Ask away, my darling.'

'Leo, could we not be married?'

He laughed aloud. 'What a forward one you are! Don't you know that it's the man who is supposed to propose?'

'Yes, but you are taking such a long time about it!'

Leo expected to share the fate of his royal master, and he was sure that Stella would fare better not as his wife but as an innocent British citizen unwittingly caught up in the struggle. Somehow or other he meant to arrange for her to journey safely to Vera Cruz and take a passage back to England. Being his wife would greatly diminish her chances. 'I have been waiting for an appropriate time,' he said, keeping these thoughts to himself, 'after we get safely away from here and can celebrate a proper wedding . . .'

'No, Leo,' she said. 'I am already your wife in all but name, and I don't want to wait to have that, too. Besides, if our time together is short, I want to spend every minute of it with you.'

'Our time together will not be short,' he said firmly. 'We have years and years ahead of us; we shall live to a ripe old age.'

'Are you turning me down, Leo?'

He could not hold out against her and, knocking over his easel, he jumped up and swept her off her feet, whirling her round. Then, setting her down, he kissed her, suddenly serious. 'No, my love, I am not turning you down. If that is what you wish, it is also what I wish.'

They were married in the chapel of the Convent of the Cross in the last week of May. Stella wore a gown Pablo had found in an attic in the city when he had been sent to find clothes for her. He had returned in triumph with a magnificent cream satin gown, encrusted with seed pearls and diamanté and with a full hooped skirt and nipped-in waist. Far too ostentatious for the conditions under which they existed, she had never worn it. It was, perhaps, the most useless trophy of the war in terms of bodily needs, but to Leo and Stella it was a symbol of love and courage and triumph over adversity, and she wore it with pride.

They knelt together at the altar, watched by Maximilian, a handful of Leo's comrades, Pablo, a few nuns and half a dozen Liberal guards sent to watch over them and foil any attempts to escape, and pledged their love and their lives to each other until death, knowing that death might be only days away. Afterwards they toasted each other in champagne, which, at the time, was more plentiful than water, and then Leo took his bride back to the room that had been set aside for them by their captors.

As soon as the door was closed and they were alone, he took her in his arms and kissed her longingly and tenderly. 'Oh, my poor darling,' he said. 'Do you know what you have let yourself in for?'

'I know exactly.'

'Together,' he whispered. 'Together, now and for always. What a deal of time we wasted!'

'Not wasted,' she said, returning his kisses one by one. 'We have come to know each other the better for the delay, don't you think? I know now why the Emperor calls you his lion-hearted friend. You are my lion-hearted husband.'

He led her to the window and they stood looking out towards the hills. 'Our destiny is almost certainly in the hands of the Liberals,' he said. 'Unless a miracle happens, we live or die according to their dictates. Do you realise that?'

'Yes.'

'And you do not mind?'

'I mind . . . I mind a great deal, but I would rather die here with you than live anywhere else without you.' She turned and held his face in both her hands. 'Remember that, Leo.'

He pulled her to him, holding her so tightly that he lifted her off her feet. 'My own star, my guiding light, my love,' he said, carrying her across to the bed and laying her down gently. 'Tonight is ours. Let tomorrow take care of itself.'

The lawyers appointed to defend Maximilian arrived and spent days closeted with him, discussing the charges, which he refused to take seriously. He would not go to the city's pink sandstone theatre to attend the military tribunal, and was sentenced in his absence to die by the firing-squad, along with Miguel Miramón and others.

Maximilian spent his last days writing letters—to his brother, to his wife, to his lawyers, to Juárez—requesting that Miramón and others of his followers such as Leo might be spared, but to that he received no answer. To Leo, who had taken Stella to visit him, he said, 'Go now, my lion-hearted friend, and leave while you can. I beg you, take advantage of the . . .' He paused, searching for the right word, then went on, smiling, '. . . ceremony, and escape. Go back to Europe before you share my unhappy fate.'

'I can't do it,' Leo said, as they left him. 'I cannot think of walking away from him now.'

'Of course not,' Stella said simply.

'But we will try to leave as soon . . . as soon as it's over,' he said. 'Pablo will be waiting just outside the city on the Vera Cruz road with a mule-cart, and, with luck, our captors will be too busy . . .' He paused, too choked to speak, then gathered himself. 'They may not be guarding the exits.' He smiled down at her. 'Wear a heavy cloak with a hood to cover your hair. You mustn't be recognised.'

'Where shall we go?'

'Wherever you like, my darling. We have the whole world to choose from. England, perhaps?'

England. Home. Grandmother. If she kept thinking of that, she might be able to endure the next twenty-four hours with the courage Leo had come to expect of her.

They were already awake next morning when the trumpets sounded Diana in the Liberal quarters—had been awake for hours—but at the signal, they rose and dressed. Leo wore the uniform of an Austrian Hussar, even knowing it might draw attention to himself. 'It is the last service I shall render him,' he said. 'He will know I did not turn away from him at the end.'

They went out into the streets that were lined by troops; the civilian inhabitants of Queretaro remained behind closed shutters. Three carriages drew up at the door of the prison and Maximilian himself emerged, dressed in black and wearing a white sombrero. Behind him came his valiant commanders, who each climbed into separate carriages, accompanied by a priest. The command to move was given and they moved slowly along the street and up the Hill of Bells to the music of the Dead March, followed by Maximilian's tiny retinue on foot.

When they were nearly at the top, they halted. Here a short adobe wall had been hurriedly built. Priests and prisoners left their vehicles and moved towards it. Three simple coffins were brought up and laid in readiness, then Maximilian directed where each of the three should stand, before turning to the officer in charge of the firing-squad.

'At your disposition, *Señor*.' When the officer saluted with his sword and began to ask forgiveness for what he was about to do, Maximilian added, 'The duty of a soldier is to obey. No forgiveness is necessary. Carry out your orders.'

He folded his hands over his heart, and said clearly, 'I forgive everyone. I pray that everyone will also forgive me, and I wish that my blood, which is now to be shed, may be for the good of the country. Long live Mexico! Long live Independence!'

There was a hushed silence, and Stella, safe in Leo's encircling arms, turned her head away; she could not look. Leo himself stood stiffly upright, staring stonily ahead at the man who had been first his friend and then his monarch, and uttered a prayer for his departing soul.

The commander of the firing-squad raised his sword high in the air. '*Listos! Apunten! Fuego!*' The sword-arm dropped.

The sound of twenty-one rifles discharged into the silent air startled Stella, and she felt Leo's arm tighten round her waist. When she looked up at him, he was still staring straight ahead at the spot where Maximilian had been standing, and the tears were running down his cheeks.

'Leo,' she said gently, when it seemed he would never move, 'we must go now.'

They turned and walked slowly down the hill. Stella became aware that there were armed Liberal soldiers walking alongside, guarding them.

'It's too late,' she whispered to Leo. 'What are we to do?'

He looked about them. 'When I tell you to run,' he said in an undertone, 'you run, as fast as you can. Find Pablo. Understand?'

'And you?'

'I'll meet you there.'

'No, Leo,' she said, guessing what was in his mind. 'I will not run away and leave you. What kind of wife would I be to do that?'

He turned to grin down at her, though he never felt less like laughing. 'An obedient one.'

She smiled back at him. 'I was never very good at being obedient.'

The guards were closing in on them now and there was no mistaking their intent; Stella and Leo were being escorted as prisoners. There would be no escape.

At the bottom of the incline they came face to face with Redford Carson. They stopped. Stella held her breath as the two men faced each other.

'Stand aside, Stella,' Leo said calmly, as he reached for his sword. His hand found only the empty scabbard. The guards grabbed his arms and held him, while he glared angrily and helplessly at the American.

'Colonel,' Stella said quietly, 'you have won. What more do you want from us?'

'Nothing. I came to say goodbye to a very courageous woman. Today the Mexican Empire came to an end, and I take no pride in its downfall, but it is done, and I am returning to Washington.' He signalled to the guards to release Leo, and waved them away. 'Safe conduct to Vera Cruz,' he added, thrusting a sheaf of papers into Leo's hand. 'For both of you, and the Mexican boy. You'll need them.' Then he turned on his heel and strode away.

'I wonder whose is the greater victory,' Leo said slowly, gazing after him. 'I think it must be Maximilian's.'

'Yes, my darling,' she said. 'Yours and Maximilian's.'

Redford Carson went back to his quarters to pack his belongings before returning to America. He had been a pawn in a political game, and he had done his work well, too well. His victory had been an empty one, because, in doing his duty, he had lost the only woman he had ever loved. He stood looking for a long time at the portrait hanging on the wall of the room he had taken in one of the town's least damaged hotels. It had been picked up by Diaz's troops on the road outside Mexico City, and passed from hand to hand until once more it had come into his possession.

It was a picture of a girl standing in front of a fairytale castle, a girl so beautiful that she took his breath away. He had coveted it when he first saw it, because, even then, he knew that Stella was the only woman he wanted. Now, having lost the girl it represented, he would keep the painting, and the spirit that shone from it would sustain him in the lonely years ahead.

'To the victor the spoils,' he said aloud, putting it carefully in the bottom of his trunk, and smiling at the irony of it.